The Policy Consequences of John Maynard Keynes

The Policy Consequences of John Maynard Keynes

Edited by Harold L. Wattel

M. E. SHARPE, INC.
Armonk, New York

Library of Congress Cataloging in Publication Data

Main entry under title:

   Papers presented at a conference held at Hofstra University, Sept. 21–24, 1983.
   Includes bibliographical references.
   1. Keynesian economics—Congresses. 2. Economic policy—Congresses.   I. Wattel, Harold L.

HB99.7.P65   330.15'6   84-23542
ISBN 0-87332-316-5
ISBN 0-87332-317-3 (pbk.)

Design by Angela Foote

Printed in the United States of America.

To
Morgan Elizabeth
and
Kaolin Fire

CONTENTS

Foreword

As Director of the Hofstra University Forum, *The Policy Consequences of John Maynard Keynes*, I wish at the outset to express my gratitude to M. E. Sharpe, Inc. for affording some of the Forum papers a wider audience than could hear them delivered. The primary purpose in convening this assembly of scholars was to celebrate the 100th anniversary of the birth of John Maynard Keynes, but in the strict meaning of the word *convene*, there was a public purpose also. We in the Economics Department at Hofstra felt that there was a need for a professional discussion of Keynesian policies in terms accessible to the interested citizen.

The nation's economy is now being guided by policies "elected" by the citizenry after a decade in which Keynesian policies seemed to have lost their effectiveness. That Keynesianism had worked earlier only served to confuse the issue. With whom did the fault lie? With government? With business? With economists? The public, it seemed, was entitled to an opportunity to learn about the theoretical economic uncertainties involved in shaping economic policies. Further, we felt, hustings were not the best places to ascertain economic truths. Hence, the convoking of a forum dedicated to studying only the public policy implications of Keynesian theory here and abroad.

Friedrich von Hayek, a dissenter from Keynesian doctrine, argues that Keynes's . . . "main aim was always to influence current policy, and economic theory was for him simply a tool for this purpose."[1]

In assaying the policy implications of Keynes's work, the conference did not intend to deny the importance of Keynes's theoretical analyses,[2] for the framework of macroeconomics was erected by Keynes, a construct ubiquitously employed by friend and foe. In the areas of both theory and policy, Keynes made revolutionary contributions.

A few words about the man are in order. He was born on June 5, 1883, the first of Florence Ada and John Neville Keynes's three children.[3] In that same year Karl Marx died, and Joseph Schumpeter, the Austrian and later American economist, was born. During Keynes's sixty-three years—he died on April 21, 1946—he wrote ten books and close to four hundred articles, reviews, reports, and pamphlets.[4] From his earliest days he was an involved citizen. It was this involvement in public affairs—recommendations for revising the treaties ending World War I, recommendations for the ending of the worldwide depression of the 1930s, recommendations to the British government on the financing of its World War II effort, and recommendations for the rebuilding of the world's international financial structure after World War II— that increases his stature in the company of scientific immortals. Samuelson measures him against Newton and Darwin.[5]

Keynes never inspired in his disciples the kind of fervor that marks the disciples of Marx and Freud. This is all to the good because it permits followers their freedom to discover newer ''truths'' without being accused of betraying the revolution. There are post-Keynesians. Are there post-Marxists? Post-Freudians? Times do change and, since time is a critical variable in both economics and psychology, should one not expect and even hope for the gradual revision of science to accommodate the change? Economics is the richer for the post-Keynesians and for the work of their critics.

Now a few more lines about the Forum. Held at Hofstra University over a three-day period, September 22–24, 1983, it presented a total of 22 papers, all but three focused on Keynesianism as applicable to developed nations, developing nations, and the international financial economy. Of the 22 papers, 11 are reprinted in this volume. The program is listed here to give the reader a view of the complete Forum. The listing of the papers is as presented, an order different from that employed in this book.

Keynote Address

James Tobin   Keynesian Policies in Theory and
                               Practice

The International Economy

John Williamson   Keynes and the International Eco-
                               nomic Order

The Developing Economies

Hans Singer   The Influence of John Maynard
                               Keynes on the Economic Policies of
                               Underdeveloped Nations

Jose Carlos Braga   The Influence of John Maynard
                               Keynes on the Economic Policies of
                               Brazil*

---

*Papers not included in this volume; they may be ordered at cost from Hofstra's Department of Economics.

*Papers not included in this volume; they may be ordered at cost from Hofstra's Department of Economics.

On two of the Forum evenings, invited speakers addressed the more personal aspects of Keynes's life. Charles Hession, on the first evening, explored the androgynous aspects of Keynes's character in a paper titled "The Peculiar Genius of John Maynard Keynes." On the second evening, Carolyn Heilbrun spoke of Keynes and his friends; her paper was titled "Keynes and Biography." John Heilbrun described Keynes's aesthetic interests in "Keynes and the Economics of the Arts."[6]

This is the place to acknowledge the help I received in mounting the Keynes Forum. I do so gratefully, well aware that these words do not fully convey to others the exceptional contributions of all those who became involved in the undertaking because of conviction or friendship or intellectual interest. I say thanks to my colleagues in the Economics Department who helped in the planning of the conference and especially to Helen Hill Updike, Lynn Turgeon, and Jacob Weissman, who also assisted with the editing of these papers. The University was generous in providing funding and support staff. Karin Barnaby, of Hofstra's Center for Cultural and Intercultural Studies, shouldered the burden of much of the administrative details associated with this undertaking. Without the additional assistance received from outside sources, however, the Forum would have remained another glorious fantasy. We are therefore in debt to the following businesses and professional groups: The Exxon Education Foundation, Inc.; Pan American World Airways; Value Line, Inc.; ARA Services, Inc.; R. H. Macy and Company, Inc.; the International Ladies Garment Workers Union; AFL-CIO; Hayt, Hayt and Landau; the Supermarket Workshop; the New York State Council for Economic Education; Harcourt, Brace Jovanovich, Inc.; McGraw-Hill Book Company; Pepperidge Farm, Inc.; and the Fiesta Nut Company.

I received cooperative and efficient help in preparing these manuscripts for publication from the staffs of the Office of the Secretary of Hofstra under the directions of Stella Sinicki and Doris Brown. As for the content of the manuscripts, the authors assume full responsibility for the ideas advanced; the reader should not infer that their ideas necessarily represent the views of the agencies with which the authors are associated.

Hempstead, New York
April 1984
Harold L. Wattel

Notes

1. Friedrich von Hayek, "The Keynes Centenary: The Austrian Critique," *The Economist*, June 11, 1983, p. 39. He also contends that Keynes never mastered the full body of economic theory.
2. Centennial celebrations focusing on various aspects of Keynes's work were held here and abroad in 1983, e.g., one on theory at Cambridge University in July.
3. There is no dearth of biographical information. R. F. Harrod's *The Life of John Maynard Kenyes* (London: Macmillan, 1951) is the standard; Robert Skidelsky's *John Maynard Keynes 1883–1920* (London: Macmillan, 1983) is the latest of the biographies.

4. These, along with letters, etc., are now available in 13 volumes published by the Royal Economic Society between 1971 and 1984.

5. Peter Drucker disagreed, concluding his *Forbes* (May 23, 1983) article on Schumpeter as follows: "No one in the interwar years was more brilliant, more clever than Keynes. Schumpeter, by contrast, appeared pedestrian—but he had wisdom. Cleverness carries the day. But wisdom endureth" (p. 128). Samuelson's verdict is somewhat different: " . . . it is in no sense demeaning to Schumpeter's high achievements to place him outside the class that contains Newton, Darwin, and Keynes" (*The New York Times*, May 29, 1983).

6. The Hession and John Heilbrun papers have not been reproduced here, but they are available at cost from Hofstra's Economics Department.

The Policy Consequences
of John Maynard Keynes

Introduction

Harold L. Wattel

The eleven papers comprising this volume focus on the policy implications of the work of John Maynard Keynes and provide an assessment of that legacy for developed economies, for developing economies, and for the international economy.

Essays focused on the American economy open the book. The lead article by James Tobin is followed by those of Peter Bernstein, Robert Lekachman, Paul Sweezy, and Norman Ture. A paper by John Kenneth Galbraith concludes the first section. Papers on the major developed European economies comprise the second section: John Eatwell's on England, Robert Boyer's on France, and Dudley Dillard's on Germany. In the third section the reader will find two studies; the first is by Hans Singer on the usefulness of Keynesian policies for developing countries, followed by John Williamson's paper on Keynes's contributions to the structuring of the international economy.[1]

Rather than summarize each author's contribution, the editor has opted to select for review and comment a few themes, which are treated variously by the authors.

Keynes's Basic Philosophy
The commonly accepted view of John Maynard Keynes is that he was primarily policy oriented. In the words of E. J. Hobsbawm: "From his dramatic entry on the public scene as a critic of the 1919 Versailles peace to his death, Keynes spent his time trying to save capitalism from itself. . . ."[2] What kinds of policies will save capitalism from itself? It is one thing to enforce the rules of the game and to foster competition through antitrust laws. It is quite another for government to impose wage and price controls to curtail inflationary pressures or to invest directly to maintain a level of aggregate spending commensurate with full employment. How far would Keynes go?

Eatwell subscribes to a portrait of Keynes as a budding socialist, prepared to institute comprehensive microeconomic controls when the conditions of an economy called for it. Lekachman also sees Keynes as a "radical" planner but as more eclectic in his selection of the devices necessary to

3

maintain full employment and to secure, in addition, a more egalitarian capitalist society. Boyer, one may infer from his article, is closer to Lekachman than to Eatwell. While Eatwell believes that Keynes would sanction microeconomic meddling, he never clearly spells out the nature of that meddling, never specifies what kinds of and how much price intervention Keynes would countenance beyond the usual monetary management of interest rates, exchange rates, and tariffs.

One can assume from Keynes's hints, according to Galbraith and Tobin, that Keynes (in Tobin's words) "expected and advocated direct government interventions in the wage setting process."[3] Nevertheless, for Galbraith and Tobin, Keynes remains the loyal capitalist, a reformer yes, but a conservative capitalist reformer. Galbraith has no doubts that "Keynes was . . . exceedingly comfortable with the economic system he so brilliantly explored . . . . He was not . . . attracted by Marx." Before judging Eatwell's effort to make Keynes into a socialist, readers may want to look again at *The General Theory*, especially pages 378–81.

If Keynesians undertake to manage the micro, the macro, and the international elements of the economy, can we conclude that business people were and are wrong in opposing Keynesian policies? Tobin muses on this: "The reasons for business interests to reject Keynes are not entirely clear." Galbraith is much more judgmental on this score:

> It was, as it remains, the perverse genius of conservatives to misunderstand the larger implications of efforts on behalf of their own salvation—to combine vehemence with a righteous commitment to their own euthanasia. Perhaps, the problem is not posed well by the question: What was Keynes' basic philosophy?

Reading these papers and rummaging again through *The General Theory*, one might rather pose the question in this way: "Should we employ, in the short run, policies which may be inimical to the ethos of the system in the long run?" Let us look briefly, therefore, at the short run policy goals of economic planners.

The papers selected for this volume reflect a deliberate attempt to portray positions along a broad economic-political spectrum. Although the authors start from different premises, a constructive exchange of ideas has resulted. Is the distance between Sweezy and Ture bridgeable? Possibly not, but Ture, qua supply-sider/rational expectationist, and Tobin, the Keynesian, do have common ground. For other authors the overlap is more obvious. Galbraith is convinced that Keynes believed " . . . that capitalism was worth saving, that it could be made to work." Ture, Tobin, and Boyer would probably agree with Keynes on this. The matter of what steps government should take to save capitalism is the point at which the authors diverge.

Examining Ture, we find the following:

> The conservative's basic policy objective is to improve the efficiency of market performance, . . .

Good public economic policy calls for reducing the government's presence in the private marketplace, for correcting the relative
price and cost distortions that government actions and policies
entail, ...[4]

Does Ture at this late date assume perpetual full employment? His
statement sounds pre-Keynesian. The Keynesian starting point that all of us
have learned is that full employment is not the "normal equilibrium" state of
a private enterprise economy! If the rational expectationists believe that government cannot return the capitalist economy to full employment earlier than
the private market would when left to its own devices, does it follow that doing
nothing is in the best interests of the system in the long run? Can any of us
ignore the economic and political instability that accompanies mass unemployment?

Tobin, on a very different tack, contends that returning an underemployed economy to full employment was and remains a first priority for all
governments in the Western world, and with a bit of irony, reminds us that the
Reagan budget deficits, born of tax cuts, increased defense expenditures, and
the eased monetary policies of the Federal Reserve Board in 1983 exerted
" . . . a powerful expansionary influence on aggregate demand." He joins
the issue raised by Ture in this way: "Whatever one may think of the distributional equity and allocational efficiency of these measures, they are increasing
private and public spending on goods and services and making jobs." In other
words, in the interest of priority number one, namely, full employment, Tobin
is willing to take on "liberals" and "conservatives" by designating as lesser
priorities both of their important goals, that is, income equalization and
allocational efficiency. Tobin's priorities are truly Keynesian, according to
Boyer in that " . . . interventions by the state should not be directed solely
toward such traditional objectives as stabilizing the purchasing power of
money or balancing public expenditure and receipts but must instead aim at
maintaining full employment, whatever may be the transitory effects of such
policies upon public accounts and money."[5] Our writers clearly differ about
how indifferent governments can be to those other issues, such as inflation and
the size of the national debt. But careful reading may reveal not only some
patches of common ground but also that Keynes, were he alive, might be less
ideological and more pragmatic and imaginative than present opponents and
disciples.

Keynes's Disciples

Marx never completed a blueprint for a communist society. Similarly,
Keynes never described policies needed to solve all the problems that might
confront government in attempting to maintain full employment or to secure
more equal distribution of income. In fact, in *The General Theory* (p. 383) he
denied any attempt to compose such a list of policies. Could he have foreseen
all the problems that have ensued or may yet ensue from implementing
macroeconomic policies? William H. Beveridge, in his 1945 *Full Employment*

in a Free Society, did explore some of the problems that might arise, such as inflation due to collective wage bargaining and noncompetitive price policies, and the problems associated with an unstable international economic order.[6,7] Would Keynes have agreed with Beveridge's formulation and suggested remedies? Does Beveridge accurately portray Keynes's preferences? Who speaks for Keynes today? By what standard may one judge? We find Ture seeing allegedly Keynesian policies as reflections not of Keynes but of Keynes's disciples. He offers the thesis that "the Keynesian influence on public policy as we see it today is the result of the application or misapplication of his views, primarily those conveyed in *The General Theory*, by his disciples." This view is supported by Richard Rahn of the Chamber of Commerce in a paper delivered at the Forum but not included here. He said, " . . . policy makers have frequently used the adjective 'Keynesian' to gain respectability for policies that Keynes himself would not have endorsed."[8]

Paul Sweezy, occupying a different place on the political spectrum, finds some so-called disciples donning robes of Keynesian policy in a harlequinesque fashion.[9] "Keynes's followers, or at any rate those who became the prophets of the New Economics, vulgarized these opinions to the point of turning Keynesianism into a cure-all for the capitalist business cycle." While Ture and Rahn would maintain that the disciples moved on too broad a front, Sweezy holds that Keynes was himself more radical than his American disciples dared to be. After all, did not Keynes espouse distributional equalization and the socialization of investments? Putting this matter of Keynes or disciples aside, does the bottom line reveal success or failure?

Have Keynesian Policies Worked?

Tobin observes somewhat caustically, "The current depression is tragic, but the coincidence of timing may be fortunate. It should help revive the credibility of Keynesian analysis and policy within the economics profession and in the broader public arena." He asserts that, in a dynamic world, one cannot expect ossified analysis and policies to work; that is, Keynesians have the responsibility for designing instruments now missing from their toolboxes in order to cope with new problems.[10]

This prescription for the future rests on Tobin's understanding of the past. He has no reservations regarding the efficacy of Keynesian policies prior to 1973. Conservative economists, however, now deny the possibility that any government intrusions into the economy can be efficacious.[11]

We turn again to Ture for a conservative position. "Government fiscal and monetary policy actions," he claims, "have no direct effect on real aggregate income or real aggregate demand. . . . Any alteration in real aggregate demand can occur only if there is a preceding increase in real output. . . ." His case against government intervention is expanded with the contention that nominal changes in income and demand only serve to distort price relationships, which destabilize the economy further. Running to the data books will not necessarily credit or discredit this case because, in the final analysis, the question in a recession is whether voluntary private action by business (borrowing more, which will increase monetary aggregates) or government spending (running deficits that will increase monetary aggregates) will generate recovery from a cyclical downturn. As Abba Lerner has written elsewhere about the Great Depression, private confidence in the economy collapsed so that only increased government spending ". . . could have been effective in increasing spending and employment until investors' confidence was restored. Hence the call for *fiscal* measures."[12]

Tobin marks the post–World War II period as "one of unparalleled prosperity," a period during which "virtually all advanced democratic capitalist societies adopted, in varying degrees, Keynesian strategies of demand management."[13] This may beg the evaluative question of whether Keynesianism is a better antideflation weapon than anti-inflation weapon. Beveridge, our Keynesian disciple quoted earlier, was willing to grant that inflation was as much an evil as deflation; but, though he did prescribe to correct cost-push inflation, he had nary a word in his book about fighting demand-pull inflation. Nor are there any policy statements in *The General Theory* on the control of demand-pull inflation. While one can construct a long list of possible reasons why demand management may not have worked well in the United States in countering inflation,[14] apparently it was stagflation "that done the bloke in." Let us take a closer look at the phenomenon known as stagflation.

Stagflation

Disenchantment with Keynesian policies in the United States developed in the mid-1970s, when the nation began to suffer simultaneously from rising prices and rising unemployment. In Britain, the malaise had set in much earlier, according to Eatwell, who, with Ture and Sweezy, lay the blame here and abroad on the shortcomings of basic Keynesian theory; others, like Tobin and Galbraith, blame the use, misuse, or nonuse of particular policy tools. Tobin grants that "Keynes did not provide, nor did his various followers over the years, a recipe for avoiding unstable inflation at full employment." This may be an overstatement or at least a statement that needs modifying. Some recipes preferred in the past have not been politically acceptable.[15] For example, would Americans buy Beveridge's remedies? Beveridge, as early as 1945, was prepared to control what we now call "profit-push inflation," one ingredient of stagflation, by policies that led from supervision or oversight (Big Brother is watching you!) to regulation (including price controls) to public ownership. To control wage-push inflation, another ingredient of stagflation, he recommended "jaw-boning" first, compulsory arbitration second, and, in cases of strikes contrary to public economic policy, the withdrawal of all public support for the strikers.[16] These steps do seem to go against the grain of American sensibilities.

Tobin, too, has composed an extensive list of anti-inflationary policy tools, which readers can discover for themselves in his paper. Galbraith and Ture clash on anti-inflation policy. Galbraith opts for a tight *fiscal* policy

because he feels, theoretically and practically, it is less damaging to investment than tight monetary policy. Ture alleges that analysis and experience
have shown fiscal policy to be without merit. Hence, he chooses tight money
policy. Is it likely that monetary policy, or fiscal policies as we have known
them, can solve the problem of stagflation? Probably not because lagging
investment is also a factor. Private investment is not always stimulated by
falling interest rates or rising incomes.

   Notable by their absence in this compendium of papers are policies for
the stimulation of investment. New ideas for restoring profit anticipations to
induce a high level of capital investment are not explored by our contributors.
We ought not to forget that Keynes identified the collapse of the marginal
efficiency of capital as the villain in any cyclical downturn. Those on the left,
presumably, would resort to the ''socialization of investment.'' Those on the
right would leave the matter to a private market renewed by lowered levels of
government intervention and taxes. The supply-side case that increasing investment would reduce unemployment and dampen inflation ought not to be
dismissed out of hand. To be sure, the inflation portion of stagnation-inflation
is not likely to be solved by new investment, since the culprit is cost-push
inflation. However, when investment falters, will it be reinvigorated by reducing the size of the federal government and federal taxes? If not, are we to
continue to rely on investment tax credits as the main tool?

   We have reports that there is a rallying of disparate persons around the
concept of industrial policy as a way to stimulate the level and direction of
investment in the American economy. Government participation appears to be
an integral part of these new policies. Lekachman mentions ''the confusions of
industrial policy.'' On the other hand, supporters of industrial policy hold that
on one issue the case is clear: government must finance the search for new
investment opportunities. According to them, our economy must seek replacements for the older industries that have fed our post–World War II
affluence, such as the automobile, the computer, drugs, and the civil-aviation
industries.[17]

   Will ''Dynamic Keynesianism'' be able to come to terms with the
problem of investment and investor perceptions? I can find only one sentence
in *The General Theory* (Chapter 12) that hints at the importance of perceptions: ''Thus if the animal spirits are dimmed and the spontaneous optimism
falters, leaving us to depend on nothing but a mathematical expectation,
enterprise will fade and die. . . .''[18]

   Were Keynes alive today, would he have policies for stimulating private
investment that are more imaginative than our contemporary Keynesians?
Would he recommend that tax revenues or government-bond revenues be
auctioned to the private sector for domestic investment even if negative rates
of interest were required? Would he suggest alternatively that these same funds
be used for the purchase of equities to provide firms with the funds to modernize moribund industries and to found new industries? There can be no doubt
that sustaining capital investment in the face of a declining marginal efficiency

of capital was Keynes's major concern. How shall we state our problem? Have previous successes in stimulating consumer demand blinded us to the fact that the Keynesian policies have not been equally effective in stimulating investment demand? Here Keynes's imagination is sorely needed.[19]

We have dwelt long on Keynes and the American economy. How does he fare elsewhere?

Keynesian Policies and the World Economy

The interconnections of economic activities are legion. That managing them on the domestic scene is beyond the ability of central planners is one of the threads in the Ture paper. When government spends to maintain full employment at home, new troubles may emerge if domestic policies are not constrained by international economic circumstances. This was of concern to Keynes. As World War II drew to a close, he participated in discussions regarding the desired shape of the post–1945 international economy. As far as he was concerned, appropriate international arrangements could be fashioned which did not interfere with domestic full-employment policies. His formulations were not always accepted; yet, as a team player, according to Williamson, he remained an enthusiastic supporter of international agencies and processes proposed by others, for example, by representatives of the United States.[20]

Keynes foresaw the need for more planned international economic management than was established in the postwar period. He was not sanguine about a renewal of a high level of international trade if it depended on a freely operating market system. In his mind there would have to be international cooperation to establish a worldwide trading and clearing system. Two agencies considered by Keynes to be vital to the development of a lively international economy were an International Monetary Fund and a World Bank. In addition, he saw a need to control capital movements and to provide backward countries with capital equipment for long-term economic development. As noted above, Keynes did not succeed in obtaining mechanisms to tackle the latter two needs. As for the two financial institutions, in his book the IMF was insufficiently disciplinary and the World Bank was insufficiently funded. Williamson certainly agrees.

Both Singer and Williamson challenge economists and our international economic institutions to shore up the crumbling system of international buying and selling, borrowing and lending. Singer, for example, laments " . . . that Keynes's original ideas were not more fully accepted and did not prevail at Bretton Woods . . . I am thinking here . . . particularly of his proposals for a world currency controlled to satisfy liquidity needs and based on primary commodities. . . ." Exchange-rate misalignments, a recurring problem, cause unfortunate economic consequences and Williamson ticks off these: loss of output, unneccessary readjustment costs, ratcheting price-level effects, and stimulation of protectionist pressures, among others. At this writing, debtor

nations, with the aid of the International Monetary Fund, are trying to resche-
dule their external debts so as not to bring down their own houses and those of
their creditors.[21]

Coda

Readers approaching these papers with an open mind may not only see
many issues in a new light but also be stimulated to read and reread the works
of Keynes, his contemporaries, and his disciples. As for finding common
ground over which all of our authors are marching, the editor suggests as one
possibility, the importance of investment.

Was not Keynes correct in attributing cyclical downturns to the collapse
of the marginal efficiency of capital? When the outlook for profit is poor, the
flow of investment is likely to be meager. In putting the issue in this way,
Keynes emphasized the significance of entrepreneurs and their motivations.
We might not have expected this of Keynes, since in *The General Theory* he
joined Smith in identifying consumption as the sole end of economic activity
(p. 104). One could have expected that he would have stressed instead Marshall's contention that in interpreting the history of man it is "the science of
activities and not that of wants."[22] In one sense, this lays at the feet of business
persons the responsibility for devising new activities.

To have supported Marshall rather than Smith would have been consistent with Keynes's later emphasis on investment demand. Supply-siders, in
one sense, remind us of the centrality of the capitalist to the system. They
protest that there can be no consumption without production. Consequently,
there must be some piece of ground here where their footprints and those of the
Keynesians cross. They diverge, however, in their assessment of the motiva-
tional aspects of investment.

Keynesians need not argue against the monetarist contention that production in a modern economy is unlikely to be increased without a prior
change in the monetary variables; this is true whether there is private expansion due to private borrowing or public expansion due to deficit spending by
government. The monetarists seem content to believe that the only good
monetary expansion is private, by the reaction of business people to changing
interest rates. Keynesians deny the ability of low interest rates to stimulate
investment in the face of a catastrophic fall in the marginal efficiency of capital
and hence lay great store in government investing instead. Leaving stimulation to private-market interest rates or publicly reduced interest rates (even to
zero) may result in no new borrowing and no new production. But the emphasis on the *investor* may not be misplaced. Keynes and the monetarists are on
common ground in identifying the investor as the key figure in the drama.
They part company, however, when the Keynesians charge the private market
with an inability to resuscitate investment during economic crises.

The rational expectationists also traverse this ground when they focus
almost exclusively on the supply side of the market equation. But they turn off
the road and head for the woods when they assume that investors and other

business people are perfectly informed and are willing and able to react to available information. Few students of the American economy are prepared to follow them into the wilderness, surely not the Keynesians.

This leaves Eatwell, Sweezy, and Lekachman closer than the more conventional Keynesians to Keynes's own analysis of the problem. They argue that there is need for the socialization of investment; for them government is *the* investor. In such a mode, what is left of capitalism? Can Keynesianism save capitalism from itself (when investors are refusing to invest) for itself (to profit)? Boyer emphasizes the evolutionary nature of Keynesianism; this evolution will have to discover new ways to stimulate investment.

Can we devise ways to stimulate investment on a sustained basis in an egalitarian society? Or have we become so egalitarian that citizens on the lower 80 percent of the income scale are unwilling to accept uninterrupted growth in real income in lieu of improvements in their relative share of the nation's real income? One critic thinks this is so, seeing government as a schizophrenic " . . . acting mindlessly, between giving priority to reducing unemployment and giving priority to reducing inflation."[23] Must it ever be so in our political system? The editor leaves you here, hoping you will find pursuit of the themes in these eleven papers as exciting as he did.

Notes

1. The sequence of papers is different from that at the Forum. See Foreword for original organization.

2. See review of Robert Skidelsky's biography of Keynes in *The Guardian*, 20 November 1983, p. 22.

3. The freedom to do so may be limited in Keynes's view, since according to Williamson, Keynes thought that domestic economic policy should be subject to some form of international market discipline.

4. Norman Ture, "Keynes's Influence on Public Policy, A Conservative View," *Infra*, pp. 52-53.

5. Robert Boyer, "The Influence of Keynes on French Economic Policy: Past and Present," *Infra*, p. 80.

6. Beveridge conceived this volume as a follow-up to his government-sponsored earlier study (1942): *Report to His Majesty's Government on Social Insurance and Allied Services* (p. 10). It followed from his belief that "The adoption of a policy of full employment by the United States would be the most important economic advance that could happen in the whole world and to the benefit of the whole world."

7. See Parts V and VI of Beveridge, *Full Employment in a Free Society* (New York: W. W. Norton, 1945).

8. Rahn's paper is available from the Hofstra University Economics Department.

9. Is Harlequin armed with an ineffective wooden sword or a glorious magic wand?

10. The same position is taken by Samuelson in his article in *The Economist* (June 25, 1983) and by Boyer in his paper herein.

11. Rational expectationists maintain that laissez-faire is the best economic government fiscal or monetary policy. This foresight, they assert, begets responses that neutralize government's therapeutic actions. But can Tobin's reading of the record of the American economy following World War II be rejected? Consider the words of Robert E. Lucas, Jr., a high priest of the Rational Expectationist School: "If all we had was the postwar data set we wouldn't know a lot, because there hasn't been enough action in this period. . . . In the old days, however, the pre-World War II period—the typical depression would imply a decrease in real output by 10 percent in a year. That's a different order of magnitude from anything we've seen in the postwar period." Arjo

Klamer, *Conversations with Economists* (Totawa, N.J.: Rowman and Alanheld, 1984) p. 43. Keynesians might well hold that their case had been made; the magnitudes were of a lesser order only because Keynesian policies made them so.

12. Abba Lerner, "From Pre-Keynes to Post Keynes," *Social Research*, Autumn 1977, p. 390.

13. Dillard finds Germany's prosperity an exception. See "The Influence of Keynesian Thought on German Economic Policy," *Infra.*, pp. 121-123.

14. One would find on such a list, inter alia, the politics of legislating tax rate increases in election years, the failure to coordinate more fully fiscal and monetary policies, the perceived threat of government growth to individualism, the leads and lags endemic to the federal expenditure process, the lack of federal-state fiscal coordination, and the lack of adequate data for accurate forecasting.

15. During the Carter administration, a letter to the editor of *The New York Times* (May 7, 1979) from John Kenneth Galbraith read: "My colleagues cannot possibly believe that they are required only to tell us that things are getting worse and that nothing can be done." A second letter from Alfred Kahn, adviser to the president on inflation, to the same paper (May 29, 1979) rejected the implied exhortation to "Don't just stand there, do something!" contending that the opposite advice was more valid: "Don't just do something; *stand* there!"

16. Beveridge, Part V.

17. See Allvine and Tarpley, Jr., *The New State of the Economy* (Cambridge, Mass: Winthrop Publishers, 1977) and Robert Reich, *The New American Frontier* (New York: Times Books, 1983).

18. *The General Theory*, p. 162.

19. See *The General Theory*, pp. 320 and 378. On the latter page we find the often alluded-to "investment socialization" quotation, but the manner of socialization is far from dogmatic:

> I conceive, therefore, that a somewhat comprehensive socialization of investment will prove the only means of securing an approximation to full employment; though this need not exclude all manner of compromises and of devices by which public authority will cooperate with private initiative. But beyond this no obvious case is made out for a system of State Socialism which would embrace most of the economic life of the community (p. 378).

20. Williamson pays Keynes a compliment by noting that it was Keynes and not Harrod who was the father of "the crawling peg."

21. Jose Carlos Braga's paper on Brazil, Salvador Kalifa-Assad's paper on Mexico, and Sayre Schatz's paper on Nigeria deal with this problem. They are not reprinted here but are available at cost from Hofstra's Economics Department.

22. Alfred Marshall, *The Principles of Economics* (New York: Macmillan, 1946), p. 90.

23. Herschel Grossman, "Rational Expectations, Business Cycles, and Government Behavior," in Stanley Fischer, *Rational Expectations and Economic Policy* (Chicago: University of Chicago Press, 1980), p. 9.

1

Keynes's Policies in Theory and Practice

James Tobin

The hundredth anniversary of the birth of John Maynard Keynes occurs, like the publication of *The General Theory*, during a world depression. History has contrived to call attention to Keynes just when his diagnoses and prescriptions are more obviously credible than at any other time since the Great Depression of the 1930s. The current depression is tragic, but the coincidence of timing may be fortunate. It should help revive the credibility of Keynesian analysis and policy within the economics profession and in the broader public arena. It may even enhance the prospects for recovery in this decade, and for stability and growth in the longer run.

Of course we have a long way to go, both to restore prosperity to the world and to restore realistic common sense to discussion and decision about economic policy. But the beginnings of recovery that have brightened the economic news this year, mainly in the United States, can be credited to Keynesian policies, however reluctant, belated, or inadvertent. Our Federal Reserve finally took mercy on the economy about a year ago and suspended its monetarist targets. Its easing of monetary policy saved the world financial system from dangerous crisis and averted further collapse of economic activity. At the same time, American fiscal measures began to exert a powerful expansionary influence on aggregate demand. This Keynesian policy was, of course, fortuitous in its timing and unintentional in its motivation. It was a combination of tax cuts, rationalized by anti-Keynesian supply-side arguments, and increased defense spending. Whatever one may think of the distributional equity and allocational efficiency of these measures, they are increasing private and public spending on goods and services and creating jobs. Every business economist and forecaster knows that, even if his boss's speeches deplore federal deficits as the principal threat to recovery.

In the battle for the hearts and minds of economists and of the thoughtful lay public, the tide may also have turned. The devastating effects of Thatcher policies on the United Kingdom, and of Volcker policies in this country after October 1979, have opened many eyes and minds. The idea that monetary disinflation would be painless, if only the resolve of the authorities to pursue it relentlessly were clearly announced and understood, proved to be as illusory as Keynesians predicted. Monetarism—both of the older Friedman version stressing adherence to money stock targets and of the newer rational expectations variety—has been badly discredited. The stage has been set for recovery in the popularity of Keynesian diagnoses and remedies. I do not mean to imply, of course, that there is some Keynesian truth, vintage 1936 or 1961, to which economists and policymakers will or should now return, ignoring the lessons of economic events and of developments in economics itself over these last turbulent fifteen years. I do mean that in the new intellectual synthesis which I hope and expect will emerge to replace the divisive controversies and chaotic debates on macroeconomic policies, Keynesian ideas will have a prominent place.

The Postwar Record

A strong case can be made for the success of Keynesian policies. Virtually all advanced democratic capitalist societies adopted, in varying degrees, Keynesian strategies of demand management after World War II. The period, certainly until 1973, was one of unparalleled prosperity, growth, expansion of world trade, and stability. Unemployment was low, and the business cycle was tamed. The disappointments of the 1970s—inflation, stagflation, recessions and unemployment resulting from anti-inflationary policies—discredited Keynesian policies. But after all, the Vietnam inflation occurred when President Johnson rejected the advice of his Keynesian economists and refused to raise taxes to pay for his war. The recoveries of 1971–73 and 1975–79 ended in double-digit inflation in the United States. But the Yom Kippur war of 1973, OPEC, and the Ayatollah Khomeini were scarcely the endogenous consequences of those recoveries or of the monetary and fiscal policies that stimulated or accommodated them. Indeed, the main reason for pessimism about recovery today is the likelihood that excessive caution, based on misreading of or overreaction to the 1970s, will inhibit policy for recovery in the 1980s. If so, we will pay dearly in unemployment, lost production, and stagnant investment to insure against another burst of inflation.

But if we Keynesians need feel no compulsion to be apologetic, neither are we entitled to be complacent. Keynes did not provide, nor did his various followers over the years, a recipe for avoiding unstable inflation at full employment. The dilemma, though it became spectacularly severe in the last fifteen years, is an old one. It was recognized and prophesied by Keynesians like Joan Robinson and Abba Lerner in the early 1940s, when commitments to full-employment policies after the war seemed likely, and it was a practical concern of policymakers throughout the postwar period. It still remains the major problem of macroeconomic policy. Keynesians cannot accept—nor will, I think, the politics of modern democracies—the monetarist resolution of the dilemma, which amounts simply to redefining as full employment whatever unemployment rate, however high, seems necessary to ensure price stability. But we cannot ignore the possible inflationary results of gearing macroeconomic policies simply to the achievement of employment rates that seem "full" by some other criterion. The politics of modern democracies will not allow that either. I shall return to this central issue later.

Keynes on Macroeconomic Policy

It is time now to say more about what Keynesian policies are. Actually, *The General Theory* itself contains little in the way of concrete policy recommendations; for the most part, those are left for the reader to infer. But Keynes was, of course, an active participant in policy debates in the United Kingdom in the 1920s and 1930s. One evident purpose of *The General Theory* was to provide a professional analytical foundation for the policy positions he had been advocating in those debates.

Keynes opposed Britain's return in 1925 to the 1914 parity of sterling with gold and the U.S. dollar. His arguments were summarized in *The Economic Consequences of Mr. Churchill*, who was chancellor of the exchequer at the time. More from shrewd realism than from theory, Keynes based his opposition on a view he held consistently thereafter and formally expounded in *The General Theory*: the downward inflexibility of money wages. He predicted, correctly in the event, that making wage costs fall to correct the overvaluation of the pound would be difficult, socially disruptive, and economically costly. He thought that workers and their unions would accept lower real wages accomplished by a lower exchange value of sterling and higher prices for imports, while they would resist the equivalent adjustment via cuts in money wages. Once the fateful decision he opposed was taken, moreover, Keynes advocated government leadership in bringing about a smooth reduction of nominal wages. This advice, too, was ignored. Britain entered a long period of industrial strife, mass unemployment, and depression.

In 1929 the Liberal party, led by Lloyd George, proposed during its unsuccessful electoral campaign a program of public works to relieve unemployment. Keynes supported the proposal in his pamphlet with H. D. Henderson, *Can Lloyd George Do It?* There and in his later testimony before the Macmillan Committee, Keynes refuted what came to be known as the "Treasury View." In modern parlance, this view was that public-works outlays, financed by borrowing, would "crowd out" private borrowing, investment, and employment one hundred percent. The U.K. Treasury, like other exponents of crowding-out scenarios in other countries and at other times, made no distinction between situations of idle and fully employed resources. Keynes pointed out how public and private saving generated by public-works activity, and overseas borrowing as well, would moderate the crowding out the Treasury feared and how the Bank of England could be accommodative. Of course, only after the famous multiplier paper by Keynes's student R. F. Kahn, stimulated by this very controversy, could Keynes develop a full rationale for his position.

The reigning governments would neither adjust the exchange rate nor adopt expansionary fiscal measures. Keynes was therefore led for macroeconomic reasons to favor a general tariff, in effect a devaluation of sterling for merchandise transactions only. When Britain was finally forced to devalue sterling in 1931, Keynes lost interest in the tariff, though one was enacted anyway. Keynes was, of course, quite aware of the "beggar-my-neighbor" aspects of devaluations and tariffs, but in the British policy discussions he was a Briton. *The General Theory*, fortunately, is cast in a closed economy, interpretable as the whole world, and thus excludes nationalistic solutions.

The general characteristics of Keynes's policy interventions are clear from these examples. Keynes consistently focused on real economic outcomes, to which he subordinated nominal and financial variables, prices, interest rates, and exchange rates. He naturally and unproblematically attributed to governments the power and the responsibility to improve macroeconomic performance. Keynes was a pragmatic problem solver, always ready to figure out what to do in the circumstances of the time. These characteristics carried through to his policy career after *The General Theory*, his effective contributions to British war finance and international monetary architecture.

What does *The General Theory* itself say about policy? Fiscal policy, long regarded as the main Keynesian instrument, is introduced obliquely as a means of beefing up a weak national propensity to spend. Keynes warns against budget surpluses built by overly prudent sinking funds. He advocates redistribution through the fisc in favor of poorer citizens with higher propensities to consume. He welcomes public investment but deplores the political fact that business opposition to productive public investments limits their scope; nonetheless, intrinsically useless projects will enrich society if the resources directly and indirectly employed would otherwise be idle. Keynesian theory of fiscal policy was developed by others, notably Alvin Hansen and the members of his Harvard Fiscal Policy Seminar.

The Role of Money

Keynes was ambivalent on monetary policy. For fifteen or twenty years following publication of *The General Theory*, many economists, more in England than America, used the authority of the book to dismiss or downgrade the macroeconomic importance of money. Their reasons were first, the apparent insensitivity of investment and saving to interest rates during the 1930s, and second, the observed insensitivity of interest rates to money supplies in the same period. Keynes's own views were more subtle. Though he originated the "liquidity trap" and exploited it in his theoretical attack on the "classical" theory of unemployment, in his discussions of monetary policy he did not regard it as a typical circumstance or as an excuse for inaction by central banks. Neither did he regard investment decisions as beyond the reach of interest rates. His skepticism arose from his belief that the long-run expectations governing the marginal efficiency of capital are so volatile and unsystematic that central banks might well be unable to offset them by varying interest rates. Yet he thought they should try, arguing for example that mature investment booms should be prolonged by reductions in interest rates, not killed by monetary tightening.

The same view led Keynes in *The General Theory* to advocate some "socialization" of investment. This idea is not spelled out. Apparently Keynes had in mind not only public capital formation and tax policies affecting private investment, but more comprehensive, though cooperative, interventions in private investment decisions. Moreover, he had in mind not only cyclical stabilization but a long-run push to saturate the economy with capital and accomplish "the euthanasia of the rentier." Perhaps Jean Monnet's postwar "indicative planning" in France, where government sponsored a coordinated raising of sights to overcome pessimism and lift investment, is an example of what Keynes had in mind. Perhaps some of the Swedish measures designed to make investment less procyclical are another example.

Finally, I want to call attention to Keynes's habit of regarding wage determination as subject to "policy." This is evident in *The General Theory* as well as in the pamphleteering cited above. In the book, Keynes discusses stable versus flexible money wages as an issue open to social choice. He regards cyclical stability of nominal wages not only as likely but as preferable to flexibility. In a famous passage, he notes that monetary expansion and wage reduction are equivalent ways of attaining higher employment and observes that only "foolish" and "inexperienced" persons would prefer the latter to the former. His frequent references to "wage policy" do not fit very well with his attempt at the outset of *The General Theory* to build his story of involuntary unemployment on the competitive foundations of Marshallian economics. But in policy matters Keynes was a shrewd and practical observer, and it would not be farfetched to infer from his hints that he expected and advocated direct government interventions in the wage-setting process.

Keynesian Principles of Macroeconomic Policy

The theory of macroeconomic policy, the subject of bitter controversy today, really developed after World War II and after Keynes's death. The principles of what came to be known as Keynesian policies were expounded in the postwar "neoclassical synthesis" by Paul Samuelson and others. They occupied the mainstream of economics until the powerful monetarist and new classical counterrevolutions of the last fifteen years. They were the intellectual foundations of official U.S. policies in the Kennedy–Johnson years, when the media discovered them and somewhat misleadingly called them the "New Economics." They are expounded in the 1962 Economic Report of the Kennedy Council of Economic Advisers.

Let me review those principles, with particular reference to the items that are now particularly controversial, some of which are explicitly rejected by U.S. policymakers, as well as by those of other countries, notably the Thatcher government.

The first principle, obviously and unambiguously Keynesian, is the explicit dedication of macroeconomic policy instruments to real economic goals, in particular full employment and real growth of national output. This has never meant, in theory or in practice, that nominal outcomes, especially price inflation, were to be ignored. In the early 1960s, for example, the targets for unemployment and real GNP were chosen with cautious respect for the inflation risks. Today, however, a popular anti-Keynesian view is that macroeconomic policies can and should be aimed solely at nominal targets, for prices and/or nominal GNP, letting private "markets" determine the consequences for real economic variables.

Second, Keynesian demand management is activist, responsive to the actually observed state of the economy and to projections of its paths under various policy alternatives. The anti-Keynesian counterrevolutionaries scorn activist macroeconomic management as "fine-tuning" and "stop-go" and allege that it is destabilizing. The disagreement refers partly to the sources of destabilizing shocks. Keynesians believe, as did Keynes himself, that such shocks are endemic and epidemic in market capitalism; that government policymakers, observing the shocks and their effects, can partially but significantly offset them; and that the expectations induced by successful demand management will themselves be stabilizing. (Of course, Keynesians have by no means relied entirely on discretionary responsive policies; they have also tried to design and build automatic stabilizers into the fiscal and financial systems.) The opponents believe that government itself is the chief source of destabilizing shocks to an otherwise stable system; that neither the wisdom nor the intentions of policymakers can be trusted; and the stability of policies mandated by nondiscretionary rules, blind to actual events and forecasts, are the best we can do. When this stance is combined with concentration on nominal outcomes, the results of recent experience in Thatcher's Britain and Volcker's America are not hard to understand.

Third, Keynesians have wished to put both fiscal and monetary policies in consistent and coordinated harness in the pursuit of macroeconomic objectives. Any residual skepticism about the relevance and effectiveness of monetary policy vanished early in the postwar era, certainly in the United States though less so in Britain. Keynesians have, of course, opposed the use of macroeconomically irrelevant norms like budget balance as guides to policy. They have, however, pointed out that monetary and fiscal instruments in combination provide sufficient degrees of freedom to pursue demand-management objectives in combination with whatever priorities a democratic society chooses for other objectives. For example, Keynesian stabilization policies can be carried out with large or small government sectors, progressive or regressive tax and transfer structures, and high or low investment and saving as fractions of full-employment GNP. In these respects, latter-day Keynesians have been more optimistic than the author of *The General Theory*: they believe that measures to create jobs do not have to be wasteful and need not focus exclusively on bolstering the national propensity to consume. The idea that the fiscal-monetary mix can be chosen to accelerate national capital formation, if that is a national priority, is a contribution of the so-called neoclassical synthesis. Disregard of the idea since 1980 is the source of many of the current problems of U.S. macroeconomic policy, which may not only be inadequate to promote recovery but also perversely designed to inhibit national investment at a time when greater provision for the future is a widely shared social priority.

Fourth, as I observed earlier, Keynesians have not been optimistic that fiscal and monetary policies of demand management are sufficient to achieve both real and nominal goals, to obtain simultaneously both full employment and stability of prices or inflation rates. Neither are Keynesians prepared, as monetarist and new classical economists and policymakers often appear to be, to resolve the dilemma tautologically by calling "full employment" whatever unemployment rate results from policies that stabilize prices.

Every American administration from Kennedy to Carter, possibly excepting Ford, has felt the need to have some kind of wage-price policy. This old dilemma remains the greatest challenge; Keynesian economists differ among themselves, as well as with those of different macroeconomic persuasions, on how to resolve it. It may be ironically true that, thanks to good luck and to the severity of the depression—the two Eisenhower-Martin recessions of the late 1950s helped pave the way for an inflation-free Keynesian recovery in the early 1960s, and the Volcker depression may do the same—revival of inflation is unlikely during recovery in the 1980s, just when policymakers are acutely afraid of it. But it would be foolish to count on that, even more to assume the problem has permanently disappeared.

The Need for Incomes Policy

The need for a third category of policy instruments—in addition to fiscal and monetary, the "wage policy" hinted in *The General Theory*—is clear to me. We can and should push other measures to reduce the expected value of the NAIRU (the nonaccelerating-inflation rate of unemployment). These include standard labor market, manpower, and human capital policies. They include attacks on the legislative sacred cows that impart floors to some wages and prices and bias upward the price response to aggregate demand stimulus. They include encouragement to new arrangements for labor compensation, substituting shares in performances and fortunes of employers for exclusive reliance on administered or negotiated scales of pay for labor time. They include measures to make collective bargaining more responsive to those workers with greater risks of unemployment. But even if everything is done that realistically can be done, politically and economically, on these fronts, I believe we will need incomes policies in our arsenal. The challenge is to design policies that labor and management will accept in the interests of better macroeconomic performance—policies that will not be so rigid and heavy-handed in microeconomic impact as to entail heavy costs in allocational efficiency. I myself believe that guideposts, to which compliance is induced by tax-based rewards, offer the greatest promise. But the subject is still wide open.

Until Keynesians design the instrument missing from their kit of tools, we cannot press with the full conviction and confidence merited by theory and history the superiority of Keynesian policies to the anti-Keynesian policies of recent experience.

Politics and Ideology

In the near half-century since the debut of *The General Theory*, Keynesian macroeconomics has been identified politically and ideologically with liberalism, in the modern rather than the nineteenth-century meaning of that word. Although prior to 1979, conservative governments—Republican in the United States and Conservative in Britain—practiced Keynesian demand management, its main proponents have been liberal parties: Democratic in this country, Labour in the United Kingdom, social-democratic parties elsewhere. Certainly Keynes has never been accepted in the ideological pantheon of business and finance, despite the efforts of groups like the Committee for Economic Development in the United States to define a pragmatic synthesis. The lines are drawn more sharply than ever now that conservative movements with ideologies explicitly condemning Keynes and Keynesian policies have gained influence and power.

The reasons for business interests to reject Keynes are not entirely clear. Keynes himself thought the implications of his theory were moderately conservative. He found no fault with the way capitalist systems allocated employed resources. (These days, with externalities more apparent and hazardous, he might be less confident.) He wanted to employ more resources—to the benefit of claimants to profits as well as to job-seekers, as experience repeatedly testifies. The fiscal and financial shibboleths he challenged, and often ridiculed, were obstacles to general prosperity, not just to the well-being of workers. Compared to the revolutionary institutional changes threatened by other critics of capitalism's failures in the Great Depression, the reforms prescribed by Keynes were mild and conservative indeed. Perhaps the instinctive revulsion of conservatives was due to the suspicion that the liberation of government from traditional norms and the assignment to government of powers and responsibilities for overall economic performance would expose capitalists to unpredictable social, political, and economic hazards. Perhaps businessmen feared that full employment would cost them more by tilting bargaining power toward labor than it would gain them in the fruits of prosperity. Perhaps they felt intuitively that they really were being displaced from the temples of their civilization.

Organized labor has found Keynesian economics selectively congenial. Its interest in jobs coincides with the full-employment emphasis of Keynesian macroeconomic policies. But labor's support of price-increasing measures and unions' representation of senior employed workers at the expense of the unemployed worsen the agony of the trade-off and cripple full-employment policies. Moreover, it has been difficult, to say the least, to obtain and maintain labor's acceptance of incomes policies. Political parties that espouse Keynesian policies are also those which depend on nonbusiness interest groups for campaign support. The public does not make distinctions obvious to economists, and many opponents of those interests mistakenly associate Keynesian economics with all sorts of dubious microeconomic interventions.

There is, however, a sense in which Keynesian economics is a natural ally of liberalism. In the same passage where Keynes exonerated capitalism of allocational inefficiency, he faulted it for inequality of wealth as well as for chronic underemployment. There is nothing particularly Keynesian about the welfare state, which in greater or lesser degree has grown in every democratic capitalist country since World War II. Keynesian macroeconomists could take any side of controversies about social security, socialized medicine, food stamps, and the like. Nevertheless, Keynesian economics at a minimum provides a license for welfare-state measures and other government efforts toward redistribution of wealth. The license is the faith that macroeconomic stabilization and prosperity are compatible with a wide range of social policies, that modern capitalism and democracy are robust enough to prosper and progress while being humane and equitable. That faith conflicts with the visions of extreme Right and Left, which agree that extremes of wealth and poverty, of security and insecurity, are indispensable to the functioning of capitalism. Keynesian policies helped to confound those dismal prophecies in the past; I think they will do so again.

2

Wall Street's View of Keynes and Keynes's View of Wall Street

Peter L. Bernstein

Wall Street's view of Keynes is not nearly as illuminating as Keynes's view of Wall Street. Indeed, imbedded there are the central ideas that form the core of his theories about the sources of disequilibrium. We all know about the stock market and the beauty contest, of course, but that is only one facet of how Keynesian theory and the financial community are interwoven with each other. It is ironic, as I shall demonstrate shortly, that this is also where Wall Street is most stubbornly opposed to accepting what Keynes had to say.

Therefore, I must begin with a few observations about the view from Wall Street before reversing the process and looking at the matter from Keynes's vantage point. These observations stem from a questionnaire that I mailed in June 1983 to a representative group of senior institutional investors and portfolio managers, the details of which are in the appendix to this paper.

The questionnaire set forth what I consider to be the primary elements of Keynesian economics and then asked the respondents to indicate strong disagreement, disagreement, neutrality, agreement, or strong agreement. The results suggest that this generation of Wall Streeters understands more about how our economy works than their predecessors did.

Wall Streeters agree that fiscal policy is the preferred method for offsetting an excessive propensity to save, that the interest rate sets the price of liquidity rather than the price of savings, and that the stock market is a critical determinant of the rate of real investment. They are not repulsed by the thought that monetary policy is preferable to wage cuts as a means of overcoming unemployment, and on balance they are doubtful that the economy tends naturally toward high employment equilibrium with optimal conditions of costs and profits.

On the other hand, I was surprised at their clear disagreement with two statements in the questionnaire—although perhaps these disagreements reveal Wall Street's true sentiments about the sources of disequilibrium. The first statement was:

> Wealthy economies have higher savings rates than poor economies and are therefore more vulnerable to high rates of unemployment.

The second statement was:

> Since the stock market is nothing more than a beauty contest in
> which the objective is to pick the girl that everyone else thinks is the
> prettiest, its influence on the rate and direction of investment is
> for the worse, not for the better.

Ninety percent of the responses on the savings-rate statement were
strong disagreement or disagreement, even though about half the people had
agreed with the statement that the economy did not tend naturally toward full-
employment equilibrium. While admittedly unemployment is a terrible problem in the poor as well as the wealthier economies at this moment, it would be
difficult to argue that unemployment has spread from the poor nations to the
wealthy rather than the other way around. I would also admit that oversaving,
as we once described it, is an obsolete concept in today's world; nevertheless,
growth and economic development have—until very recently—been much
more rapid and consistent in the less developed economies than in Western
Europe or the United States.

Tempting as this matter may be for further discussion, I turn instead to
the second statement—the impact of Wall Street on the investment process—
because it is closer to my topic and, more important, because it is closer to
Keynes's most valuable contributions to the analysis of the sources of economic disequilibrium.

Although nearly fifty years have passed since the appearance of *The
General Theory*, with its famous chapter on long-term expectations, the leop-
ards on Wall Street have not changed their spots one bit. Well-organized and
liquid stock exchanges are still driven by professional investors, whose primary goal is not just to beat the market but, cheered on by greedy clients, to outdo
one another in a brutal, short-term performance horse race. How can these
very players fail to recognize that this process inevitably leads to mispricing
assets, when they so clearly enjoy the wild spins of the takeover game on the
undervalued side and then go on, obsessively and repeatedly, to overvalue
other companies, only to toss them overboard later when the bubble bursts and
the fad passes?

The inability of these investors to understand—or at least to accept as
valid—Keynes's parable about the beauty contest is strong evidence that Wall
Street's view of him is, in the gentlest terms, blurred. Keynes's point, you will
remember, was that, unlike direct investments by owner-managers, organized
investment markets permit frequent revaluations of old investments and that
these revaluations exert a "decisive influence" on the pace of new investment.
The difficulty arises because these revaluations

> . . . are governed by the average expectation of those who deal
> on the Stock Exchange . . . rather than by the genuine expectations
> of the professional entrepreneur (1936, p. 151). . . . We devote
> our intelligences to anticipate what average opinion expects the
> average opinion to be. (1936, p. 156)

Consequently, the mispricing of assets is not only an inevitable but also an *inherent* characteristic of liquid security markets.

The durability of Keynes's accusations is proof of how acute his perceptions were; but this was by no means all that he had to say about why the financial markets are the primary source of disequilibrium in the real economy. His entire analysis of the disruptive influence of the investment community on output and employment was his unique insight, stemming, no doubt, from his own lively experience in the world of money and finance.

Although Adam Smith, Ricardo, Malthus, and Marx had all identified various sources of difficulty in the functioning of a market-driven capitalistic economy, none of them had pointed to the financial sector for the origins of trouble. This was hinted at in the Marshallian k—idle cash balances or uninvested savings—and explored from the opposite viewpoint of excessive circulating media in Wicksell and the Austrian School. Harrod and Hawtrey, closer to Keynes, were becoming more sensitive to it, but the impact of financial markets on real economic decisions is the *central* drama of the Keynesian system. It is on Wall Street and Lombard Street, not in the factories or on the farm or even on Pennsylvania Avenue and Westminster, that the critical decisions are made.

This view was not special to *The General Theory*. I am unaware of any of Keynes's work in economics that does not concentrate on financial or monetary matters. Furthermore, he concentrates less on the mechanics of monetary and security transactions than on their institutional and psychological features. Generally, he finds that their influence on the real economy leads to a "job-. . . likely to be ill-done," precisely because the psychological motivations of the participants lead to unwanted outcomes.

I have already touched on his view of how the liquidity of the stock exchange illustrates this unfortunate tendency, and I shall shortly show how the same view permeates the rest of his theoretical structure, but two additional brief comments on the functioning of the stock market may be helpful.

The ratio of the dividend paid on a stock to the price of the stock in the market, which we conventionally refer to as the yield on the stock, is considered by most people to be determined by investors, who presumably set the price that they will pay for the dividend. This view, however, ignores the two-sided aspect of a ratio. Investors may set the price, but corporate managements set the dividend. Thus, both parties participate in the determination of the yield. A dividend change reflects a shift in management's view of the future; a price change reflects a shift in the investor's view.

Since yields are variable over time, it is clear that prices and dividends move independently of each other. Or, to put it another way, managements and investors frequently disagree about the value of companies traded on the exchanges. What this means, in sum, is that Keynes was absolutely correct in asserting that liquid exchanges lead to valuations that will differ significantly from valuations made by owner-managers.[1]

Second, as Keynes believes that the liquidity provided by the exchanges leads them to acquire the characteristics of a casino, he suggests that they should, ''in the public interest, be inaccessible and expensive.'' He wants a high ''jobber's turn'' and transfer taxes. Precisely the opposite has occurred in Wall Street, where brokerage commissions on large transactions are now essentially *de minimus* and where trading activity is dominated by investors exempt from capital-gains taxes. As a result, the reasons for his concerns are, if anything, more compelling today than they were fifty years ago.

Inherent obstacles to optimal outcomes are by no means limited to the stock market. Its senior sibling, the bond market, provides its fair share of distortions as well. The source of the difficulty is in fact identical: the psychological motivations of investors in an environment of liquid markets and daily revaluations of assets.

Although Keynes's discussion of interest rates and the incentives to liquidity in Chapter 15 of *The General Theory* never refers back to the state of long-term expectations analyzed in Chapter 12, he describes the nature of the problem in almost the same words:

. . . the rate of interest is a highly conventional, rather than a highly psychological, phenomenon. For its actual value is largely governed by the prevailing view of what its value is expected to be. *Any* level of interest which is accepted with sufficient conviction as *likely* to be durable *will* be durable. (1936, p. 203)

This means that the rate of interest can remain for long periods of time at levels that are too high to lead to and sustain full employment, particularly with ''a fickle and highly unstable marginal efficiency of capital'' (1936, p. 204).

The causes of an excessively sticky long-term rate of interest go deeper than the beauty-contest syndrome. Remember that interest, in the Keynesian system, is a reward for parting with liquidity or, to use another of his phrases, ''the current earnings from illiquidity.'' These earnings are more than a reward. They are ''a sort of insurance premium to offset the risk of loss on capital account.'' As the rate of interest declines, therefore, the lender faces more than just a shrinkage in the reward he might earn. Much more important, the lower interest income provides less protection against losing principal if interest rates should rise after the investor has bought the bond.

This is the genesis of the liquidity trap, in which the long-term rate of interest refuses to fall below some minimum level, no matter how much money the central bank pumps into the system. In view of the volatility of long-term bond prices, in other words, lenders will refuse to part with long-term money unless they are assured of a minimum flow of coupon income sufficient to cover capital losses if they need their money back prior to the maturity of the bond. In a deeply depressed economy, this required return may well be higher than the marginal efficiency of capital.

The trap in which we find ourselves today is even more vicious than the liquidity trap of the 1920s because it will catch us at both ends. No one has figured out how to wriggle out of it.

From 1951 to 1981, bond investors suffered large nominal losses, but their losses in real terms were far worse. As this painful experience entered the memory bank of these investors, their minimum required return grew larger and larger. At each successive trough in long-term bond yields—that is, at the peaks of the brief bull moves in bond prices that interrupted the extended bear market—the level of yields was consistently higher than at the preceding bull-market peak. It was also systematically higher, reflecting the magnitude of the capital losses in the intervening bear move. The bigger the beating, the more modest the subsequent recovery in bond prices (see Bernstein, 1980, 1981, and 1982).

Thus, Keynes was correct in identifying the long-term interest rate as something more than a reward for parting with liquidity. The psychological and conventional features of long-term interest rates have built in an insurance premium to offset losses on capital from bond-price declines so that, on a total-return basis, the investor can hope to come out whole even in a bear market. These features, however, tend to make long-term interest rates much stickier than short-term rates.

This explains the painful trap in which we find ourselves at this very moment. Just as in the 1930s, long-term interest rates hang in far above the current rate of inflation, reflecting the determination of lenders to avoid repetition of the ghastly losses of real wealth and income inflicted on them during the past thirty years.

On the other hand, unlike the 1930s, we are unable to treat this malaise by pumping a great supply of money into the system. This only agitates painful memories of the past and threatens to drive nominal interest rates to levels even more ridiculous relative to inflation than they are now.

Keynes hit it right on the button. If ever we had to live with a level of interest rates "accepted as *likely* to be durable," it is this one. It is indeed "a highly conventional phenomenon."

But if Keynes recognized a profound source of disequilibrium in the psychological and conventional features of the bond market, that was child's play compared to what he perceived in the role of money itself. Money is the mother lode of all the diseases with which the financial sector infects the real economy. Whereas classical economic theory takes a cool view of money as a means of exchange and Marshall recognized its qualities as a store of value, Keynes condemned money as being the residue of anxiety and uncertainty. Otherwise, he asks, why "should anyone outside a lunatic asylum wish to use money as a store of wealth?" (1937, p. 216).

In a marvelous passage, he goes on to conclude that "The possession of actual money lulls our disquietude; and the premium which we require to make us part with money is the measure of our disquietude" (1937, p. 213).

Hyman Minsky, who has so effectively linked Keynesian theory to the analysis of financial disorder, has elaborated on this concept of money by bringing it right back to the heart of the financial community and Wall Street.

He points out that the principal motive for holding money is that payments are due in the future; he who has no payments to make has no need for money. The necessity to make those payments is usually certain, but

> . . . cash flows depend upon system behavior [so that] both bankers and their borrowing business clients want margins of safety. . . . Liquidity is the attribute of assets that enable them to provide margins of safety and *the liquidity of any asset other than money depends upon the behavior of financial institutions and markets* (1984, p. 7, emphasis added).

Wall Street is very much in the business of making liquidity the attribute of assets that might not have much liquidity without it—stocks, bonds, and short-term paper, to say nothing of bank balances and longer-term obligations denominated in nondollar currencies. The trouble is that Wall Street is not a central bank: Wall Street is a community of profit-seeking organizations that share the needs, drives, uncertainties, and disquietudes of their customers.

These are precisely the reasons why "the job is likely to be ill-done." The interposition of money and related financial instruments between the accumulation of real capital assets and the production of goods and services for final use is almost bound to lead to instability and even chaos on a periodic basis.

If you take these observations as brickbats thrown at Wall Street, you miss the whole point. Quite the contrary. What distinguishes the economics of John Maynard Keynes from the economics of his predecessors and from most of his followers is *the explicit recognition of uncertainty as the inescapable companion to the human condition.* As he put it in a famous passage on the difficulties of foretelling the future, "We simply do not know" (1937, p. 213). Liquidity—our uses for it and the institutions we have created to provide it—is an integral component of our defenses against uncertainty.

There are two related ways to confront uncertainty. One is to make decisions that are reversible so that we can deal with surprise. The other is to hold assets whose nominal value is certain, or even better whose real values are certain, so that the passage of time will not matter.

What Keynes has made us recognize is that we deal with uncertainty by creating institutions that can make real economic decisions reversible and then we make them reversible into cash. If Wall Street were a source only of *finance* for enterprise, the system would function differently. Wall Street, however, is much more than that: it is also a source of *liquidity* that enables us to meet our financial obligations as they fall due.

The ultimate source of trouble is that Wall Street does not create liquidity. It can only mobilize liquidity and then trade its inventory of it with those who need it. In an uncertain world, where equity decisions are based on distorted beauty contests, where lending decisions are biased by memories of past errors, where money is both limited in supply but subject to unlimited demands for its use, the miracle of it all is that the job is done as well as it is!

Note

1. I have analyzed this phenomenon in detail in a paper in the Fall 1983 issue of the *Journal of Post Keynesian Economics*.

References

Bernstein, Peter L. "Collective Memories and Long-Term Interest Rates." Presentation to the Financial Analysts Federation Investment Workshop, Princeton, July 22, 1980.
————. "The Limits and Consequences of the Bull Market in Bonds." Memorandum to clients, December 1, 1981.
————. "The Gibson Paradox Revisited." *The Financial Review*, Fall 1982.
Keynes, J. M. *The General Theory of Employment, Interest, and Money*. New York: Harcourt Brace and Company, 1936.
————. "The General Theory of Employment." *Quarterly Journal of Economics*, February 1937, pp. 209–223.
Minsky, Hyman P. "Frank Hahn's *Money and Inflation*: A Review Article." *Journal of Post Keynesian Economics*, Vol. VI, No. 3, Spring 1984.

Appendix

To conduct the survey of institutional investment managers, we mailed a questionnaire to 192 subscribers to *Institutional Investor* magazine, the most widely read and authoritative publication in the field. We selected the names at random.

We received 21 replies. The questionnaire and the breakdown of the responses appear at the end of this appendix.

This is a test that could hardly stand up under the rigid scrutiny of statistical significance: the sample was small to begin with, and only 11 percent responded. On the other hand, the answers discussed in the text were so clearly distributed that they do deserve serious consideration as being representative. The distribution of institutions responding also suggests that the answers are generally representative of Wall Street opinion. Of course, the small response may simply indicate that Wall Street's view of Keynes is a blank!

Among those respondents who signed their names, we find the head of one of the biggest insurance companies; chief investment officers of a major mutual-fund complex, one of the largest trust companies, and a top-ranking investment-counsel firm; a vice-president of Merrill Lynch; several directors of research; the pension officer of a large industrial company, and a private investor.

Wall Street's Views on Keynes and Keynesian Policies

	Strongly Disagree	Disagree	Neutral	Agree	Strongly Agree
1. Our economy, left to itself, does *not* have a natural tendency toward equilibrium at full employment with optimal conditions of costs and profits.	4	3	3	8	3
2. The best was to assure that the rate of investment at least equals and, preferably, exceeds the amount that households and business firms want to save is through the use of fiscal policy.	1	3	8	8	1
3. The rate of interest is the price that equalizes the demand for liquidity with the supply of money. It does not equalize savings and investment.	2	3	1	13	2

	Strongly Disagree	Disagree	Neutral	Agree	Strongly Agree
4. In conditions of high unemployment, an increase in the supply of money will be a more effective instrument than cutting nominal wages if we want to raise the level of employment.	0	5	5	7	2
5. Long-term interest rates are relatively unimportant to business managers when they decide whether or not to acquire new plant and equipment.	0	5	5	7	2
6. Fears of capital losses on long-term bonds mean that there is a limit below which long-term interest rates are not likely to fall. Therefore, fiscal policy will be a much more potent instrument than monetary policy for controlling economic growth.	1	8	6	4	1
7. Wealthy economies have higher savings rates than poor economies and are therefore more vulnerable to high rates of unemployment.	7	12	1	1	0
8. The stock market has a significant impact on business decisions to invest in capital goods.	0	3	6	8	4
9. Since the stock market is nothing more than a beauty contest in which the objective is to pick the girl that everyone else thinks is the prettiest, its influence on the rate and direction of investment is for the worse, not for the better.	7	13	1	0	0
10. If I were forced to choose between Keynes and Milton Friedman as Chairman of the Council of Economic Advisers, I would choose Keynes.	5	4	1	6	5
11. If I were forced to choose between Keynes and Hayek as Chairman of the Council of Economic Advisers, I would choose Keynes.	4	2	7	3	4

All responses to this questionnaire are confidential, and are for the exclusive use of Peter Bernstein. However, it is often useful to know the identity of the respondent. Accordingly, we would appreciate your providing the additional information requested below—on a completely confidential basis:

Name of organization: _____

Your name and title: _____
Return to:
  Institutional Investor
  Attn: Statistical Department
  488 Madison Avenue
  New York, New York 10022
  (212) 832–8888 x 282

3

The Radical Keynes

Robert Lekachman

Since 1971 the Royal Economic Society, which Keynes served as secretary and editor of the *Economic Journal* during almost all his professional career, has been issuing with all deliberate speed two or three volumes in most years of Keynes's collected writings, so far as they pertain even tangentially to economics. As this centennial year draws to a close, the edition touches the number of thirty, complete save for a general index and bibliography.

I propose to concentrate upon the most fascinating portions of the collection, the thirteen volumes that deal with Keynes's activities. The general editors, Donald Moggridge and Elizabeth Johnson, appear to have collected almost every letter their hero wrote—fortunately for the history of economic ideas, their man kept carbon copies. The treasure trove within the "Activities" volumes include, in addition to the correspondence, memoranda, counsel to politicians, over two-hundred pages of testimony to the Macmillan Committee in 1929 and 1930, and an equal number immortalizing the frequently acrimonious relationship with Kingsley Martin, the durable editor during the 1930s of *The New Statesman*. As a frequent contributor to this journal and a member of its board, Keynes kept an impatient eye upon the twists and turns of an editorial policy that simultaneously opposed Hitler and British rearmament.

Here my objective is to distinguish the Keynes who palpitates through some thousands of pages of "Activities" with the textbook caricature. Here, I do discover myself in astonishing agreement with Norman Ture, though again on a single point, that Keynesians really are quite separable from Keynes. As Joan Robinson, who sadly no longer is available to speak sharply for herself, was wont to phrase it, the textbook writers have "bastardized" Keynes. Their Keynes turns out to be a rather mild fellow, willing to tinker with monetary and fiscal policy, the better to preserve capitalist arrangements with which he was for the most part content.

The Keynes who speaks to me resembles much more closely Joan Robinson's malcontent, critic of free enterprise, and independent radical. The literary style of this essay is about to improve dramatically because I plan to quote Keynes copiously in his own defense.

II

Even as a young man when, presumably, he was most influenced by the august Alfred Marshall and the only minimally less august A. C. Pigou, Keynes was strikingly skeptical about the wonders of free markets, the sanctity of the gold standard, and even—horrors!—the perfections of free trade. In 1914 he emitted these positively rude sentiments about gold:

> If it proves one of the after effects of the present struggle that gold is at last deposed from its despotic control over us and reduced to the position of a constitutional monarch, a new chapter of history will be opened. Man will have made another step forward in the attainment of self-government, in the power to control his fortunes according to his own wishes.''[1]

Or savor a more general statement of distaste for capitalism uttered two decades later in 1933:

> The decadent international but individualistic capitalism in the hands of which we found ourselves after the War, is not a success. It is not intelligent, it is not beautiful, it is not just, it is not virtuous—and it doesn't deliver the goods.[2]

I wish that I had said that.

Notoriously, scandalously, Keynes lacked faith in that essential of free-market doctrine, flexibility of wages and prices. In 1930 he dismissed wage cuts as the sovereign remedy for lingering depression: "It is not possible for the Bank of England to carry out a policy of producing enough unemployment to bring down wages."[3] Lord knows, they tried, much as our own Federal Reserve did in 1980, 1981, and most of 1982.

As for the miracles of equilibrium, I can do no better than quote from the master's posthumous article, an *Economic Journal* contribution dated June 1946:

> I do not suppose that the classical medicine will work by itself or that we can depend upon it. We need quicker and less painful aids of which exchange variation and overall import control are the most important.[4]

The radical Keynesians centered in Cambridge can cite their leader here as in a great many other instances to excellent effect.

As these and many dozens of other possible citations demonstrate, Keynes was a planner from quite a tender age. It is customary to retell old jokes about his inconsistencies. As the grandfather of the genre runs: Put five economists in a room and they will in short order produce six opinions, two of them Mr. Keynes's. The critics, friendly or malicious, miss the thread of consistency that runs through Keynes's policy recommendations over time and topic. Keynes was ready to intervene, to float a plan, invent a device, write a pamphlet, coax a politician, and tailor a program to resolve almost any difficulty. As an activist, Keynes sought the same ends: prosperity, growth, and high employment by whatever means shifting politics and economic circumstances seemed most likely to achieve them. Of course, Keynes was at times a free-trader, at others an advocate of revenue tariffs, and at still others an exponent of more complex policies. He never seemed to suffer guilt about intervening in the operations of markets whose perfections regularly eluded him.

Recall, for instance, his pamphlet *How to Pay for the War*, reprinted from several long articles in the London *Times*. The thrust of the argument was the use of forced savings as a check upon potential wartime inflation. Simultaneously Keynes grasped an opportunity to advance toward another goal, redistribution of postwar British national income in a more egalitarian fashion.

Plan, plan, plan. Harking back to the 1920s, when the British Depression began, nearly a decade in advance of the American phenomenon—in the north of England and Scotland where declining old industries like textiles, shipbuilding, and coal mining were concentrated—we encounter Keynes's remedy under the explicit rubric of "industrial policy." Keynes advised cartels, modernization of equipment, shrinkage in size, and government help. How often must the wheel be reinvented by our Rohatyns and Reichs? In the 1920s he advocated sectoral planning.

But he was perfectly agreeable to the contemplation of planning of wider scope. Here he is on the eve of World War II:

> In contemporary conditions we need, if we are to enjoy prosperity and profits, so much more central planning than we have at present that the reform of the economic system needs as much urgent attention if we have war as if we avoid it. The intensification of the trade cycle and the increasingly chronic character of unemployment have shown that private capitalism was already in its decline as a means of solving the economic problem. [5]

At the start of the same decade, Keynes commented approvingly upon a manifesto released by Sir Oswald Mosley, on the verge of leaving the Labour party en route to a career as a fascist and anti-Semite:

> But I like the spirit which informs the document. A scheme of national economic planning to achieve a right, or at least a better, balance of our industries between the old and the new, between agriculture and manufacture, between output for export and output for home consumption, between home development and foreign investment; and wide executive powers to carry out the details of such a scheme. That is what it amounts to.
>
> For the important question today . . . is the question whether those are right who think that the course of prudence and proved wisdom is to trust to time and natural forces to lead us with an invisible hand to the economic harmonies; or those who fear that there

is no design but our own, and that the invisible hand is merely
our own bleeding feet moving through pain and loss to an uncertain
and unprofitable destination.[6]

Keynes left no doubt that he vastly preferred "to substitute for the operation of
natural forces a scheme of collective planning."[7]

Ever on the lookout for action, Keynes even had a good word to spare for
Hjalmar Schacht and the Nazi economic policy that Schacht for a spell directed. What intrigued Keynes was the bilateral barter deals that Schacht negotiated with other countries. Could one stray further from the ethos of comparative
advantage than that?

In the context of Keynes's interventionist heresies, one should cite
Keynes's services on the Macmillan Committee in 1929 and 1930. That body
was charged with saying something constructive about antidepression policy.
Keynes played a dual role, as a committee member and as a witness. For six
days in the second capacity, he treated his colleagues to a masterly policy
presentation, in the course of which he worked his way through almost any
conceivable political therapy and arrived at conclusions that he had no doubt
reached before he began. There were two things to be done: one was a massive
public-works program, which reiterated the message of his electioneering
pamphlet for Lloyd George, *Can Lloyd George Do It?*, also a 1929 production.

His second recommendation was a revenue tariff. A year or two after the
Macmillan Committee disbanded, he justified his protectionist heresy in these
terms:

> There was a time when I denied the temporary usefulness of a
> tariff as a means of combating unemployment. I still think that a
> worldwide system of tariffs will increase unemployment in the
> world as a whole. But I should now admit that if we put on a tariff at
> a time of severe unemployment it would be likely to shift on to
> other countries some part of our own burden of unemployment.[8]

As with trade, so with investment as an activity equally eligible for
public control. Here is a representative 1943 comment:

> If two-thirds or three-quarters of total investment is carried out
> or can be influenced by public or semi-public bodies, a long-term
> programme of a stable character should be capable of reducing
> the potential range of fluctuation to much narrower limits than for-
> merly, when a smaller volume of investment was under public
> control and when even this part tended to follow, rather than to cor-
> rect, fluctuations of investment in the strictly private sector of the
> economy.[9]

And of course those of us who stayed the course to Chapter 24 of *The General
Theory* will recall Keynes's allusions, as almost throwaway lines to a "somewhat comprehensive socialisation of investment" and a redistribution of Brit-

ish income in the desirable direction of diminished inequality.

As a person and as an economist, Keynes never freed himself, nor desired to free himself, from the values of Bloomsbury. To this group his loyalty never flagged. His affectionate memoir, *My Early Beliefs*, delivered to a circle of intimates in the aftermath of a severe heart attack from which he was incompletely recovered, made it clear that Bloomsbury's exaltation of beauty and friendship comprised still his underlying "religion." Bloomsbury often set the tone of his economic utterances. Here is a 1942 sample of his attitude toward the values of life after war ends:

> Where we are using up resources, do not let us submit to the vile doctrine of the nineteenth century that every enterprise must justify it- self in pounds, shillings and pence of cash income, with no other denominator of value but this. I should like to see that war memorials of this tragic struggle take the shape of an enrichment of the civic life of every great centre of population. Why should we not set aside, let us say, £50 millions a year for the next twenty years to add in every substantial city of the realm the dignity of an ancient university or a European capital to our local schools and to their surround- ings, to our local government and its offices, and above all perhaps to provide a local centre of refreshment and entertainment with an ample theatre, a concert hall, a gallery, a British restaurant, canteens, cafés and so forth. Assuredly we can afford this and much more.[10]

On tariffs, Bloomsbury impelled him to transcend mundane demonstra- tions of benign employment consequences:

> For anyone who does not imprison his mind in a strait-jacket, must know, as well as you and I do, that the pursuit of agriculture is part of a complete national life. I said above that a prosperous motor industry was a national necessity, if only to give an opening to one kind of typical Englishman. It is true in the same way that another kind needs as his pursuit in life the care and breeding of do- mestic animals and contact with the changing seasons and the soil. To say that the country cannot afford agriculture is to delude oneself about the meaning of the word "afford." A country which cannot afford art or agriculture, invention or tradition, is a country in which one cannot afford to live.[11]

No wonder Keynes had little patience with his colleagues and seldom rated economists very high. There is his frequently cited aspiration for the profession that they will one day become as useful as plumbers, technicians who appear to fix up the small troubles of our households. Here is Keynes in 1932 on the same theme:

> For the next twenty-five years . . . economists, at present the most incompetent, will be nevertheless the most important, group of

scientists in the world.[12]

Keynes, a usually optimistic soul, obviously underestimated the "horrid! interval, when these creatures matter."

Let us demolish the canard that toward the end of his life Keynes became, like lesser men as they age, more conservative. In support of this allegation, there is a frequently recalled compliment to the still-living Hayek. In 1944, soon after Hayek's *Road to Serfdom* appeared, Keynes wrote a pleasant letter to its author; possibly he had in mind all the unpleasant things he had said about Hayek over the years. Here is the blurb at issue: " . . . it is a grand book. We all have the greatest reason to be grateful to you for saying so well what needs so much to be said."[13] Did Keynes really endorse Hayek's individualistic apprehensions about state action and the slippery slope downward from social security to fascism? Listen, if you will, to some other sentiments in the same letter:

> I should . . . conclude your theme rather differently. I should say
> that what we want is not no planning, or even less planning, indeed, I
> should say that we almost certainly want more. But the planning
> should take place in a community in which as many people as possi-
> ble, both leaders and followers, wholly share your own moral po-
> sition. Moderate planning will be safe if those carrying it out are
> rightly oriented in their own minds and hearts to the moral is-
> sue.[14]

One hopes that for Hayek's peace of mind he stopped reading after the compliments ended.

It is wrong to impute a party line to the fierce individualists within the Bloomsbury circle. E. M. Forster's celebrated hope that, put to the choice, he would find the courage to betray his country rather than a friend probably echoed the sentiments of most of G. E. Moore's disciples. Keynes was not one to swallow whole even *Principia Ethica*, Moore's guide to proper conduct. Early and late, and never more intensely than during World War II, Keynes was an unashamed British patriot of a quite traditional variety. On October 14, 1939, in *The New Statesman*, he aired his disgust at some of the things that very journal was printing:

> The intelligentsia of the left were the loudest in demanding that
> the Nazi aggression should be resisted at all costs. When it comes to
> a showdown, scarce four weeks have passed before they remem-
> ber that they are pacifists and write defeatist letters in your columns,
> leaving the defence of freedom and of civilisation to Colonel
> Blimp and the Old School Tie, for whom Three Cheers.[15]

As a planner, partisan of the Bloomsbury vision of human bliss, and inveterate activist, Keynes was a man who, early and late, notwithstanding the evidence of folly that littered the political landscape, hewed to confidence in the eventual triumph of reason. At times of course, it was necessary to scream at politicians to get their attention. In 1928 Keynes wrote to Winston Churchill in this vein: "Dear Chancellor of the Exchequer: What an imbecile currency bill you have introduced!"[16] With rare meekness, possibly related to a bad case of influenza, Churchill responded: "Thank you so much for your letter. I will read your article enclosed and reflect carefully, as I always do on all you say."[17]

With Americans Keynes was more tactful. Although he had a low opinion of Roosevelt's intellect, he was as usual quite willing to repair the gaps in his economic education. In 1933 he wrote an open letter to FDR, duly featured in *The New York Times*. It began sweetly:

> You have made yourself the trustee for those in every country who seek to mend the evils of our condition by reasoned experiment within the framework of the existing social system.
>
> If you fail, rational change will be gravely prejudiced throughout the world, leaving orthodoxy and revolution to fight it out.
>
> But if you succeed, new and bolder methods will be tried everywhere, and we may date the first chapter of a new economic era from your accession to office.[18]

The same Keynes who counseled the mighty at home and abroad did not neglect the unwashed multitudes who read popular magazines. Thus in December 1934 he answered the *Redbook* query "Can America Spend Its Way into Recovery?" in the plainest of terms:

> Why, obviously!—is my first reflection when I am faced by this question. No one of common sense could doubt it unless his mind had first been muddled by a "sound" financier or an "orthodox" economist. We produce in order to sell. In other words, we produce in response to spending. It is impossible to suppose that we can stimulate production and employment by *refraining* from spending. So, I have said, the answer is obvious.[19]

Although Keynes had trouble suffering fools gladly, he was by every account and memoir an enormously persuasive negotiator, quite willing to settle for the attainable, however distant that might be from the ideal. During World War II, when he had incompletely recovered from a severe heart attack suffered in 1937, he was deeply involved in lend-lease, Bretton Woods, and, as a final service to his country, the American loan.

Those who watched him in action, opponents as well as disciples, had difficulty responding without uncontrolled enthusiasm. A typical effusion was contributed in 1944 by a certain F. G. Lee, a member of the British Treasury's Washington delegation to lend-lease discussions:

> Maynard's performance was truly wonderful. . . . He was an inspiration to us all: it is no exaggeration to say that we felt like Lucifer's followers in Milton, "Rejoicing in our matchless chief." . . .I doubt whether he has ever written or spoken with more

lucidity and charm. . . . Take Harry White, for instance—that difficult nature unfolds like a flower when Maynard is there.[20]

Varying the celestial imagery, Lionel Robbins, a neoclassicist usually at intellectual odds with Keynes, commented in the same year on Keynes's handling of the projected World Bank:

> In the late afternoon we had a joint session with the Americans at which Keynes expounded our views on the Bank. This went very well indeed. Keynes was in his most lucid and persuasive mood; and the effect was irresistible. . . . The Americans sat entranced as the God-like visitor sang and the golden light played around them. When it was all over, there was very little discussion. But so far as the Bank is concerned, I am clear that we are off with a flying start.[21]

It sounds as though a moment of silent prayer would have been in order after this.

Conclusion

I am tempted to offer further samples in demonstration of the theme I have been pursuing: that Keynes was consistently skeptical about the merits of the capitalist order and persistent in his attempts to accelerate its mutation into a more egalitarian, better-arranged, quasi-socialist higher state. But enough has already been said elsewhere to convince all but the blind. As a writer, theorist, visionary, and speaker of genius, Keynes used the talents of an economist to free the world of his tribe. He looked to a future free of material want, one in which ordinary folk could enjoy such delights as Bloomsbury offered Keynes.

Like Joan Robinson's hero, my Keynes is an independent radical, an idiosyncratic socialist. It is a pity that legions of students have encountered Keynes only as half of the neoclassical synthesis. For the real-life Keynes was a bold spirit, attracted to experiment, public intervention, planning, and redistribution of wealth, income, and power.

Indeed those of us who search for recipes for structural improvements in our society far beyond the narrow frontiers of fiscal and monetary policy need seek no further than the vibrant prose in these thirty volumes. The Keynes there identifiable would be hardly likely to settle for an economy operating at a ''natural'' unemployment rate of 6–7 percent; nor would he have been terrified by the Humphrey-Hawkins unemployment targets, the confusions of industrial policy, or the necessities of incomes policy. The unaccustomed modesty with which mainstream economists now view the possibilities of public policy could hardly be more distant from the spirit of activity and invention that animated Keynes all his professional life.

Let the radical Keynes live forever. Let the textbook Keynes disappear as rapidly from memory as students in search of mental health can arrange.

Notes

1. Vol. XI, p. 320.
2. Vol. XXI, p. 239.
3. Vol. XX, p. 223.
4. Vol. XXVII, p. 445.
5. Vol. XXI, p. 492.
6. Vol. XX, pp. 473–474.
7. Vol. XX, p. 475.
8. Vol. XXI, p. 207.
9. Vol. XXVII, p. 322.
10. Vol. XXVII, p. 270.
11. Vol. XXI, pp. 209–210.
12. Vol. XXI, p. 37.
13. Vol. XXVII, p. 385.
14. Vol. XXVII, p. 387.
15. Vol. XXII, pp. 36–37.
16. Vol. XIX, Part 2, p. 750.
17. Ibid.
18. Vol. XXI, p. 289.
19. Vol. XXI, p. 334.
20. Vol. XXIV, p. 188.
21. Vol. XXVI, p. 56.

4

Listen Keynesians!

Paul M. Sweezy

There is a remarkable consensus among economists of all ideological and political persuasions—conservative, liberal, and radical—that capitalist economies must grow to be healthy and that the key to growth lies in the capital-accumulation, or savings-and-investment process.

Accepting this view, we have long been arguing in effect that capitalism, like living organisms, undergoes a natural aging process from birth through adolescence to maturity. In the early period when society's capital stock—mostly means of production and transportation—is being built up from scratch, the opportunities for capital accumulation appear to be virtually unlimited. The more resources that can be diverted from the production of consumer goods (savings), the more can be devoted to production of means of production (investment). Growth is rapid, interrupted only by financial blockages and demand-and-supply disproportionalities. After these blockages and disproportionalities have been eliminated (a function performed by crises and depressions), accumulation and growth resume what soon comes to be assumed to be their normal course.

So it was during capitalism's youth. This was also of course the period of the rise and refinement of political economy (later called economics) as the science of capitalism's laws and tendencies, a period that can be dated from the time of Adam Smith in the last quarter of the eighteenth century to that of Alfred Marshall, which extended into the third decade of the twentieth century. With negligible exceptions the economists of this period, reflecting the historical reality around them, saw vigorous growth as the essential characteristic of the system and interruptions of growth as a temporary and self-correcting illness.[1]

In this vision of capitalism, there was no need for a special theory of the demand side of the investment process. The presence of what was for all practical purposes an unlimited demand for additional means of production could be taken for granted. The determination of the actual rate of accumula-

This paper, which served as the basis for Paul Sweezy's speech at the Hofstra Keynes Forum, originally appeared in the January 1983 issue of *Monthly Review*.

tion was therefore shifted entirely to the supply side of the equation. Marshall's handling of the problem was fairly typical. In a 20-page chapter entitled "The Growth of Wealth," he devoted less than a page to the demand for capital and most of the rest to the supply of savings. On the former he said in part:

> As civilization has progressed, man has always been developing new wants, and new and more expensive ways of gratifying them. The rate of progress has sometimes been slow, . . . but now we are moving on at a rapid pace that grows quicker every year; and we cannot guess where it will stop. On every side further openings are sure to offer themselves, all of which will tend to change the character of our social and industrial life, and to enable us to turn to account vast stores of capital in providing new gratifications and new ways of economizing effort by expending it in anticipation of distant wants. There seems to be no good reason for believing that we are anywhere near a stationary state in which there will be no new important wants to be satisfied; in which there will be no more room for profitably investing present effort in providing for the future, and in which the accumulation of wealth will cease to have any reward. (Alfred Marshall, *Principles of Economics*, 8th edition, 1920)

The belief in the existence of an unlimited demand for additional capital goods has survived to this day in textbooks, popular economic writings, and most strikingly in the supply-side theory, which provides the ideological rationalization for the Reagan administration's economic policies. According to this theory, the malfunctioning of the U.S. economy in recent years stems from too much spending and not enough saving, a combination that is supposed to have produced a low growth rate, with its attendant evils of stagnation, falling profits, rising unemployment, and all the rest.

But at just about the time Alfred Marshall was issuing the eighth and final edition of his famous *Principles*, capitalism was well into a transitional period from adolescence to maturity, climaxed by the post–World War I boom of the 1920s in the United States, by then the world's leading capitalist nation. This boom, like others before it, was fueled by a surge of investment, this time especially in the automobile and related sectors (oil, rubber, glass, highway construction, suburban housing). But the boom also displayed new features reflecting fundamental economic changes. Most important were (1) the burgeoning of consumer credit as a booster to the final demand for the products of these leading industries, and (2) a gradual downdrift of the manufacturing capacity utilization rate after 1925. These were clear signs that despite the injection of strong debt-generated demand for consumer goods, the rate of investment that powered the boom of the 1920s was unsustainable. The crisis of 1929 was a crisis of *overaccumulation*.

Previous capitalist crises had also involved overaccumulation in the sense that investment in the preceding booms had, for largely speculative-financial reasons, outrun demand. But this imbalance between investment and demand in earlier crises turned out to be a temporary phenomenon. After a period of deflation and price readjustments, the investment process resumed its stimulative role: the conventional wisdom which took for granted an unlimited underlying demand for investment was thus empirically supported and became ever more firmly entrenched.

That there was something fundamentally different about the crisis of 1929, that in this case overaccumulation was more than a temporary phenomenon and in fact marked a decisive change in the functioning of the system—this was not apparent to anyone in the early years of the Great Depression. It is hardly an exaggeration to say the the entire economics profession at the time expected growth, rooted in the accumulation process, to resume as it always had in the past.[2] To be sure it was soon recognized that the downturn precipitated by the crisis was unusually sharp and that the recovery would probably be slow and lengthy. But that had happened before—in the 1870s and 1890s—and it was not hard to find what seemed to be satisfactory explanations in the unique events surrounding World War I and its aftermath.

What finally drove home the message that things really had changed, that (in our metaphor) capitalism's transition from adolescence to maturity had been completed, was the recession of 1937–38. This event was quite unprecedented. It was not a mere short-term setback but a sudden and steep decline at a time when the upswing from the depression that began in 1933 still had a long way to go to reach what by the standards of past business cycles could be considered full recovery. The unemployment statistics tell the essential story. In the United States the peak rate of unemployment was registered in 1933 at 24.9 percent of the labor force. This declined by 1937 to 14.3 percent, and then jumped up again to 19.0 percent in 1938. What these figures describe was at the time something new under the capitalist sun—a steep recession in the midst of a deep depression.

How could this be explained? No one had any doubt about the proximate cause—the breakdown of the capital-accumulation process. In the first years of the depression, net investment not only disappeared, it was actually replaced by net disinvestment, the using up of more capital than was produced. And such positive investment as did take place in the recovery beginning in 1933 was mainly to replace what had been lost. When this was accomplished, the steam went out of the process again, precipitating the relapse of 1937–38.

Not surprisingly, a generation of economists brought up on the assumption of an unlimited demand for investment (as exemplified in the above-quoted passage from Alfred Marshall's *Principles of Economics*) was at a loss to account for such strange goings-on. Could the trouble be not in the *demand* for real investment but in the *supply* of money capital to finance investment? Hardly. That finance was available was evident from the fact that interest rates had fallen to purely nominal levels (treasury-bill rates were 0.14 percent and the Federal Reserve rediscount rate was 1.50 percent in 1936); and any real pickup in the rate of investment would have boosted corporate profits, thus generating the funds for further investment. What the recession of 1937–38 revealed was thus the total inability of bourgeois economic theory to cope with the new phenomenon of capitalist maturity. We repeat: underlying this theory, insofar as it related to economic growth and the nature of economic fluctuations, was the usually implicit assumption of an unlimited demand for investment. Given this assumption, interruptions of growth could be caused only by failure of the institutional (financial, governmental) mechanism of the system to function properly. The very idea that such interruptions might flow from the inherent logic of the system itself rather than from the faulty functioning of its mechanism was ruled out in advance.

The first serious challenge to this deeply ingrained orthodoxy came in the form of Keynes's *General Theory of Employment, Interest, and Money*, published in 1936, shortly before the recession that began late the following year. For the first time the possibility was frankly faced, indeed placed at the very center of the analysis, that breakdowns of the accumulation process, the heart and soul of economic growth, might be built into the system and non-self-correcting. Although it has not been widely recognized, it was this feature of *The General Theory* which more than anything else marked it as a turning point in the development of bourgeois economic theory. The stage was thus set for a sweeping reconsideration of the whole theory of investment.

What *The General Theory* dealt with as a theoretical problem was posed as an intensely practical problem by the recession of 1937–38. The combination sent shock waves through the economics profession, touching off a debate that could and should have developed into the most searching and significant intellectual confrontation the United States had experienced since the antislavery struggle of a century earlier. The debate was initiated by the publication in 1938 of Alvin Hansen's *Full Recovery or Stagnation?* and the issue was joined the following year in the second volume of Joseph A. Schumpeter's monumental treatise on *Business Cycles*.[3] Hansen and Schumpeter were probably the two most prestigious American economists of the 1930s, and the fact that they took the lead in debating this most crucial of all current economic problems seemed to guarantee that one of those ''splendid tournaments'' in the history of economic thought of which Marx had written was about to take place.[4]

But it was not to be. Ominous war clouds gathered over Europe in 1938 (Hitler annexed Austria in March, and the Munich Pact sacrificing Czechoslovakia was signed in September), and the outbreak of hostilities in 1939 completed the shift of attention, in the United States as elsewhere, from depression to war preparation. It soon turned out that the two were alternatives not only as objects of public attention but in practice as well. The unemployment rate, which remained over 17 percent in 1939, dropped rapidly thereafter until it reached its wartime low of 1.2 percent in 1944.

Not surprisingly, the debate that had begun so auspiciously in the wake of the recession of 1937–38 receded into the background and died out completely after the war. The all but total lack of attention paid by the economics profession to Josef Steindl's penetrating work *Maturity and Stagnation in American Capitalism* (1952) proved, if indeed proof was needed, that the trauma of the 1930s had been forgotten. It is not true, however, that Keynes was forgotten. What did happen in the new postwar conditions was that the emphases of Keynesian theory, as it had been interpreted by Hansen and his followers in the 1930s, were drastically revised. The problem of the long-run demand for investment, on which Keynes differed from Marshall, gave way to concern over fluctuations in demand for investment in the course of the business cycle. And Keynes's great achievement was now seen not as a highly original contribution to the understanding of capitalism's basic *modus operandi* but as the invention of a set of clever recipes to counteract the ups and downs of the business cycle. In the depression phase, monetary policy should aim to lower interest rates, while fiscal policy should deliberately create government deficits in order to stimulate aggregate demand for goods and services, the market being left to determine which goods and services and in what proportions. In the prosperity phase of the cycle, this policy mix should be reversed to forestall "overheating" of the economy (a favorite expression): interest rates should be increased, government spending reduced, and taxes raised, with the resulting budgetary surplus being used to repay the debt incurred to finance the preceding deficit.

This was the gist of what gradually came to be called the New Economics. Joan Robinson and some others among Keynes's followers from an earlier period called it Bastard Keynesianism.

The reason why the emerging debate of the 1930s was interrupted and forgotten while Keynes was being turned into a quite ordinary purveyor of business-cycle remedies is obvious: for some three decades after the beginning of World War II, capitalism seemed to have recaptured its youth.[5] Recessions were mild, and after every setback investment bounced back at least as vigorously as during any comparable period in the earlier history of capitalism. The old orthodoxy of the unlimited demand for investment, which had been briefly challenged in the 1930s but never overthrown, simply reasserted itself as an unstated axiom of the New Economics. The truth is that, apart from claims to be able to control the business cycle, the New Economics is fundamentally no different from the old economics. And when the problems of the 1930s—the breakdown of the accumulation process, the onset of stagnation, the soaring of unemployment—began to reappear in the 1970s, the New Economists showed themselves to be as helpless as their pre–World War II ancestors.

One consequence of this failure of the New Economics was to open the door to the inane dogmas of monetarism and supply-side economics and their misbegotten offspring, Reaganomics. Put into practice—to the extent that a combination of incompatible and contradictory policy prescriptions can be put into practice—this monstrosity has made matters worse. The other main consequence is that the large body of respectable and respected economists who are too intelligent and/or too honest to buy the rubbish that has to be taken seriously in Washington these days are at a loss to offer meaningful advice to policymakers or to contribute to the formation of an intelligent public opinion on many of the most important issues of our time.

Just how bad the situation has become is well illustrated by the effort of one of the best of the younger economists to find a way out of the impasse we have been discussing. In a remarkably outspoken article in *The New York Times Magazine* ("The Great Stagnation," October 17, 1982), Lester Thurow, Harvard-trained professor of economics at MIT, presents a grimly accurate description of the present worldwide capitalist crisis, concluding:

> All of which adds up to this: The world economy is likely
> to continue sinking into the quicksands. We are likely to have more of
> the rising unemployment and increasing financial distress we
> have been experiencing for the last three and a half years. There is
> simply no indication that the Western nations, individually or
> jointly, have any program or any approach that is capable of turning
> the tide.

What follows in the article's last paragraph, however, deserves to be awarded the prize for Anticlimax of 1982: "From the perspective of this economist . . . the solution lies in old-fashioned Keynesian stimulus. Until we are willing to practice it, America and the world are likely to remain mired in what might be called the Great Stagnation." One rubs one's eyes in wonderment. Talk about practicing stimulus! During the 1970s, the decade in which the Great Stagnation set in, there was not one year in which the federal budget was balanced, and the aggregate deficit in the twelve years 1970–81 was over $400 billion. And the Reagan administration, for all its railing against its big-spending predecessors, has set out on a course of tax cuts for the rich and handouts to the Pentagon that promises to make them look like pikers: latest budget estimates project deficits of well over $200 billion a year for a long time to come. Nor is this the only kind of stimulus that has been practiced in recent years: monetary and related banking policies have been crucial ingredients in the unprecedented explosion of private debt that has characterized the entire post–World War II period. And yet all these multifaceted forms of stimulation have dismally failed to reinvigorate the accumulation process, which Thurow, like all other economists, recognizes to be the key to the health of capitalist economies.

Talk of old-fashioned Keynesian stimulus thus turns out to be as irrelevant as the nonsensical chatter of the monetarists and the supply-siders. But this doesn't mean that Keynes is irrelevant. As we noted above, his *General Theory* of 1936 set the stage for a sweeping reconsideration of the whole theory of investment. Unfortunately, this reconsideration never materialized. The late Michal Kalecki, the Polish economist who has justifiably been credited with "inventing the Keynesian Revolution" before Keynes, commented on this subject shortly before his death in the following terms:

> Why cannot a capitalist system, once it has deviated down-

wards from the path of expanded reproduction [growth], find itself in a position of long-term simple reproduction [no growth]? In
fact we are absolutely in the dark concerning what will happen in
such a situation so long as we have not solved the problems of the determinants of investment decisions. Marx did not develop such a
theory, nor has this been accomplished in modern economics. Some
attempts have been made in the development of the theory of cyclical fluctuations. However, the problems of the determination of investment decisions involving . . . the long-run trend are much
more difficult than in the case of the "pure business cycle.". . .
One thing is clear to me: the long-run growth of the national income involving satisfactory utilization of equipment is far from obvious. (*Social Science Information*, December 1968)

We do not mean to suggest that what is needed is simply a "theory of the
determinants of investment decisions": the problem is much broader and
includes a crucially important historical dimension, which has received some
attention in recent years from economists attracted by the hypothesis that
capitalist development during the last two hundred years or so has taken place
in long cycles. All we are saying is that this is a much neglected and underdeveloped area of economic inquiry, which can no longer be neglected by any
economist who wants to be taken seriously on the most important problems of
our time. As far as bourgeois economics is concerned, Keynes started it, and it
would seem appropriate for his followers to take up where he left off.

But there are also other reasons why Keynes is relevant. A large part of
The General Theory was devoted to showing how and why classical and
neoclassical economics alike were wrong in assuming that there are built-in
tendencies in capitalist economies to operate at full employment and hence to
self-correct any deviations from full employment. But he didn't stop there. He
went on to give his views on how the state in capitalist societies could, and in
his opinion should, remedy this lack of an automatic regulatory mechanism. In
the postwar period, as noted previously, Keynes's followers, or at any rate
those who became the prophets of the New Economics, vulgarized these
opinions to the point of turning Keynesianism into a cure-all for the capitalist
business cycle.

Keynes himself, however, while of course concerned with the business
cycle, went much further. Anyone who will take the trouble to read the last
chapter of *The General Theory*, entitled "Concluding Notes on the Social
Philosophy Towards Which the General Theory Might Lead," will recognize
a mind that carries on in the tradition of critical bourgeois thinkers of the
past—those whom Marx, in the preface to the second edition of the first
volume of *Capital*, called "disinterested inquirers" as opposed to "hired
prize-fighters." Keynes saw clearly that capitalism contained what in the long
run was a potentially fatal flaw, and he wanted to eliminate it, not merely patch
it over with a Band-Aid. And in pursuit of this end, he was willing to contem-

plate reforms as radical as the far-reaching equalization of the distribution of income through the eventual elimination of rentier incomes (interest and rent) and through the "somewhat comprehensive socialization of investment." He recognized that the enlargement of the functions of government these reforms would entail "would seem to a nineteenth-century publicist or to a contemporary American financier to be a terrific encroachment on individualism," a proposition that, if made today, would have to be rated a terrific understatement.

"Is the fulfillment of these ideas a visionary hope?" Keynes asked in a concluding section. "Have they insufficient roots in the motives which govern the evolution of political society? Are the interests which they will thwart stronger and more obvious than those they will serve?" To which he replied: "I do not attempt an answer in this place. It would need a volume of a different character from this one to indicate even in outline the practical measures in which they might be gradually clothed."

We are not suggesting of course that Keynes had the answers or that he would have come up with them in the sequel to The General Theory if it had been written. What is important is that if he pursued this line of thought, he would have had to confront the basic issue of the power of the ruling class. Whether he would have done so, in view of his ideological attachment to capitalism, is naturally a matter for speculation. Readers of Monthly Review know that, in contrast to Keynes, we have an entirely different view of what it will take to liberate the enormous latent power of today's advanced economies from the stranglehold of capitalist control. But unlike the establishment economists of our time, including his latter-day followers, Keynes at least knew that there were real and deadly serious problems to be dealt with, and he was not afraid to tackle them. He was a disinterested inquirer, not a hired prizefighter. Are there any of them left today?

Notes

1. Some students of the history of economic thought might contend that the preceding summary is contradicted by the forebodings of the classical economists beginning with Ricardo and Malthus, which earned early nineteenth-century political economy its reputation as the "dismal science." This is more apparent than real, however. These thinkers, Ricardo foremost among them, argued on the basis of two presumed natural laws, the law of diminishing returns and the Malthusian law of population, that the accumulation of capital would eventually run out of steam because wages and rent would so far eat into profits as to leave capitalists with neither the wherewithal nor the incentive to continue accumulating. It is important to recognize that there was a very strong political-ideological element in this argument: it was more or less deliberately designed to bolster the case for free trade. The abrogation of the corn laws (agricultural protectionism) would effectively repeal the law of diminishing returns as far as England was concerned and thus liberate the accumulation process from its shackles. This goal was attained in 1846, after which the economists stopped worrying about threats to the future growth of capitalism.

2. This comes through very clearly in two detailed studies of the period: William E. Stoneman, A History of the Economic Analysis of the Great Depression in America (New York: Garland Publishing, 1979); and Dean L. May, From New Deal to New Economics: The American Liberal Response to the Recession of 1937 (New York: Garland Publishing, 1981).

3. See "Why Stagnation?" *Monthly Review* 34 June 1982, pp. 1–10.
4. Preface to the second edition of volume 1 of *Capital*. Marx was referring specifically to the "quarrel between industrial capital and aristocratic landed property," which elicited the participation of England's outstanding economic thinkers in the decade of the 1820s.
5. See "Why Stagnation?."

5

Keynes's Influence on Public Policy: A Conservative's View

Norman B. Ture

Let me preface this discussion by distinguishing between Keynes and his work, on the one hand, and his disciples and their work on the other. Keynes was a great creative artist in economics. His major works provided a grand scheme of thought about how the economy works—or doesn't work, as the case may be. But the Keynesian influence on public policy as we see it today is the result of the application or misapplication of his views, primarily those conveyed in *The General Theory*, by his disciples. As is often the case, with the passage of time an ever-widening gap opens between master and followers. In the debate on "Does money matter?" is it conceivable that Keynes would have spoken for the negative, with so many of his U.S. protagonists? Would he have perceived the seemingly endless arithmetic exercises aimed at determining, for instance, the size of the multiplier as key questions of theory as applied to policy, important enough to have consumed so much of the profession's intellectual energies and so many pages of its journals?

I have little doubt that what is today considered "Keynesian" goes beyond the intellectual or policy legacy of John Maynard Keynes. But argument on either side of this contention is merely speculation, to little useful purpose. What we are addressing here is the influence of Keynesianism, rather than of Keynes, on public policy.

Keynesianism, I believe, has exerted a significantly antiprogressive influence on public policy. The indictment of Keynesian-tilted policies is long; even a modest cut at it calls for a far more extended discussion than this paper permits. I shall therefore identify only a few of the policy offenses for which Keynesians bear the onus.

Foremost among these offenses is the highly successful effort to persuade policymakers—and through the media's eager cooperation, the public at large—that government can, should, indeed must, manage the economy by manipulating fiscal and/or monetary policies to control aggregate demand. No matter one's "school" of economics, we can all share the view that government policies and operations exert some influence on how effectively the economy performs, in terms of criteria relevant to us as practitioners of a rigorous intellectual discipline and/or as makers of public policies. But Keynesianism far exceeds this recognition of the fact that no impenetrable wall separates the government from the economy; it overleaps to the unwarranted conclusion that skillfully designed and adeptly executed policies can fine-tune the economy's performance in the short run to produce the sort of results idealized in a Humphrey-Hawkins's statement of what public economic policy is all about. Presumably the "right" combination of monetary ease and fiscal constraint can be designed to produce that level and rate of increase in aggregate demand which will provide the desired degree of price-level stability, employment, and growth. And the "right" inventory of government expenditure programs and the "right" tax structure, combined with the "right" regulations, will provide us the "right" distribution of income and wealth, the "right" allocation of resources, and the "right" rate of satisfying the "great, unmet social needs."

When and insofar as public policy has been guided by these Keynesian persuasions—and it has done so far too often—the results at best have fallen far short of expectations and more often have been qualitatively different from them. Policy "misfires" have not been the consequence, as Keynesian apologists have claimed, of failure by the administration and/or the Congress to follow the prescriptions of their economists. Nor does the fault lie primarily, as often asserted, in the lags between the onset of the economy's deviation from some optimum performance path and the perception of the deviation (in the inadequacies of economic forecasting), between the perception and the corrective action, and between the corrective action and its economic effects. The fault stems rather from the fundamental Keynesian misconception that manipulation of fiscal or monetary aggregates can affect real aggregate demand, hence real output and income, by altering disposable income; and, as a corollary, it stems from treating these alleged income effects as the first-order effects of fiscal and monetary policies, with relative price effects relegated to second-order status, if not ignored entirely. In fact, government actions have no direct impact on real aggregate demand; indeed they affect nominal aggregate demand directly only as they rely on changes in the stock of money or its income velocity. The first-order effect of government policies and actions are relative price effects; income effects are second order, depending on the allocative responses to the first-order price effects.

Changes in real aggregate demand derive from changes in real total income, which result from changes in real output. Unless one believes in magic, one must recognize that changes in output occur only in response to changes in the amount of production inputs used in production and/or in the intensity or effectiveness of their use. If government actions were to have a direct or first-order effect on aggregate income, hence aggregate demand, they would have to alter directly the amount or effectiveness of inputs committed to production. No government action does that. Changes in the amount of production inputs committed to production result only if the real rewards for their use, the real net price received per unit, are changed.

To hold otherwise is to assume either that people persistently confuse nominal with real changes in prices or that the opportunity costs for providing labor or capital services are constant in the short run, i.e., that short-run factor-supply curves are horizontal. Neither assumption is acceptable in theory, and neither assumption is supported by the evidence of people's behavior.

Government fiscal and monetary policy actions, to repeat, have no direct effect on real aggregate income or real aggregate demand. Indeed, fiscal actions, taken by themselves, have no direct effect even on *nominal* aggregate demand although they are certainly likely to alter the composition of spending and the identity of the spenders. Changes in the stock of money, whether undertaken by themselves or as accompaniments to changes in fiscal variables, do alter *nominal* aggregate demand but, even if unanticipated, are extremely unlikely to have any direct effect on *real* aggregate demand. Any alteration in real aggregate demand can occur only if there is a preceding increase in real output, in turn depending on an increase in production inputs or the effectiveness of their use. To assert that changes, anticipated or not, in the money stock and consequent changes in nominal aggregate demand result in changes in the amount or efficiency of production inputs is to assert that factor supply functions are infinitely elastic with respect to their real prices or that the suppliers are consistently and persistently unable to distinguish nominal from real price changes. Neither view is an acceptable basis for public policy.

The consequences of Keynesian efforts to fine-tune aggregate economic performance have been to entrench an inflationary bias in economic policy and economic outcomes, along with increasing biases against market-directed personal effort and saving and investment. The mistaken focus of fiscal and monetary policy instruments on manipulation of aggregate demand in pursuit of "full employment" has led to concentration on the size and sign of the gap between fiscal aggregates, in substantial disregard of the really relevant attributes of fiscal actions—their effects on relative prices. As a consequence, over most of the forty-some years of Keynesian dominance of fiscal policy, tax increases have been concentrated on business and upper-bracket individual taxpayers, while tax reductions have been concentrated on lower-bracket individuals. There have been, we must gratefully acknowledge, exceptions, but despite these, there can be little question that there has been a continuing shift of aggregate income tax burdens into the upper income brackets, along with a continuing increase in the marginal tax rates applicable to the real incomes of the majority of individual taxpayers.

The antieffort, antisaving consequences of these trends have been enhanced by the sustained, rapid growth of transfer payments. The expansion of these payments was deemed to serve two Keynesian policy objectives: the redistribution of income and the expansion of aggregate demand, typically confused with economic growth. Virtually ignored in the process was the effect of much of these transfer payments in reducing the cost of being unemployed while raising the cost to the employed.

These government spending and tax policies have combined to discourage growth in factor supplies and use. In an era in which acceleration of the capital-to-labor ratio was needed to maintain growth in labor's productivity and real-wage rates, hence to provide acceptable increases in demands for, and supplies of, labor services, public policies have generally tilted toward burdening capital formation, slowing the growth in the stock of capital. The principal impact of this tendency has been to decelerate productivity growth in manufacturing and goods-processing industries, contributing to an accelerating shift in employment to services, finance, and trade. Certainly we would have little to complain of in these developments if they were the outcomes of efficiently operating markets; in fact, they are much more the inadvertent consequences of public policies that have been substantially blind to their effects on relative prices and the allocative responses thereto while chasing after elusive aggregate-demand objectives.

An outgrowth of this Keynesian concentration on management of aggregate demand was the notion that there is some optimum mix of fiscal and monetary policies that will effectuate a pursuit of the short-run stabilization and the long-run growth-in-capacity objectives. The broad outlines of the policy-mix thesis may be summarized as follows. The "easier" the monetary policy, the lower the level of interest rates and the higher the level of investment. To prevent the desirably high level of investment, with its attendant multiplier effects on aggregate demand, from exerting an untoward inflationary influence, an adequately restrictive fiscal policy is called for. Because government-spending programs, with the exception of defense, aim at meeting the "great unmet public needs," restrictive fiscal policy by and large calls for tax increases, which, equity demands, should fall on upper-bracket individuals and corporate businesses. The effects of such taxes on the relative cost of saving, hence the cost of capital, may be safely ignored because saving is "interest inelastic" and because the easy-money policy's effect in lowering interest rates more than offsets any adverse effect on business investment demand from higher taxes on the returns on investment.

Virtually every element in this scenario has been demolished analytically and by the evidence of the economy's performance, but the policy-mix myth continues to beset public policy. Its contemporary exposition is to be found in the "crowding-out" thesis, with its insistence on raising taxes to reduce government deficits which, competing with private borrowing for some given amount of "loanable funds," "credit," or some such, allegedly raise interest rates and depress capital formation.

Finally, by virtue of its focus on aggregate demand as the principal concern of economic policy, Keynesianism generated a policy paradox, the Keynesian resolution of which, when implemented, has resulted in further impairment of allocative efficiency. In the Keynesian policy scenario, the conditions of aggregate supply are treated as substantially unresponsive to public policy in either the short or long run. It is only a modest simplification to state that, at least until recent times when Keynesians deemed it judicious to coopt rather than oppose "supply-side economics," the Keynesian analysis treated conditions of supply as determined by factors lying beyond the reach of public policies. Given conditions of supply, the outward positioning of the aggregate-demand curve resulting from expansionary policies may result in intersection of aggregate demand and supply schedules at a point on an upward sloping portion of the latter—in the range of "bottlenecks," capacity "shortages," and what have you. Moreover, this upward tilting of the aggregate supply schedule might begin short of "full" employment. Thus, growth in output, more consequentially in employment, and in price-level stability are likely to be at war with each other, except when the economy is operating below its "capacity."

Resolution of this Phillips-curve dilemma presumably calls for an "incomes policy," a euphemism for price and wage controls of varying degrees of severity. In essence, any such policy purports to flatten the aggregate-supply curve beyond the point at which it would otherwise begin to slope up in order to permit further increases in employment and output without increase in the price level. The view that any factor-supply condition can be converted into an infinitely elastic curve in the short run is, of course, an analytical absurdity, implying utterly unreal properties of the underlying utility functions. The distortions of the market system's measure of relative prices which the application of any such scheme entails is either ignored or deemed to be of so little consequence as to represent no deterrent to government determination of appropriate rates of compensation and of output prices. These distortions, however, have not been inconsequential. They have accentuated economic instability. Combining excessively expansionary aggregate-demand policies with governmental repression of wage and price increases has a perverse effect on factor supplies and inputs; and when controls are eased or removed, the eruption of the previously bottled-up output and factor-price increases impels either the imposition of contractionary policies, such as tax increases, which raise the costs of supplying capital and labor inputs, or reimposition of controls. Market functions are, of course, impaired.

In each respect touched upon in the preceding discussion, the influence of Keynesianism on public policy has been regrettable. Public policies have misidentified the barrier to economic progress as inadequate or misdirected aggregate demand, when the very policies framed to overcome this inadequacy have far too often imposed adverse impacts on the costs and rewards for providing the inputs upon which economic growth depends. The pursuit of these policies, moreover, has been associated with an ever-increasing presence of government in the economy, a presence that far more often than not has masked or distorted market signals and impaired market functions.

The policy innovations initiated in 1981 gave promise of a basic reorientation of public economic policies in a free-market, conservative context. The conservative's basic policy objective is to improve the efficiency of market performance. For the most part, the conservative identifies the impediment to efficient market performance as one or another government intrusion, whether in the form of purchases of goods and services, transfer payments, regulations, tax laws, or monetary actions. Virtually all of these intrusions can be expressed in terms of their excise effects, the way in which they distort the relative costs and prices that would otherwise prevail. Good public economic policy calls for reducing the government's presence in the private marketplace, for correcting the relative price and cost distortions that government actions and policies entail.

Some progress has been made along these conservative lines, although policy developments in 1982, particularly the reacceleration of monetary and federal expenditure growth and the irresponsible, counterproductive Tax Equity and Fiscal Responsibility Act of 1982 were a substantial setback. Whether the strong pace of economic recovery can afford the setting for resumption of the policies initiated in 1981 or whether there will be a continuing restoration of Keynesian influence in economic policy is difficult to predict with confidence. The long-run well-being of the economy surely requires the policies initiated in 1981.

6

Keynes, Roosevelt, and the Complementary Revolutions

John Kenneth Galbraith

History has its more than modestly impressive coincidences; one has been manifest in these last two years. Within that time we have celebrated the anniversary of the two men with whose names in this century, along perhaps with that of Lloyd George, the English-speaking world associates the word revolution. The year 1982 was the hundredth anniversary of the birth of Franklin D. Roosevelt, the author of the Roosevelt Revolution. 1983 was the hundredth anniversary of John Maynard Keynes of the Keynesian Revolution. It is my purpose here to comment on these two great movements, but particularly that associated with the name of Keynes, as they were seen at the time but not excluding a word as to their more durable effects.

My qualification for the exercise just mentioned is evident and increasingly rare; it consists in durability, the fact that, in some slight measure, I was there. I knew both Roosevelt and Keynes, though in the greatly subordinate role of the much younger man. In the spring of 1941, I was put in charge of price-control operations as these were made necessary by the emerging threat of war. My job involved a fairly impressive exercise of economic power, one of the greatest associated with the wartime mobilization. It has always been my impression that, amidst the preoccupations of the time, the president, whom of course I met, was, nonetheless, only marginally aware of my existence. My connection with Keynes was greater. In 1937, I went to Cambridge to study under him, attend the famous Keynes seminar. It was the year of his first heart attack; he did not appear at the university during the ensuing months. (It was for me a disappointing but not wholly grave deprivation; I had, in his place, Joan Robinson, R. F. Kahn, and Piero Sraffa, who were as privy to Keynes's thought and system as Keynes himself and, indeed, talked of nothing else.) In later years in wartime Washington I did meet him, partly to discuss price control strategy and again as one of the young Keynesians who sought to bring his ideas into the Roosevelt administration. As I have elsewhere told, the Keynesian ideas came to the United States and to Washington by way of Harvard, an avenue that numerous Harvard graduates did not fail to see at the time, to their sorrow and grave alarm. It was my good fortune to be in both places in those years, one of the closely associated group that sought to carry the Keynesian ideas from Cambridge, Massachusetts, to the capitol. It was a convocation, I might note, that Keynes regarded with much satisfaction, as he once made clear to Walter Salant, one of its members. There was nothing quite like it in London.

Roosevelt the Conservative

The Keynesian and the Roosevelt revolutions were, in singular measure, complementary. Yet, as between the two great principals, there was very little by way of overlapping thought and concern. With Roosevelt in the United States, as earlier with Lloyd George in England, came the much-resisted recognition that capitalism could not survive its own cruelties. Massive, despairing, and penniless unemployment, the deprivations of old age and infirmity, great inequality, the failure when left to the market of specific industries such as housing and health care and the intractable problems of others, notably agriculture, all required ameliorative intervention by the state. There was need also in the United States to reform and make secure the banking system and to minimize the more disastrous consequences of speculation and corporate pyramiding, thimblerigging, and other aberrations. This was the Roosevelt Revolution. It was, in the most compelling sense, conservative in character; without it capitalism would surely not have survived. It was, as it remains, the perverse genius of conservatives to misunderstand the larger implications of efforts on behalf of their own salvation—to combine vehemence with a righteous commitment to their own euthanasia. This, I will note presently, was a principal unifying factor as between the Keynesian and the Roosevelt revolutions.

The Roosevelt Revolution and Franklin D. Roosevelt's own perceptions stopped well short of any developed design for the macroeconomic guidance of the modern economy. From the mid-thirties on, there were, indeed, individuals in his administration, notably Marriner Eccles and Lauchlin Currie of the Federal Reserve, who had anticipated Keynes in their ideas; their minds were on a larger fiscal management of the economy. With unemployment and idle plant capacity they accepted and urged public borrowing and expenditure—a deficit—as a necessity superior to all available alternatives. They did not, at any time, persuade FDR. Nor did the later Keynesians. It is my view, supported by the weight of modern historical judgment, that Roosevelt remained committed to the deeper canons of conservative finance—the broad principle of the balanced budget—until the advent of war swept this issue aside. He did not reject the Keynesians who sought to persuade him; he regarded them as individuals uniquely skilled in rationalizing the inevitable. The inevitable here was the absence of any alternative to a large (for the time) excess of public expenditure over revenue.

How Keynes Persuaded the
Economists

Where Roosevelt stopped, Keynes began. Perhaps partly because Britain was more advanced in such matters, he did not share the Roosevelt commitment to social amelioration and reform. These were not at the center of his thought and system. Central, instead, was the use of the fiscal instruments of the state to raise and stabilize the levels of production and employment and counter the adverse movements of the business cycle.

For understanding Keynes's influence on these matters, it is essential first to understand the anthropology of the economics profession. The basic Keynesian ideas and the resulting policies were relatively simple and forthright; by the standards of the profession, unfortunately so. Say's Law, the dictum that supply always creates its own demand, was at the time an essential of nearly all professional belief and instruction. "Contemporary thought," Keynes observed, "is still deeply steeped in the notion that if people do not spend their money in one way they will spend it [that is, save and invest it] in another." This being so, there could be no organic tendency to a shortage of demand in the economy; there being no possibility of such shortage, there could be no logical basis for a policy committed to the management of demand. Central to Keynes's case was his dismissal of Say's Law; there could, indeed, be an insufficiency of demand; this, in turn, could pull down production, income, and employment until a new underemployment equilibrium was established by the minimal demand induced by, among other things, the spending compulsions deriving from hardship. It followed that demand could be supplemented (and hardship alleviated) by public expenditure uncovered by taxation—by a government supplement to aggregate demand. This was the central point of Keynes's famous open letter to Roosevelt at the end of 1933, urging, before all, the importance of increasing aggregate purchasing power by public expenditure financed by public borrowing—by deliberate resort to deficit financing. "[N]othing else counts in comparison with this."

This was not quite all of the Keynesian public-policy system; one needed a persuasive case as to why consumption and investment expenditure could be insufficient to clear markets, including the labor market, and an understanding of what made the deficiency cumulative. And there needed to be knowledge of the multiplier effect of different kinds of public expenditure. And of the relationship of fiscal to monetary policy. But the essence was here, and had Keynes confined himself to this, his public-policy recommendations would have passed unnoticed or, at best, have been dismissed with scorn. It was Keynes's genius that he added to these elements an array of intricate, sophisticated and, at times, incomprehensible ancillary propositions. These, in turn, caught and held the attention of economists; in thus occupying themselves with the diverse minutiae of Keynes's argument—with the marginal propensity to consume, liquidity preference, the coincidence of saving and investment, the baffling complexities involving movements in real and money wages—they became committed all but unconsciously to his far simpler policy design.

In the autumn of 1936, or possibly the winter of the following year, my younger colleagues at Harvard proposed an evening seminar on *The General Theory*, over which it was my rather modest privilege to preside. It was the nearly endless opportunity to discuss Keynes's ancillary propositions and to differ over what he really meant that allowed our sessions to continue. Had we been confined to what was relevant for public policy, we would have been through, alas, in a couple of weeks. In using complexity, obscurity, and not infrequent contradiction, Keynes was in the great tradition of Karl Marx and the Holy Scriptures, and it is not certain that Keynes was entirely without understanding and purpose in this matter. In the preface to *The General Theory*, he says, '' . . . I cannot achieve my object of persuading economists to re-examine critically certain of their basic assumptions except by highly abstract argument and also much controversy.''

I have said that Keynes was not centrally interested in reform—in softening the sharp edges of capitalism. That he saw this as an underlying requirement for the survival of the system I do not doubt; he did not, in the depression years, want it to take precedence over the management of output as a whole. In the open letter to President Roosevelt to which I earlier adverted, he not only criticized NRA—"An error in choice"—but worried lest the reforming thrust of other features of the Roosevelt Revolution be undermining business confidence. Nothing was of such social consequence as higher production and employment. His fears about business confidence would today, I trust, be better understood. We have come to accept that an expressed concern for business confidence is the cover story for resistance to unwelcome social reform just as the need for improved incentives is the accepted cover story for the natural wish of the affluent for more after-tax income to enjoy. Keynes's different social orientation notwithstanding, the Roosevelt and the Keynesian revolutions were wonderfully complementary.

The Balanced-budget Totem

Again the matter is starkly simple. The Roosevelt reforms, almost without exception, required money. This was especially so of those—CWA, PWA, WPA, CCC—that involved relief and job creation. This money the Keynesian Revolution provided without the need to increase taxes. It came from benign public borrowing, a desirable public deficit. Thus the complementarity. However, I must not exaggerate. This complementarity, at least until the late thirties, was extensively unrecognized—in all the early Roosevelt years there remained a strong commitment to the balanced budget, even at the cost of politically difficult and economically repressive tax action. The delayed recognition of the fortunate association between the Roosevelt and the Keynesian designs was, indeed, one of the more remarkable circumstances of the depression decade. One cause, which I have mentioned already, was Roosevelt's own doubts. More important were those of the reputable economic community and the general world of business and finance. The balanced budget was for them, as for some it remains, not an economic concept but a religious totem. In violating it, one invited punishment of untold severity in a world to come. And at a less theological level, it was thought to risk inflation. Nothing in retrospect is more remarkable than the concern in those years of the great economists and the esteemed financial minds over the danger of inflation amid the most severe and enduring deflationary movement in all economic experience.

Out of the totemic commitment to what were called "sound principles of finance" came the political and ideological excoriation of Keynes. By the late thirties, this was not greatly less than that accorded Roosevelt; it rivaled that of Marx. Some may have sensed that the Keynesian ideas were somehow symbiotic with Roosevelt reforms. They concealed their true and proper cost; nothing resists social-welfare expenditure like a tight budget. Some of the excoriation derived from the youth and adverse personality of the Keynesian advocates; on grave financial matters, young and dubiously tailored scholars were not meant to intrude. But again the cause was mostly the perverse conservative psyche.

Keynes was, as an individual, exceedingly comfortable with the economic system he so brilliantly explored; it had also served him well in practical pecuniary terms. He was not, as he told George Bernard Shaw, attracted by Marx. So the broad thrust of his efforts, like that of Roosevelt, was conservative; it was to help ensure that the system would survive. But such conservatism in the English-speaking countries does not appeal to the truly committed conservative. It is the singular and enduring characteristic of the true conservative that he (or she) places principle above performance, orthodoxy over accommodation, constancy over change. Better to accept the unemployment, idled plants, and mass despair of the Great Depression, with all the resulting damage to the reputation of the capitalist system, than to retreat on true principle. Neither then nor in our own time can we understand the true conservative—the truly committed banker, business executive, economist, or more occasional politician—unless we know how firm can be the controlling faith. In its defense, individuals will accept the suffering of others and, on less frequent occasions, their own. There is a basic rule for survival in the economic world: when someone in an important economic policy position is described as a person of high principle, all should promptly batten down the hatches and prepare for the worst.

A Willingness to Change

Keynes, as others have rightly remarked, was an economist of the depression. But he had no inflexible commitment to dogma; it was his greatest quality that he accommodated his ideas to change. He saw economic life as an historical process, not as a manifestation of static rules. It was the depression that caused him in *The General Theory* to depart from, indeed extensively reject, the far more orthodox view that he had manifested in his earlier *Treatise on Money*. (Few authors have more effectively destroyed their own classic.) When World War II came, and inflation became a danger as distinct from a specious excuse for inaction, he went promptly on to advocate an incomes-and-prices policy. He accepted the inflationary dynamic of the wage/price interaction, the need for stabilizing union wage claims and the prices of what could then still be called wage goods. Given this response, there can hardly be doubt that he would have continued to see an incomes-and-prices policy as part of the larger strategy of modern macroeconomic management. No one, certainly, would have been more amusingly contemptuous of the claim that such action somehow interferes with resource allocation in a world where corporations and unions have long used their market power to invade and influence market allocation in their own interests.

Nor would Keynes have been surprised at the heavy social cost of the recent American and the continuing British commitment to astringent monetarism. *The General Theory* was a retreat from his earlier fascination with monetary policy and the required functional magic. He would not have applauded the recent rise to eminence of Professor Friedman and the exceedingly painful consequences from which we are just emerging. But perhaps he would not have been wholly surprised by this experience. He spoke strongly of the influence of economists ''both when they are right and when they are wrong,'' and he never doubted a willingness to inflict pain and suffering in pursuit of these ideas. That which we have recently endured from the monetarists would not to him seem exceptional, although not for that reason more forgivable.

While Keynes would also have applauded the recent retreat of the Reagan administration from the monetarist commitment, he would, one imagines, be impressed by the eloquence of the new disciples he now has in Washington and their insistence that deficits are not only benign but deeply in accord with the highest Republican principles.

There is obvious danger, however, in this line of argument. One is strongly tempted to attribute to Keynes what one wishes to believe oneself. I would hope, were Keynes back in life, that he would raise his voice against the fatuous nonsense about ''crowding out''—of the danger, even the inevitability, of public borrowing displacing private capital borrowing to the grave disadvantage of the latter. The issue is one of Federal Reserve policy. We will have such crowding out only as the Federal Reserve raises interest rates to suppress private investment, to restrain investment spending. This, in turn, will be in response to the renewed danger of inflation. I cannot think this unlikely. But it does not mean that there is some explicit pool of investment resources which, on being sucked dry, will bring automatic interest rate effects. The problem of the budget deficit, to repeat, is the problem of inflation and resulting Federal Reserve policy.

Monetary versus Fiscal Restraint

There are other problems of current policy where the world has moved beyond the age of Keynes. Keynes wrote at a time when interest rates, by modern standards, were at insignificant levels. It not being possible much to reduce interest rates, fiscal policy remained as the only active instrument of demand management. I would now urge the advantage of combining a more relaxed monetary policy with, in the not distant future, a much more conservative fiscal policy. Fiscal restraint is far less damaging to economic performance than monetary restraint made effective, as it must be, by high interest rates. This last, however, is the likely policy. There will be a strong temptation to counter the deficits that will survive recovery and the resulting demand-induced inflation with higher interest rates and reduced investment, rather than by adequate taxes and the resulting restraint on consumer demand. That, of course, is because the resort to investment restraint is politically far easier than the resort to taxes. This is supported by the curious myth that monetary policy is socially neutral, a proposition manifestly in conflict with the tendency for people who lend money to have more than those who borrow money. An active policy of monetary restraint is affirmatively damaging to economic efficiency, productivity, and growth. And this is no longer a matter of theoretical faith. It is the exceedingly practical lesson of the monetarist experiment of these last years in the United States and Britain.

I return in conclusion to my larger point. It was the deeper conviction of Keynes that capitalism was worth saving, that it could be made to work. His enemies and antagonists should have been those who were committed to its demise. For some of those, some Marxians, he was, indeed, a regressive bourgeois apologist, the architect of an ineffective design for perpetuating an outworn system. But this opposition to Keynes was of slight consequence; his great conflict was with those whom he sought to save. It was there that the real passion was aroused. This, I venture to think, is the continuing lesson of Keynes as also of Roosevelt, and the lesson for our own day. Those who have the greatest stake in the system are most resistant to the measures by which its hardships are mitigated and its performance improved and made tolerable to people at large. When capitalism finally succumbs, it will be to the thunderous cheers of those who are celebrating their final victory over people like Keynes.

7

Keynes, Keynesians, and British Economic Policy

John Eatwell

I

Keynes was the most practical of economists, concerned throughout his life with issues of economic policy. Even the intricate theoretical discussion of the *Treatise on Money* was directed toward the formulation of coherent monetary policies to deal with the depressed state of the British economy. Yet, for all his concern with the real world, Keynes was keenly aware of the crucial role played by economic theory in the formulation and implementation of economic policy. The well-known assertion that

> . . . the ideas of economists and political philosophers, both when they are right and when they are wrong, are more powerful than is commonly understood. Indeed the world is ruled by little else. Practical men, who believe themselves to be quite exempt from any intellectual influences, are usually the slaves of some defunct economist. Madmen in authority, who hear voices in the air, are distilling their frenzy from some academic scribbler of a few years back. (Keynes, 1936, p. 383)

is overstated to the point of willful misrepresentation. Economists' ideas do not typically lead events; they follow them. Economic analysis *is* important, however, in political controversy. A group putting forward a particular point of view will try to show not only that it has a uniquely correct understanding of how the system works but also that, as a consequence, its policies conform to "natural justice" or are "in the national interest." Then, once a particular interpretation has been invented of how the system works, it may be transformed and developed in a way that is totally independent of the conflict in which it originated. An idea that began as an argument in a particular cause acquires a "scientific aspect." It appears to be independent of political controversy and so becomes a yet more powerful weapon. So, economic ideas and concepts do provide the raw material of policy debate, the categories used in discussion and in the collection of data that define the economy. And while recent events have encouraged some cynicism on this score, intellectual coherence can play a leading, though not decisive, role in determining the direction of economic policy. Thus, there exists a natural action and interaction between the development of economic theory and the changing balance of political forces.

In this essay I will attempt to illustrate this mutual interaction by examining the influence of Keynes's theories on the development of British economic policy from World War II on. I will therefore be dealing with the impact of *The General Theory* and *How to Pay for the War* rather than any of Keynes's earlier contributions to policy debate such as *The Economic Consequences of the Peace, A Tract on Monetary Reform*, or *Can Lloyd George Do It?* It is, after all, in *The General Theory* that we find Keynes's distinctive ideas.

Prior to 1936 Keynes, in common with Pigou and Robertson, had argued, on entirely orthodox grounds, that unemployment was due to the obstruction of the market mechanism by institutional and social imperfections such as sticky money wages or the pursuit of inappropriate policies by the monetary authorities. The case for public works (as in *Can Lloyd George Do It?*) was consequently based on the need to circumvent these imperfections in the short run—though the short run could, as Keynes put it in the *Treatise*, last "long enough to include (and perhaps to contrive) the rise and fall of the greatness of a nation." Whatever its practical merits, an argument based on such foundations is analytically very weak. If unemployment is caused by short-run imperfections that inhibit the normal operations of the market, will not government action to expand demand simply reinforce those imperfections? Would it not be better to take action to eliminate them and hence reap the benefits of an efficient market? The argument becomes an issue of what is practicable rather than what is correct.[1]

In *The General Theory* Keynes changed his theoretical position entirely. A key element in his transition from the *Treatise* to *The General Theory* was the argument that unemployment is not due to short-run imperfections of the market mechanisms, but rather to its normal long-run operation:

> There are . . . I should admit, forces which one might fairly well call "automatic," which operate under any normal monetary system in the direction of restoring a long-period equilibrium between saving and investment. The point upon which I cast doubt—though the contrary is generally believed—is whether these "automatic forces" will . . . tend to bring about not only an equilibrium between saving and investment, but also an optimum level of output. (*JMK*. XIII, p. 295)

As a result then, the task of Keynes's new theory was:

> to explain the outstanding feature of our actual experience: namely, that we oscillate, avoiding the gravest extremes of fluctuations in employment and in prices in both directions, round an intermediate position appreciably below full employment and appreciably above the minimum employment a decline below which would endanger life. (Keynes, 1936, p. 254)

TABLE 1
Growth rates of gross domestic product,
gross domestic product per head of population,
and manufacturing output per person-hour, 1950–80 (percentages)

Gross Domestic Product

	UK	USA	FRG	FRANCE	ITALY	JAPAN
1950–60	2.6	3.2	7.6	4.4	5.9	8.1[a]
1960–70	2.8	3.8	4.1	5.6	5.5	11.1
1970–80	1.8	2.8	2.8	3.7	4.0	5.3

Gross Domestic Product Per Capita

	UK	USA	FRG	FRANCE	ITALY	JAPAN
1950–60	2.2	1.6	6.5	3.5	5.3	7.0[a]
1960–70	2.2	2.6	3.3	5.0	4.7	10.0
1970–80	1.8	1.7	2.7	3.6	3.2	4.0

Manufacturing Output Per Person-Hour

	UK	USA	FRG	FRANCE	ITALY	JAPAN
1950–60	2.0[b]	2.4[b]	6.0[b]	3.9[b]	4.1[b]	n.a.
1960–70	4.0	2.9	5.7[c]	6.8[c]	6.6[c]	12.1[c]
1970–80	2.4	2.9	3.9	4.8	4.5	6.4

Notes:

[a]1953–60.
[b]Total output (sum of all
sectors) per person-hour.
[c]1963–1970.
n.a. Not available.

Sources:

A. Maddison, Economic Growth in the
West; OECD, National Accounts;
OECD, Industrial Production;
National Institute Economic Review.

The intellectual justification for an interventionist policy could now be derived from a theory of the normal operations of the market. The scale and content of such a policy would depend upon the circumstances of the economy at a given time. But the foundations of an entirely new theory of economic policy were laid in *The General Theory*—or so it seemed to Keynes and his followers. These foundations are one element in our story. A second element must be the actual achievements of economic policy since World War II.

By virtually any criterion, British economic policy since World War II has been a failure. There have, of course, been some relatively short periods in which the economy appeared to have broken out of its steady decline relative to other major Western economies, but these have proved to be short-lived. Thus, while the economy achieved what were for Britain historically high rates of growth of GNP in the fifties and sixties, these growth rates were significantly below those achieved elsewhere (see Table 1).[2] The growth of productivity

TABLE 2
Shares of world exports of manufactures, 1960–80 (percentages)

	UK	USA	FRG	FRANCE	ITALY	JAPAN
1960	12.7	17.9	14.8	7.4	3.9	5.3
1970	8.6	15.3	15.8	6.9	5.7	9.3
1980	6.8	11.8	13.9	6.8	5.5	10.4

Sources: *Cambridge Economic Policy Review*, 1979; *National Institute Economic Review*, various issues.

in British manufacturing was also notably slow, and one important consequence of this has been a steady decline in Britain's share of world trade in manufactures (see Table 2). The outcome of these trends has become only too evident in the past five years: since 1979, output in manufacturing industry has fallen by 16 percent to a level approximating that of 1967 (a recession year); unemployment has reached approximately 14 percent, with a further 2 1/2 percent of the labor force engaged in government make-work schemes; and, despite the low level of domestic activity, the balance of payments on current account is barely in balance. Even so, the full extent of Britain's economic decline has been masked by the bounty of North Sea oil. From virtually nothing in 1975, oil production has risen to approximately 90 million metric tons per year, exceeding that of Kuwait. Oil exports accounted for 19 percent of the value of British exports in 1982. Without oil the balance of payments would be £5.8 billion in deficit, with a deficit on manufactures of £3.3 billion—this in a country that has traditionally enjoyed a surplus on trade in manufactures. Oil production has now peaked and within two to six years is likely to begin a steady long-term decline. Even if there were a significant upturn in world trade, the long-term prospects for the U.K. economy are very poor indeed. So the conditions that in the fifties and sixties determined a poor *relative* performance now contain the potential for absolute decline.[3]

It is against this background of failure, that the role of Keynes, and more generally of Keynesian economics, in the formation of the theory and practice of economic policy must be evaluated. The basic theses I will attempt to maintain are as follows:

1. The basic precept underlying the formation of economic policy in Britain since World War II has been what Andrew Shonfield (1965, p. 88) called "arm's-length government." Shonfield argued that "Britain's post-War experience provides [an] illustration of the way in which a living tentacle reaches out of past history, loops itself round, and holds fast to a solid block of the present. The striking thing in the British case is the extraordinary tenacity of older attitudes towards public power. Anything which smacked of a restless or over-energetic state, with ideas of guiding the nation on the basis of a long

view of its collective economic interest, was instinctively the object of suspi-cion'' (ibid). Nothing that has happened since Shonfield wrote leads me to amend his conclusion; indeed in the past decade a key element in British economic policy has been a desire to reduce intervention by the state at macroeconomic as well as microeconomic levels. Ultimately the rationale for a noninterventionist policy rests on a belief in the efficient operation of free markets. Inherited from the glittering era of British nineteenth-century eco-nomic success, this belief is deeply ingrained in British economic thought *and in British economic and political institutions*.

2. The implications for the economic role of the state that might be drawn from Keynes's *General Theory* were a threat to this established order. If, as Keynes argued, the normal functioning of the market was incapable of ensuring an adequate volume of investment to maintain the economy at full employment, there is a clear role for state expenditure. But the argument may be taken further. The volume of investment is but one aspect of the general process of accumulation. If the market cannot ensure a satisfactory volume of investment, who is to say that the *composition* of investment will accord with social objectives? Within Keynes's critique there lay the potential rationale for a *dirigiste* economic strategy, geared not only toward maintaining the level of activity but also toward guiding the structural development of the economy. Any such *dirigiste* interpretation of Keynes's analysis clearly failed to make headway against established opinion despite the apparent success of Keynesian methods in the formulation of fiscal policy. Keynes's ideas were confined to a ghetto labeled ''macroeconomics''; ''microeconomics'' remained the pre-serve of orthodox pre-Keynesian economics, and much of economic policy.

3. Much of the responsibility, if that is the appropriate word, for this limitation of Keynes's analysis to macroeconomic policy rests with political forces and traditions within British society. However, a major contribution to the limitation of the impact of Keynes's ideas is to be found in crucial failings in the ideas themselves. These failings enabled orthodox principles to be resuscitated in the form of the so-called neoclassical synthesis, which in turn provided the intellectual rationale for the mix of short-term macroeconomic adjustments and essentially free-market industrial strategies that characterized postwar economic policy.

4. The outcome is an extraordinary paradox: it was the apparent success of Keynesian macroeconomic policy that enabled orthodox theories of the market mechanism to survive the humiliation of the thirties and then reemerge in the seventies to the discomforture of the rump of Keynesian ideas. The revival of monetarism is therefore not so much a reinstatement of belief in the market mechanism as the triumphant resurgence of a belief that never went away.

A full development and justification of these theses would go far beyond the scale of this essay; only the bare outlines are possible here.[4] Nonetheless, the essence of the case is, I think, clear: the theoretical message of *The General Theory* has been reconstructed to provide a safe haven for pre-

Keynesian ideas which, fitting best with the social and political forces of the British economy, have played a major role in forming the economic policy of the past thirty years.

The discussion will proceed in three stages: first, a schematic overview of the formation of British economic policy since 1939, in which the "Keynesian" and "non-Keynesian" elements are identified; second, a discussion of the theoretical limitations of *The General Theory* that weakened Keynes's argument and resulted in his theory being absorbed into the corpus of the orthodox analysis he had attempted to overthrow; and finally, an attempt to draw together the threads of the discussion to justify the four theses just outlined.

II

The theory and practice of economic policy in Britain since the war fall into four distinct phases: (1) the war economy and reconstruction, 1939–51; (2) the resurgence of the market, 1951–61; (3) planning discredited, 1961–76; (4) the triumph of monetarism, 1976 to the present.

War Economy and Reconstruction

At the outbreak of the war, Keynesian concepts had not penetrated the Treasury. Budgetary policy was still directed toward the financial needs of the government rather than the balance of resource utilization. The thirties had witnessed a significant reversal of many traditional aspects of British economic policy, notably the abandonment of free trade and the institution of a comprehensive system of industrial protection. But the cheap-money policy that had been the other characteristic of the immediate prewar years was based on the supposedly firm foundation of a budget surplus, albeit reinforced by strict controls on foreign investment. The crucial events in the development of Keynesian policy were the publication of *How to Pay for the War* and the accession of Churchill to the post of prime minister in May 1940, which brought Keynes into the Treasury. The importance of *How to Pay for the War* lay not so much in the idea of compulsory saving to limit the pressure of wartime demand on resources, but rather in the budgetary framework used. Keynes demonstrated in a practical, empirical manner how to express the budget decision in terms of effective demand. Henceforth, instead of being narrowly concerned with government finance, fiscal policy would be seen as an important balancing item in the larger whole comprising the flow of national income and output and the external balance of payments (see Winch, 1969, p. 261). The first budget to be formulated on Keynesian lines was presented by Sir Kingsley Wood in 1941, and among the papers accompanying the budget statement was Stone and Meade's estimate of national income and expenditure. The pattern of budget calculation was set for the next thirty-five years.

The new approach to budgetary policy was, however, to play a subsidiary role in the organization of the war effort, in which direct quantitative controls over production, allocation of materials and labor, and consumption, were to be the principal means of economic organization; financial issues were secondary. Nonetheless, the success of budgetary policy may be gauged precisely by the fact that ''those responsible for organising Britain's war effort were never forced to feel that financial policy was important'' (Sayers, 1956, p. 21). Monetary policy was directed solely toward the maintenance of a low interest rate (3 percent) in order to minimize the cost of financing the deficit.

Commitment to the postwar pursuit of full-employment policies was stated in the famous White Paper of 1944, of which the first sentence declared that ''the Government accept as one of their primary aims and responsibilities the maintenance of a high and stable level of employment after the War.'' A new era of state intervention in economic affairs in peacetime had apparently begun. But the White Paper was not all it seemed, for it was also argued:

> Both at home and abroad the handling of our monetary problems is regarded as a test of the general firmness of the policy of the Government. An undue growth of national indebtedness will have a quick result on confidence. But no less serious would be a budgetary deficit arising from a fall of revenue due to depressed industrial and commercial conditions. Therefore, in controlling the situation, especially in the difficult years after the war, the Government will have equally in mind the need to maintain the national income, and the need for a budgetary equilibrium such as will maintain the confidence in the future which is necessary for a healthy and enterprising industry. (H. M. Treasury, 1944, pp. 25–26)

It is evident that the Keynesian conception of budgetary policy had not been universally accepted in the Treasury.

The immediate postwar era may be divided into two distinct periods: Hugh Dalton's chancellorship, characterized primarily by the cheap-money policy, the severe shortages of the winter of 1947, and the convertibility debacle of 1947; and the later recovery under the direction of Sir Stafford Cripps, which laid the foundations for the attainment of levels of consumption in excess of prewar levels and successfully completed the process of postwar reconstruction to such an extent that a ''bonfire of controls'' was possible in 1950—their task was done.

Austin Robinson has argued that the period after 1947 marked an era of long-term planning, utilizing the controls inherited from the war to effect the structural transformation of the economy (Robinson, 1967). But the general consensus seems to be that the measures adopted were essentially *short run* and that no general long-term interventionist strategy was in fact implemented (Shonfield, 1965, pp. 89–99; Dow, 1964, pp. 13–54; Winch, 1969, pp. 282–87). Nor was economic policy notably Keynesian, direct controls rather than budgetary policies being the key determinants of general economic balance.

Taking the period as a whole, it may be argued that the major influence of Keynesian ideas was on the presentation of budgetary policy and the construction of the statistical apparatus that made that presentation possible. The cheap-money policy and the use of direct controls to achieve essentially short-term objectives were pre-Keynesian devices. And beneath the surface there rumbled the ever-present belief in the efficiency of the market mechanism, a belief shortly to be fully reaffirmed in the economic policies of the Conservative party.

The Resurgence of the Market

The true flavor of economic policy in the fifties may be judged from the chapter headings of Christopher Dow's study *The Management of the British Economy, 1945–60*. Apart from a brief discussion of the reconstruction policy, "management" consists entirely of fiscal and monetary policies. All the discriminatory policies and controls that had played an important, if short-run, role in the policies of the Labour Government were dismantled as rapidly as possible.

The emphasis of government policy was now to be on macroeconomic management, with a renewed role for monetary policy as a regulator of activity and a brake on inflation. This latter revival was particularly well received in the financial press (Dow, 1965, p. 69). Nor was this all. By the mid-fifties the Treasury was seriously considering a policy whereby exchange controls would be abolished and the volume and direction of economic activity would be determined by the unimpeded play of world market forces, with domestic influences confined to monetary policy and exchange-rate manipulation. The idea was dropped (Shonfield, 1965, pp. 100–101), but similar vestiges of pre-Keynesian orthodoxy were evident in the monetary policies of Mr. Thorneycroft in 1957.

But it was broad macroeconomic management, notably confined by balance-of-payments considerations, that dominated the period. It was the period of the policy application of the neoclassical synthesis, in which it was believed that fine-tuning of fiscal and monetary policy, allied with free markets, would achieve not only full employment but an efficient allocation of resources. It was also the era of "stop–go," in which successive waves of fiscal expansion were halted by deterioration of the balance of payments. But despite the clear constraint imposed upon the economy by the external position, the only devices deployed to deal with the problem were macroeconomic. There was no significant attempt to tackle the problems as a structural issue. Indeed, the manner in which fiscal and monetary policy were used to manipulate the balance-of-payments position (including speculative flows) was such as to discourage any long-term perspective in investment planning—the very thing required to arrest the decline in competitiveness.

The fifties—often summed up in Harold Macmillan's famous phrase "You've never had it so good,"—were years of economic failure, a failure partially masked by the rapid expansion of the world economy.

Planning Discredited

The evident failure of the British economy in the fifties to perform as well as Britain's European neighbors led, in the early sixties, to a reappraisal of the objectives and methods of economic policy. The remarkable rates of growth achieved by France and Germany encouraged the idea that French and German institutional devices might be imported to good effect. Since construction of an industrial banking system along German lines would trespass on the prerogatives of the economically and politically most powerful group in British society, the financial interest, it was the French model that commanded attention. The National Economic Development Office was established by the Conservative government in 1962 as a British version of the Commissariat Général du Plan, though it was placed carefully outside the apparatus of government and its main instruments were exchange of information and moral suasion. The Labour government's *National Plan* of 1965 was similarly toothless. As Austin Robinson pointed out (1967), it contained neither a clear analysis of what the problems of the British economy might be nor any instruments with which to achieve its vague objectives. Even the pretense of long-term planning disappeared in the balance-of-payments crisis of 1966.

Other interventionist strategies pursued in this period included the establishment of the Industrial Reorganization Corporation in 1966 as a means of rationalizing British industrial structure (in other words, it promoted mergers) and some government attempts to invest in research and development. Neither policy had any major impact, and both were wound up by the 1970 Conservative government (see Meadows, 1978; Mottershead, 1978). The only really influential planning organization set up in this period seems to have been the National Enterprise Board, established in 1975, when operating under the aggressive leadership of Tony Benn as minister of industry. However, Benn's determination to effect major structural changes in British industry soon ran into fierce political opposition, and he was removed from his post following the financial crisis of 1976.

Taken as a whole, the sixties were a period of desperate experiment in economic institutions, but experiment guided by no particular theory of economic behavior other than the orthodox theory of the efficient market. Attempts at planning, such as they were, were based on the theory of indicative planning. The idea was that the market would work efficiently if only some barriers to its operation, especially information about future investment and production decisions, could be overcome. So the role of the indicative plan was to facilitate the exchange of information. This elevated the exchange of information above any conception of what should be done.

The Triumph of Monetarism

From the end of World War II, whatever might have been the vicissitudes of interventionist thinking, the broad lines of budgetary policy, and indeed of monetary policy, had been formed on Keynesian lines. The role of the budget and of monetary policy was to ensure that the level of effective demand was appropriate to the full utilization of resources, with due regard for the rate of inflation and the foreign balance.

All this ended in 1976. The transformation had been foreshadowed by changes in the mechanisms of monetary control inaugurated by the Bank of England's consultative paper *Competition and Credit Control*, published in May 1971. Tew has argued that no fundamental break in policy was then involved (Tew, 1978). However, the new framework for monetary policy was complementary to the more dramatic changes of 1976. Then Labour Chancellor Denis Healey, under considerable pressure from the IMF, changed the entire orientation of British budgetary policy. Henceforth, instead of budgets being conceived as the means of adjusting the level of effective demand to the available resources, they were to be geared to the dictates of a preconceived rate of monetary expansion. The mechanisms of Keynesian calculation, let alone Keynesian methods or objectives, were decisively abandoned in favor of what was believed to be monetary probity.

The collapse of any pretension to Keynesian methods was confirmed by Mrs. Thatcher's Conservative government. However the outcome of the fiscal and monetary policies of recent years might be interpreted—the relationship between declared objectives and outcomes has been a matter of dispute—the theoretical foundations of those policies have been pre-Keynesian. Faith in the market mechanism has been forcefully asserted by government attempts to withdraw from any form of interventionist activity and by the introduction of sharply deflationary budgets in a period of distinctly depressed activity. The Keynesian influence on economic policy has shrunk to the level of a statistical office.

Taking the whole postwar period together, two elements are particularly prominent: (1) the preservation of the fundamental British commitment to free trade and laissez-faire, the policy of the two most influential segments of British political life—the large companies operating on an international perspective and the financial institutions of the city of London; (2) the comfortable coexistence of macroeconomic *nondiscriminatory* economic policies and the version of Keynesian theory that dominated academic and policymaking debates. It is the substance of that theory which is, I believe, the key to the rise and decline of "Keynesian" economic policy.

III

If Keynes's *General Theory* contained anything new, it had to be something other than an analysis of the short-run fluctuations of a market economy from a long-run (be it ever so mythical) full-employment equilibrium—fluctuations that might be created and perpetuated by market imperfections such as sticky money wages, inappropriate monetary policies, or the destabilizing effects of uncertainty and expectations. "Imperfectionist" theories of short-run disequilibriums based on such pragmatic inhibitions to the operation of the market mechanism had been the norm since, at least, Marshall's discussion of the trade cycle and financial pessimism (Garegnani, 1978, pp. 41–43). And yet it is exactly in terms of such imperfections that Keynesian economics is presented today, whether they be the traditional sticky money wages (Hicks, 1937; Modigliani, 1944), failure of information (Clower, 1965), false conjectures (Hahn, 1977), or generally lethargic adjustment processes (Tobin and Buiter, 1976).

That Keynes's new theory of output—the principle of effective demand—may be so readily incorporated into the corpus of the very theory he attempted to refute derives from two closely related failings in *The General Theory*:

1. Keynes failed to present any significant critique of orthodox theory. His criticism consisted of either propositions that were untrue (for example, that orthodox theorists *assume* full employment or fail to notice that savings always equals investment) or the juxtaposition of his own theory to that of his predecessors (for example, the claim that the rate of interest was a monetary and not a real phenomenon was not a critique, it *was* Keynes's theory of the rate of interest. Although this theory might be *compared* to orthodox theory, it did not constitute a demonstration that orthodox theory was false).

2. Keynes incorporated into his own theory an important element of the orthodox view: the elastic demand schedule for investment. The marginal efficiency of capital schedule (together with the presumption of a well-behaved demand curve for labor) proved to be the Achilles' heel of the Keynesian system (Garegnani, 1978, 1979). For if the volume of investment is an elastic function of the rate of interest, then there must be some rate of interest corresponding to a full-employment volume of investment. Despite Keynes's later claims that his theory of the rate of interest was an afterthought (Keynes, 1937, p. 250), it came to be the cornerstone of the entire system, for "in the absence of money and in the absence—we must, of course, also suppose—of any other commodity with the assumed characteristics of money, the rates of interest [on financial and real assets] would only reach equilibrium when there is full employment" (Keynes, 1936, p. 235).

In the orthodox theory that Keynes had sought to refute, the determination of quantity equilibrium and the determination of equilibrium prices are explained by one and the same theory. With respect to the analysis of employment, this may be expressed in terms of two propositions: (a) that there exists a set of prices at which all markets, including the labor market, clear; and (b) that variations in relative prices are associated with variations in output such that the economy tends toward the market-clearing equilibrium.[5]

In the light of the role that Keynes has assigned to the rate of interest, it would appear that Keynes was resting his theory of employment on a denial of proposition (b) rather than any denial of (a). In other words, he was following in a more elaborate manner exactly the path trod by his orthodox predecessors and leaving the core of orthodox theory intact (for an elaboration of this argument, see the introduction to Eatwell and Milgate, 1983). It is then not particularly surprising to find that with some minor modification (notably the transformation of liquidity-preference theory into a demand for money function), Keynes's theory could be presented in the manner with which we all are now familiar: not as a critique, but as a pragmatic analysis of short-run disequilibria.

Today the deficiencies in Keynes's argument may be remedied, to the ultimate benefit of what he saw as the main thrust of his theory: that variations in output maintain equality between savings and investment and that there is no tendency, even in the best of all possible worlds, for the level of output to correspond to full employment. The missing critique of orthodox theory is to be found in the outcome of the debate over the neoclassical theory of distribution and, in particular, over its treatment of "capital" as a "factor of production" on a par, so to speak, with land and labor. While this debate is seen by many as a rather esoteric controversy in the more abstract realms of economic theory, its implications are more far-reaching than has hitherto been appreciated. The central conclusion of the debate may be summed up broadly as follows: when applied to the analysis of a capitalistic economy (that is, an economic system where some of the means of production are reproducible), the neoclassical theory is logically incapable of determining the long-run equilibrium of the economy and the associated general rate of profit whenever capital consists of more than one reproducible commodity. Since, in equilibrium, relative prices may be expressed as functions of the general rate of profit, the neoclassical proposition that equilibrium prices are determined by demand and supply (or, more generally, by the competitive resolution of individual utility maximization subject to constraint) is also deprived of its logical foundation (see Garegnani, 1970).

The relevance of this critique of the neoclassical theory of value and distribution to the problem of the missing critique of the neoclassical theory of output and employment should be apparent from what has already been said. Because the neoclassical analysis of the determination of prices and the determination of quantities is one and the same theory (that of the mutual interaction of demand and supply), the critique of the neoclassical theory of value is simultaneously a critique of the neoclassical theory of output and employment. Therefore, proposition (a) must, on the grounds of the requirement of logical consistency alone, be answered in the negative. Proposition (b)—from which neoclassical theory derives the idea that under the operation of the market mechanism there is a long-run tendency toward a determinate full-employment equilibrium—is rendered superfluous.

But this is not all. If the general (or long-run) case of the neoclassical model has been shown to be logically deficient, then all imperfectionist arguments—which are derived by examining the implications of the introduction of particular (or short-run) modifications into the general case—are incapable of providing a satisfactory analysis of the problem of unemployment. This is not to say that many of the features of the economic system cited by the imperfectionists will have no role to play in a theory of employment based on foundations quite different from those adopted by the neoclassicists. After all, much of the credibility of imperfectionist arguments derives from their pragmatic objections to the direct applicability of the assumptions of the more abstract versions of demand-and-supply theory. But pragmatism is not enough. The implications of more realistic hypotheses must be explored in the context of the general theoretical framework within which they are applied. Since the account of a self-regulating market mechanism that operates according to the theory of demand and supply is unacceptable on the grounds that it is logically inconsistent, any analysis of unemployment that takes its rationale from that model is also unsatisfactory.

Not only is the orthodox theory of employment, with its derivatives, now shown to rest on inadequate logical foundations, but also the marginal efficiency of capital schedule, which is derived from orthodox capital theoretic propositions, is now deprived of any logical coherence. With no marginal efficiency of capital schedule, there is no role for liquidity-preference theory as a means of preventing the rate of interest from falling to a full-employment level, there being no such thing! What remains, thrown now into stark relief, is the proposition that the level of activity is determined by the level of effective demand.

This argument has an important corollary. Keynes's theory of effective demand rests on the denial of a mechanism by which supply-and-demand theory ensures the mutual adjustment of savings and investment and of demand to capacity. But this denial involves the rejection not only of some macroeconomic implications of neoclassical theory but of the very core of neoclassical theory itself. Not only does the market mechanism fail to ensure an optimum level of output, but it necessarily fails to ensure an optimum composition of output, too.

IV

The interpretation of *The General Theory* that suggests that an efficient economic policy concern itself only with the maintenance of effective demand in as nondiscriminatory and noninterventionist a manner as possible, leaving the content of economic activity to be determined by the market, not only fitted well with the traditional British abhorrence of an active state, but also appeared to be derived from Keynes's own vision of the implications of his theory.

If we suppose the volume of output to be given, *i.e.* to be determined by forces outside the classical scheme of thought, then there is no objection to be raised against the classical analysis of the manner in which private self-interest will determine what in particular is produced, in what proportions the factors of production will be combined to produce it, and how the value of the final product will be distributed between them. (Keynes, 1936, pp. 378–79)

This famous argument was, as we have seen, a consequence of Keynes's

failure to work through one implication of his own theory. But the absorption
of Keynes's analysis into the neoclassical synthesis carried much weightier
implications. Keynes's belief that "a somewhat comprehensive socialisation
of investment will prove the only means of securing an approximation to full
employment" (1936, p. 378)) could now be replaced by an appropriate monetary policy, and if that were not forthcoming, an incomes policy, to ensure the
requisite relationship between money wages and the available money supply.
Arguments for fiscal manipulation of the economy now were conducted on
empirical or practical grounds, the locus of debate being the relative elasticity
of IS and LM curves.

The traumas of the thirties made politically impossible an immediate
return to the policies, even the modes of thought, of that decade. The orthodox
view of the market mechanism and of the appropriate parameters of monetary
and fiscal policy had been completely discredited. The election of the Labour
government in 1945 appeared to herald a new era not only in politics but in
economics as well. But the shift in the balance of political power proved to be
an illusion. The same interests that had dominated British political life for the
past century continued to assert themselves. Fundamental ways of doing
things were not changed.

The economic problems facing Britain at the end of the war were formi-
dable. Short-run problems of demobilization and debt rescheduling were dealt
with by Cripps's reconstruction policy and by Marshall aid. But the more
deep-seated, long-term problems were not dealt with at all. The rise of the
United States as the major exporter of manufactures merely exacerbated the
steady decline of U.K. industry, which had begun at the end of the nineteenth
century. Britain's competitors—France and Germany, as well as the United
States—had forged new financial and governmental institutions in order to
catch up with and surpass British industrial performance. Now a similar
institutional realignment was needed to effect the structural transformation
required of Britain. It did not take place.

Why the needed changes did not occur, and why the preconditions for
deindustrialization were so firmly established (Singh, 1977), are matters of
considerable dispute, involving historical, ideological, and economic dimensions. But it is clear that the new Keynesian doctrines of noninterventionist
macroeconomic policy allied with a free-market microeconomic policy reinforced those elements opposed to structural reforms. This union of theory and
political practice defined the economic consensus of the fifties and sixties.
Both Conservative and Labour governments, however committed to "modernization" they might be, did not regard interventionist industrial policies—or
indeed fundamental reform of the financial system in its relationship to industrial investment—as being on the agenda.

The coexistence of Keynesian theory (even in a "bowdlerized" form)
and neoclassical theory was always uncomfortable. The monetarist revival
resulted in the demise of Keynesianism. Once-discredited ideas were not
reinstated as the bases of the formation of economic policy. The Keynesian

resistance was theoretically weak primarily because the Keynesians of the neoclassical synthesis *shared* the underlying theoretical conceptions of the monetarists. The debate over economic policy reverted to the prewar discussion of practicalities.

The failure of Keynesianism, indeed the contribution of Keynesianism to its own demise, derived from a failure to elucidate the truly radical theoretical propositions implicit in Keynes's analysis. If this had been done, then Keynesianism could not have become a quasi–free-market doctrine. Instead, it would have clashed directly with the interests vested in free markets and free trade. It is not Keynes that has failed but Keynesianism. The essential message of Keynes—that the market mechanism does not work to establish a social optimum—is more relevant today than at any time since the thirties. But it must be a message of microeconomic interventionism, with national and international dimensions, as well as macroeconomic control.

Notes

1. The characterization of "sticky money wages" or even "sticky interest rates" as short-run phenomena, the long-run determination of which may be explained along orthodox lines, is clear enough. Unless it is argued that prices are completely arbitrary, any particular level must be determined somehow. The position of "uncertainty and expectations," the most frequently cited source of market imperfection, is less easily disposed of. There is no reason to suppose a priori that uncertainty will "disappear" in the long run. Indeed, uncertainty concerning the future is a condition of life; hence, a model of expectations formation should be an integral part of any satisfactory analysis of the market economy. However, as rational-expectations theorists have demonstrated, this does not imply that uncertainty may be imposed upon orthodox theory as an imperfection inhibiting the normal workings of the market mechanism (see Milgate and Eatwell, 1983).

2. As is evident from Table 1, the relative failure of the British economy has been to some extent mirrored in the United States, particularly with respect to the rate of productivity growth in manufacturing. Nonetheless, in the past decade not only has the United States achieved a higher rate of productivity growth than the United Kingdom, but total output in U.S. manufacturing was 40 percent higher in 1981 than in 1970, whereas manufactured output in the United Kingdom was 9 percent *lower*.

3. It is of the utmost importance not to regard the dramatic declines of the last few years as a short-run phenomenon attributable largely to the policies of Mrs. Thatcher's government. While I would argue that recent government policies have exacerbated Britain's economic problems, they have not created them. The weak competitiveness that is the key to the problem is the product, as we shall see, of the economic policies of successive governments since the end of the war. In the fifties and sixties the persistent trend decline in trade performance was masked by the very large surplus in manufactured trade at the beginning of the period and by the buoyancy of the industrial economies of the world taken as a whole. As is the way with exponential trends, however, the trend has asserted itself with steadily greater force, to which has been added in recent years the slowdown and then stagnation in world trade.

4. The theses of this paper are developed at greater length in my book *Whatever Happened to Britain?* and, with respect to theoretical issues, in *Keynes's Economics and the Theory of Value and Distribution*, edited by Murray Milgate and myself.

5. The fact that neoclassical theory lacks an adequate analysis of stability is a fundamental weakness of the orthodox approach. However, this issue will be ignored in what follows so that we may concentrate on the main point.

References

Blackaby, F., ed. 1978. *British Economic Policy, 1960–74* (Cambridge: Cambridge University Press).

Clower, R. 1965. "The Keynesian Counter-revolution." In *The Theory of Interest Rates*, edited by Hahn and Brechling (London: Macmillan, 1965).

Dow, J. C. R. *The Management of the British Economy, 1945–60* (Cambridge: Cambridge University Press).

Eatwell, J. 1981. *Whatever Happened to Britain?* (London: Duckworth. New York: Oxford University Press).

Eatwell, J. and M. Milgate, eds. 1983. *Keynes's Economics and the Theory of Value and Distribution.* (London: Duckworth. New York: Oxford University Press).

Garegnani, P. 1978, 1979. "Notes on Consumption, Investment and Effective Demand, I. II." *Cambridge Journal of Economics*, as reprinted in Eatwell and Milgate (1983).

Garegnani, P. 1970. "Heterogeneous Capital, the Production Function and the Theory of Capital." *Review of Economic Studies.*

Hahn, F. 1977. "Keynesian Economics and General Equilibrium Theory." In *The Microfoundation of Macroeconomics*, edited by Harcourt (London: Macmillan, 1977).

Hicks, J. R. 1937. "Mr. Keynes and the 'Classics.' " *Econometrica.*

Keynes, J. M. 1936. *The General Theory of Employment, Interest, and Money* (London: Macmillan).

———. 1937. "Alternative Theories of the Rate of Interest." *Economic Journal.*

———. *The Collected Writings of John Maynard Keynes.* 30 vols. (London: Macmillan). (Roman numeral indicates volume number.)

Meadows, P. 1978. "Planning." In *British Economic Policy, 1960–74*, edited by F. T. Blackaby (1978).

Milgate, M., and J. Eatwell. 1983. "Unemployment and the Market Mechanism." In *Keynes's Economics and the Theory of Value and Distribution*, edited by J. Eatwell and M. Milgate.

Modigliani, F. 1944. "Liquidity Preference and the Theory of Interest and Money." *Econometrica.*

Mottershead, P. 1978. "Industrial Policy." In *British Economic Policy, 1960–74*, edited by F. T. Blackaby (1978).

Robinson, E. A. G. 1967. *Economic Planning in the United Kingdom* (Cambridge: Cambridge University Press).

Sayers, R. S. 1956. *Financial Policy, 1939–1945* (London: H. M. Stationery Office).

Shonfield, A. 1965. *Modern Capitalism* (Oxford: Oxford University Press).

Singh, A. 1977. "Britain in the World Economy: A Case of De-Industrialization?" *Cambridge Journal of Economics.*

Tew, B. 1978. "Monetary Policy." In *British Economic Policy, 1960–74*, edited by F. Blackaby (1978).

Tobin, J., and W. Buiter. 1976. "Long-run Effects of Fiscal and Monetary Policy on Aggregate Demand." In *Monetarism*, edited by J. L. Stein (Amsterdam, North Holland).

Winch, D. 1969. *Economics and Policy* (London: Hodder and Stoughton).

8

The Influence of Keynes on French Economic Policy: Past and Present

Robert Boyer

Keynes brought to economics a new conception regarding the positive roles social and political organizations could play in promoting economic change, in eliminating crises and stimulating growth. He intended his conception to replace the older order, which held that natural laws governed social and economic activity, that these laws were not to be tampered with, and that governments could only deduce them and utilize them.

That Keynesian policies have failed of late to maintain full employment free of distortions and inflation is attributed by anti-Keynesians to policies that violate these laws.[1] Some Keynesians disagree. Some argue that Keynesian policies have failed because governments have not followed Keynes faithfully. Others contend that new problems brought forth by Keynesian policies could be solved by innovative use of his analysis. At the present time, public opinion and governments are philosophically closer to the anti-Keynesian position, believing that inflation, unemployment, and deficits stem from Keynesian errors.[2]

Against this backdrop the French case is interesting because it represents a reformulation of economic policy using some Keynesian inputs. In the period extending from World War II into the 1960s, Keynesian policies contributed to French rehabilitation and modernization. Is it possible to evaluate the efficacy of these policies?

The Keynesian Revolution cannot be evaluated in the abstract. It is not so much a matter of monitoring a simple application of a scientific theory as watching an ongoing political attempt to govern capital formation in order to remove the system's instabilities.

It is now recognized that in the success of Keynesian policies lay the seeds of their own destruction: for example, new demands on profits adversely affected investment and productivity; the resolution of distribution inequities fed inflation; diverging inflation rates in OECD countries imperiled the fixed exchange-rate system. And there are limitations on national economic policies for a nation increasingly involved in international trade. All these problems have troubled policymakers in France during the last decade.

The departure from Keynesian orthodoxy in France cannot be attributed solely to the shift of government toward conservatism. Mitterand used some Keynesian policies after May 1981 but without success. Inflation persisted. Inflation lagged. France's rising external debt was aggravated by worldwide economic deflation. Hence the revival of pre-Keynesian concepts is not simply a matter of propaganda or ideology. However debatable are the policies of monetarist, supply-side, or rational-expectations schools, they do point to the presence of real macroeconomic problems.

This then is the challenge Keynesians face today. What is needed is innovation and extension of Keynes's line of analysis to the present crisis. These are the main themes in this paper.

The first part is an attempt to clarify the nature and significance of Keynesian conceptions concerning the functioning of modern economies and the adequacy of economic policies. The second part describes the original form Keynesianism took after World War II, with special reference to the French case. The third part analyzes the limits encountered since the early seventies by traditional stabilization policies. The strategy applied by the Socialist government after May 1981 raises a particularly interesting question: What are the consequences of a leftist variant of Keynesian expansionary policy? The fourth part focuses on the limits of the Socialist strategy. The concluding fifth part stresses the main topics on the Keynesian agenda and the need for new tools and theoretical formulations toward a positive solution of the present crisis.

The Many Ways of Being Keynesian

Before examining the Keynesian aspects of French economic policy, one must define Keynesian policy. After all, in the period of postwar prosperity, almost everybody declared himself or herself to be a follower of Keynes. Were there not significant differences between the successive conceptions of Keynes through his numerous writings, as well as between *The General Theory* and the various theoretical constructs elaborated by Hicks, Kalecki, Robinson, Kaldor or Samuelson, Tobin, Clower, Leijonhufvud, Davidson, and Minsky? It may be useful to distinguish two broad conceptions in Keynes's contributions and hence two approaches to economic policy.

The Fundamentalist Keynesian Reformist. At the core of most of Keynes's writings, one finds a central theme presented as a matter of fact and as a theoretical conclusion: namely, pure market mechanisms are unable to maintain full employment and, more generally, growth and stability. This follows from the accumulation process under modern capitalist conditions. At a first level of analysis, a low marginal efficiency of capital, interacting with a moderate propensity to consume—due in particular to unequal income distribution—leads to a deflationary adjustment of production and hence employment. At a second and more profound level, investment activity cannot be maintained steadily at its full-employment level in a fully developed monetary economy; business expectations tend to be rather myopic or erratic, so that they stimulate the boom through speculation and aggravate the slump. For the same reasons, an unemployment state, once prevailing, will be stable, since expectations governing investment decisions tend to be self-fulfilling.

Such profound imbalances can only be countered by a vast program of reforms and a complete reformulation of the ends and means of state intervention. The Keynesian reformism, which logically results from the fundamentalist view, aims, therefore, at an innovative policy strategy as an alternative to both laissez-faire and socialist programs. Government should try to create the general legal and institutional framework in which private production decisions and income distribution can be determined more efficiently by private self-interest. Toward this objective, Keynes proposed in his *General Theory* a series of reforms in three key areas: first, progressive taxation and social services to increase the propensity to consume, reducing the saving of the rich and augmenting the consumption of the poor; second, centralized control over the monetary system to promote an adequate stimulus to investment decisions; and third, if necessary, a direct influence upon investment through public works or control over private investment. These moves toward greater equality in income distribution, the euthanasia of the rentier,[3] and a comprehensive socialization of investment[4] should be complemented by the dissemination of data relevant for business decisions. The public provision of data necessary for investment decisions can be conceived as a kind of socialization in expectations formation or indicative planning.[5]

France adopted many of the central themes identified with fundamentalist Keynesianism for postwar modernization. Nevertheless, it is important to present briefly a more restricted conception of Keynesianism (effective-demand Keynesianism, or effective-demand management), since it has been at the heart of the monetarist-Keynesian controversy during the sixties and in subsequent attacks by neoclassical economists.

A More Limited View: Effective-Demand Keynesianism and Fine-tuning Policies. Whatever the positions adopted by the different Keynesian schools on the principal questions, there existed a simplified but representative Keynes macromodel. In the limited view the rejection of Say's Law is manifest from the possibility that planned saving and planned investment need never be equal. During the sixties this simplified Keynesian model, exhibiting the multiplier effects of "autonomous demand" (as presented in the first chapters of Hansen's *A Guide to Keynes* and in the IS-LM formulation by Hicks), became widely accepted as Keynes's legacy. Moreover, almost every macroeconometric model incorporated this effective demand Keynesianism as an essential component. French economists accepted this conception, and the first completely formalized macromodel built for the Treasury in the mid-sixties was clearly based on the framework of effective-demand Keynesianism.[6] (Other labels for this line of analysis included Leijonhufvud's income expenditure theory, Barrère's circuit theory, and Coddington's hydraulic Keynesianism.)

It is not really surprising that such a precise but limited formulation of Keynes's complex and multifaceted ideas led to very definite conceptions regarding economic policy. First, interventions by the state should not be directed solely toward such traditional objectives as stabilizing the purchasing power of money or balancing public expenditure and receipts but must instead aim at maintaining full employment, whatever may be the transitory effects of such policies upon public accounts and money. Second, fiscal and monetary instruments must be used for demand management—namely, such expansionary policies as extension of public spending, tax cuts, and low interest rates— when effective demand is less than necessary to support full employment; restrictive policies—the same instruments reversed—as soon as excessive demand triggers an inflationary process. Thus, business cycles could be reduced in their duration and amplitude. Through steady investment, growth could be stimulated and the budget balanced over the course of the cycle. In fact, such fine-tuning policies appear as the direct consequence of effective-demand Keynesianism, at the very least in the form it took in the sixties.[7]

In an even more limited sense, Keynesianism was sometimes further reduced to the notion that fiscal policy was far more efficient than monetary policy in controlling the level of economic activity, due to the existence of a liquidity trap in money holdings or a very low interest-elasticity of investment. This hyperrestricted Keynesianism, generally considered in juxtaposition with an equally unsophisticated monetarism, could define a final, simplistic conception of Keynesian economic policy, that is, mainly budgets matter. This third and rather extreme statement will be considered only incidentally in the present text.

Given these introductory classifying definitions, let me now describe the evolution of Keynesianism in France since World War II.

French Economic Policies After 1945: A Long Tradition in an Original Form of Keynesianism

During the interwar period, classical theory and traditional conceptions of economic policy predominated. Nevertheless, as the crises of the thirties appeared deep and lasting, there was analysis leading to alternative policies to laissez-faire. The so-called purchase-power theory expected increases in wages to stimulate demand and reduce underutilized capacities.[8] A recurrent proposal during the period of crisis was to promote public works in order to give jobs to the unemployed. In many other countries during the thirties,[9] one can find economists groping after the same theory as Keynes, without direct reference to or knowledge of his various analyses.[10]

In fact, before World War II, Keynes's writings—and in particular *The General Theory*—had not been translated into French. That Keynes was an opponent of German reparations and ostensibly unfavorable to French interests, moreover, seems to have limited the influence of the British economist on French public opinion.[11] It is generally accepted that the policy pursued by the

Front Populaire after 1936 owed much more to an implicit purchasing-power theory and to the observation of foreign experiences—the New Deal in the United States and Schacht's policy in Germany—than to a direct influence by Keynes.[12] But the short-lived Front Populaire was not sufficient to promote a way out of the crisis. A conservative coalition came back to power, benefiting from the financial and social objections to Blum's program. His institutional reforms covering labor-management relations, minimum wages, the social-security system, taxes, and public interventions required a long period before they could stimulate a new economic and social dynamic. Unfortunately the program lacked a sufficiently complete and coherent framework. Such a framework, the compatibility of the various components, and an adequate statistical apparatus were present after World War II. Keynesianism appeared then as a powerful means for unifying and clarifying a vast program of social and economic reforms. Let me stress the four features of this complex process of transforming economic policy.

The Prominent Role of Higher Civil Servants in the Diffusion and Implementation of Keynesianism. Few people in France seem to have read the English version of *The General Theory* or the earlier works of Keynes.[13] A French translation by Jean de Largentaye (an *inspecteur des finances*, a top-level official in Treasury) was available in 1942. Even though the book reviews were laudatory and favorable, *Théorie Générale* did not become a best-seller. Some of those who did read it came to play prominent roles in the reorganization of the Treasury, in the introduction of National Accounts Statistics, and in the development of new forecasting tools. Last but not least, these high-ranking government officials were participating actively in economic policy decisions and trying to influence politicians' economic thinking. The history of the small group of young economists at the origin of the creation of SEEF, a service of financial and economic studies within Treasury, is testimony to the major impact they had on the financial and economic policies that emerged during the fifties and lasted until the early seventies.

In order to assure its importance in the civil service, the initial group spread its influence by teaching modern methods of public management at ENA (National School for Administration, which trains top-level government officials), making forecasts, writing analyses of the economy and proposals to the chancellor of the exchequer, and organizing institutions for public discussion of economic matters (Commission des Comptes de la Nation, Commissariat Général du Plan, and so forth). In the fifties and sixties, Claude Alphan, Simon Nora, Jean Saint-Geours, Jean Cerise, Jean Ripert, and Pierre Uri—all former SEEF economists—became key figures of a new generation of top-level civil servants, usually labeled ''technocrats,'' in the appreciative sense of the term. Particular personalities turned out to play major political roles. Pierre Mendès-France, who backed these efforts from the beginning, exerted a lasting influence, even if he remained in power as president of conseil only for a short period.[14] Valéry Giscard d'Estaing, who became acquainted with national accounts and macroeconomics early in his career, was undersecretary of the Treasury in 1959, then chancellor of the exchequer during the sixties, and finally president de la République from 1974 to 1981. Michel Rocard, initially head of the division in charge of annual forecasting at the Treasury, is usually held responsible for reconciling the political Left with economic assessment and management. Minister for planning after May 1981, he is now minister of agriculture.[15] Each proposed a new synthesis between traditional political motives and a coherent economic strategy, both for Center-Right coalitions and the parties of the Left.[16]

So, compared with other countries, in France Keynes's ideas appear to have been disseminated among top civil servants, government officials, and, to a lesser extent, academics.[17] This is not to underestimate the role of such pioneers as François Perroux, Alain Barrère, and many others who introduced the newer English theories and particularly the Keynesian paradigm. For a long period, until the end of the sixties, undergraduate courses presented classical, neoclassical, and Keynesian approaches successively, without any clear discussion of their complementarities or antagonisms.[18]

This pragmatic orientation of the Keynesian tradition in France explains a second uniqueness.

More a Fundamentalist than a Mere Effective-Demand Keynesianism. The economic situation after World War II was, in fact, quite different from that of the thirties.

The main objective in France was the reconstruction and modernization of the productive sector in the face of a huge increase in consumer demand. Of crucial importance in that early period was the directed allocation of credit, equipment, goods, and raw materials in order to promote a more or less balanced growth of the different sectors. The government's basic analytical tool was a rough approximation of input-output matrices.[19] Effective-demand management was the complement, not the core, of this strategy. From 1945 to 1954, the recurrent and important question was how to control excess demand and external imbalances, not how to stimulate reluctant investors.[20]

This radical change in contexts from 1929 to 1939 explains the second uniqueness. The "inflationary gap" between productive capacities and demand was such that the stable-price hypothesis implicit in the most simplified versions of the Keynesian model was no longer tenable. Thus, an "inflation multiplier" (and a price-wage spiral) replaced the "employment multiplier." In this situation of full employment, however, Keynes himself conceded that *The General Theory* had little new to offer. The inflationary bias of reconstruction, much more acute in France than in other developed countries, was not without consequences. At times, devaluation was a necessary complement to the pursuit of reconstruction and rapid growth.

A third institutional peculiarity points out a real difficulty in applying the standard effective-demand model. The nationalization of the main commercial banks after 1945 completely transformed the banking system and resulted in state funding of a large part of investment. It also gave the Central Bank a prominent role in controlling credit and creating money. Hence,

Treasury officials could not rely on models that ignored the monetary sector too explicitly or reduced the financial process to a pure market determination of the interest rate. In France during this period, the quantitative and selective control of credit by the state constituted an instrument at least as powerful as the public budget. Moreover, availability of statistics concerning some key financial flows made possible, if not easy, a very detailed modeling of the financial sector. Thus, the first attempts at macromodeling were, especially by comparison to the IS-LM approach, quite original.[21] They initiated a "French approach" to monetary policy, in which the Keynesian circuit and multiplier effects were linked to credit creation and destruction.[22]

At this stage, French technocrats were more "fundamentalist" than "effective-demand" oriented. The inherent instability of capital accumulation in a context of a sophisticated financial system prone to rapid shifts in expectations is the core of most of the private–public interactive analysis associated with "Budget Economiques." The idea of growth as a mercurial process, potentially subject either to cumulative depression or explosive inflation, was frequently expressed during the fifties. Consequently, the proposed remedies were far more ambitious than the fine-tuning policies based on tax or public-spending policies. They aimed at a complete transformation of the institutions inherited from nineteenth-century capitalism in order to promote mass consumption, a socialization of a large part of investment, and managed credit money.

A last but crucial argument is that France was one of the rare advanced countries to implement a system of indicative planning of the type imagined by Keynes in his "End of Laissez-Faire." While no one can give a precise enough evaluation of the impact of this complex process, various researchers have suggested a positive role in French dynamism.[23] Who remembers today that many foreign social scientists came to France in the sixties to study "the French miracle"? The progressive decay of planning since then and the present disillusionment may lead to underrating the past achievement. Before proceeding, let me point to two additional characteristics of Keynes's legacy in France.

A Fusion of a New Social Alliance, a Modernist Project, and Keynesian Reformism. Given France's seemingly far-reaching conception of Keynesianism, one may well wonder if the use of Keynes was nothing but a convenient way to dress up its old interventionist tradition. Unlike most other advanced societies, a large part of French public opinion has tended to blame its economic problems on the "free market" and to advocate state intervention through law enforcement, detailed regulation, credit controls, subsidies, public-spending programs, tax exemption, and other measures. So, in France the Keynesian revolution could easily be viewed as evolutionary rather than revolutionary. This would, however, contradict the belief widely held during the sixties that the then prevailing, uniquely encouraging conditions in OECD countries (rapid growth, quasi-full employment, the disappearance of cumulative depressions, and the smoothing of cycles) were due mainly, if not exclusively, to countercyclical policies based on the scientific skills of macroeconomics.

Using what little historical research there is, this writer presents a less one-sided interpretation. After World War II, Keynes's analyses and proposals did change economic policy conceptions, but their influence was only a part of a far-reaching technological, economic, social, and even political transformation occurring in France.

It is difficult to demarcate cleanly the rapid modernization of the economy from the emergence of Keynesian reformism. The parallels between the medium-term strategy expressed in the first plans and the short-term stabilization policies inherent in the Budgets Economiques were clearly established in the statements of politicians, as well as in the analytical works of economists and the ex-post accounts by historians.[24] In fact, after "Liberation," the common objective of the various groups allied in power was to avoid repetition of the catastrophic interwar period, when the diffusion of new technologies and products, scientific management methods, and a more modern way of life had been blocked. For them it was necessary to go beyond the basically conservative behavior of most corporate owners. The overriding of corporate power, after the nationalization of a significant part of the industrial and banking sectors (both political, as a reaction to their attitude during the Vichy regime, and economic), allowed for a new investment strategy. Through direct intervention in key sectors and selective credit allocation, modernization became the prime objective of the industrialists and government officials. Support for their objective came from the workers and their unions, heretofore reluctant or strongly opposed to Taylorist methods, under the pressures for reconstruction. Labor was content to confine itself to bargaining for its share of the productivity gains; it left the methods for obtaining those gains to management.[25]

All these changes resulted in a new pattern of development. A high rate of investment fostered rapid productivity increases, which were to sustain a continual growth in real wages and consumption. The buoyant demand coupled with a good profit outlook and low real interest rates in turn stimulated new rounds of investment.[26] For twenty-five to thirty years, this powerful engine engendered remarkable growth—unprecedented in its rate and stability.[27] Short-term stabilization policies were used alternately to keep inflation under control and to minimize the amplitude and duration of recessions. Stabilization policies can be thought of as "governors" of a system, not as replacements for an economic system. Such a distinction is clear in the experiences of the U.K. economy during the last thirty years and of almost all the OECD countries since the seventies.

An important factor for understanding the success of the modernist Keynesian policies was the wide acceptance in France of a new social-democratic accord. Wage earners shared the objective of modernization under the condition of sharing the "dividend of growth."

On one side, wage determination has been gradually transformed structurally from a highly competitive wage mechanism, with unemployment as a major determinant, to an administered wage-determination system based on past consumer-price increases and expected medium-term productivity gains.[28] The relative insensitivity of wages to moderate disequilibriums in the labor markets in the late fifties confirmed Keynes's conceptions about nominal wages. But far from being a datum inherited from the interwar period, this development was mainly a consequence of the post-1945 accord.[29]

On the other side, the expansion of the wage earners' proportion of the total population and the political pressures of unions and left-wing parties led to new forms of socialization of revenue. A comprehensive social-security system was introduced after 1945, with the consequence that for the first time in history, transfer income became a notable part of household income.[30] This also created an automatic stabilizer of considerable importance, one possibly as powerful as discretionary taxes or public-expenditure policies.[31]

As a result of these two changes, the majority of workers was able to develop forms of mass consumption, a necessary complement to the mass production techniques made possible by scientific management and new technologies. Thus the circuit of investment–production–employment–consumption was closed in a very growth-dynamic mode. The modernist Keynesian strategy also had major social consequences, most significantly, the integration of blue-collar workers into society and the rapid growth of white-collar workers in both the private and the public sectors.[32]

So French Keynesianism is much more akin to Keynesian reformism than to simple fine-tuning policies. Additional evidence for this point is found in the radical changes after 1945 in the volume and structure of public expenditures and taxes. After World War I, the share of public expenditures of the gross national product remained moderate during the twenties but increased during the thirties despite the efforts of conservative governments to check it. Therefore, a unique aspect of the post-1945 period was the rapid rise of this share to record levels and then its quasi-stability from 1955 to 1974. During the last decade, and once again amid a deepening crisis, state intervention has expanded significantly.[33] A state's redistribution of almost half of national income in accordance with various institutionalized rules has introduced a counterbalance to the pure market mechanisms and may largely explain the new private-public interactive pattern during the last thirty years. The change in the relative weights of different state activities is important too. Beyond the general functions of justice, defense, and diplomacy, three major areas are responsible for the surge in public expenditures. Immediately after 1945, there were *subsidies to industry*. During the whole period there were steady increases for both education and social transfers. Surveys and econometric studies conclude that these changes managed to increase the marginal propensity to consume, to reduce distributional inequality, and to stabilize investment at least in the nationalized sector.[34] At the same time, the tax system was reformed to stimulate productive efficiency and the reinvestment of profits and speculative gains. The replacement of various excise taxes by a tax on

Value Added (VAT) exemplified this effort of adapting state intervention to a medium-term strategy of development. The discretionary measures of a countercyclical nature, however significant at any particular moment, seem rather secondary by comparison with these longer-term structural reforms implemented by the French modernist-Keynesians.

Two conclusions can be drawn from this historical retrospective.

First, it would be erroneous to reduce the Keynes legacy in France to that of mere fine-tuning policies. In fact, the group of new higher civil servants, government officials, and leading ministers acted collectively as Keynes probably would have. Their objectives were to check, through far-reaching structural reforms, the inherent instability of capital accumulation in the pure market system and to utilize a pragmatic approach toward fashioning medium- and short-term economic policies.

Second, the impact of the purely economic component of Keynes's policy proposals is not easy to assess since the post–World War II period was characterized by important and simultaneous transformations in almost every sector of French society. The "dynamism" of the new vintage of industrialists, the willingness of workers to accept technological change and the "American way of life," the use of the power of the State for accepted economic objectives, the emergence of a "modern" elite in politics and civil service, the implementation of "unique" public measures, and the availability of adequate statistical data and forecasting tools, all combined to produce a fundamental renovation of the French economy.[35] France was not alone in achieving this "miracle." It was a common experience throughout Western Europe, with the exception perhaps of the United Kingdom. What is specific to France is the prominent role of the state in promoting and organizing the high level of economic activity. Traditional French interventionism, previously conservative and defensive, became modernist and aggressive. In this context Keynes's ideas fitted well into the overall emphasis on reconstruction and growth by providing a theoretical synthesis with which to formulate and legitimate the underlying changes necessary for policymaking.

But, as shown by a significant body of historical research, the objectives, the tools, and the efficiency of economic policy may depend crucially on the underlying social and economic environment.[36] This is confirmed by the subsequent evolution from general acceptance to some disillusionment with Keynesian economics. This is the main focus of the rest of this paper.

The Mid-Sixties, the Heyday of Keynesian Ideas and Economic Policies. The very ambitious character of the modernist-Keynesian policies required a long period to produce the expected consequences. As a matter of fact, it took more than a decade to rebuild and modernize French industry, to promote adequate mechanisms for wage-and-price determination, to expand the social-transfer system in order to cope with the rapid growth of wage earners, and to adapt money creation to the decline of direct public financing of investment. Foreign trade and financial flows tended to be more or less in equilibrium, giving French economic policymakers relative autonomy.

So it was only after 1958—a year marked by a series of further modernization reforms, the inception of the Fifth Republic, and de Gaulle's arrival to power—that France's economic and social structure finally began to correspond to the various hypotheses implicit in the narrower Keynesian system. Following the inflationary boom of 1963, a restrictive policy was pursued, resulting in lower productive-capacity utilization due to only moderate growth of effective demand. But the French economy suffered no longer from structurally insufficient supply or imbalances among various industrial branches.[37] The modernization of industry improved competitiveness and allowed a slight gain in France's world-market share. With the then fairly stabilized system of trade and international monetary relations, foreign trade stimulated growth and facilitated policymaking.

Once the economy seemed to be on a fast-growth path, the main question for the Treasury was to optimize its interventions in search of a compromise between full employment and inflation. For perhaps the first time in French history,[38] Keynesianism appeared mainly as a restricted application of effective-demand Keynesianism rather than the application of fine-tuning policies. Nevertheless, the double objective of quasi-full employment and low inflation was difficult to achieve in a country in which recurrent struggles of social groups over income distribution created inflationary pressures often validated by monetary authorities. As in the United States, the Keynesians called for a form of incomes policy, but the social and political process rapidly blocked attempts in that direction.[39] In any case, traditional instruments were proving sufficient to moderate inflation, although at the cost of a reduction in economic growth.

Leaving this problem aside for the moment, the observer must be impressed by the "Keynesian unanimity" that prevailed during the sixties. Did not the everyday reality confirm the predictions of the theory?

One cannot overstate the value of the improved statistical apparatus put in place by government. Many surveys and much new data were integrated into the French national account system. This system provided a complete description of the Keynesian circuit, from production to incomes via monetary and financial flows. The debates on macroeconomic policy benefited from a more accurate statistical base. Even some important sectoral choices or pinpoint reforms could be analyzed in terms of their consequences at the macro level. The traditional theory of public choice was thus improved by taking into account variations in capacity utilization.[40] One may get the impression that the Keynesian approach was reforming micro theory.[41]

As a consequence of the availability of rather long economic series and the improvement in computational facilities, macroeconomics modeling entered a new area. In 1966 the joint work of the Statistical Institute and the Forecasting Unit of the Treasury produced France's first fully formalized model. At its core was a Hansen-type multiplier of autonomous demand. Nominal wages were exogenous, and the financial sector was not taken into account.[42] This model, even though unpublished, played a significant role because it was used within Treasury to analyze the possible consequences of various measures of economic policy under discussion. Hence, during the sixties, economists and civil servants seem to have referred more and more to a restricted Keynesianism, even if the modernist–Keynesian-reformist approach was still present in the medium-term strategy expressed by the Commissariat General du Plan.

During the same period, the preparatory work for the Fifth Plan (1966–70) marked the heyday of indicative planning. Never since then has there been such a close interaction between a series of technical studies and the social and political bargaining process.[43]

Even politicians began to incorporate the Keynesian message more and more into their utterances. The necessity of stabilizing measures and the rationale for transitory public deficits were clearly admitted, irrespective of the orientation of political leaders. Take two examples.

The chancellor of the exchequer during the major part of the sixties was none other than Valéry Giscard d'Estaing. Although in the beginning of his political career, Giscard d'Estaing's orientation had been rather conservative, increasing acquaintance with Keynesian methods and ideas progressively modified his economic policy proposals. By the mid-sixties, public opinion came to consider him as the model of a modernist and well-informed politician. His intellectual and practical references to Keynes were an essential part of his strategy.

Parties of the Left incorporated into their programs their own interpretations of the Cambridge economist; for example, redistributive measures and social reforms could spur growth, given a significant underutilization of capacities. In their opinion, only the timidity and conservative orientation of the parties in power prevented such a program, which was favorable both in social and economic terms.

Thus Keynesianism, although oversimplified and subject to different interpretations, provided a new legitimacy for political programs. The success of the New Economics in the United States, as embodied in Kennedy's programs, constituted a final argument for its widespread acceptance.

The sixties were the age of Keynes in the universities, too. Following the evolution occurring in the rest of the world, and under the pressure of professional economists working for the Treasury, Commissariat Général du Plan, or the Statistical Institute, universities modernized the programs of their economics departments.[44] What emerged was a clear distinction between micro and macro theory. On one side, courses on microeconomics usually presented axiomatic versions of the Walrasian system. On the other, textbooks on macroeconomics included elements of national income accounting, Keynesian short-term models (of Hansen or IS-LM type), and finally some key models in growth theory. For example, Hansen's *Guide to Keynes* (1953) was not translated and edited into French until 1967. In the same year we had the publication of the first version of Lionel Stoleru's book on macroanalysis. It proposed a brand-new and attractive survey of the main concepts and methods in macroeconomics. It contributed greatly to the diffusion of an eclectic Keynesian-neoclassical synthesis.[45]

Finally, the economic evolution up to May 1968 seemed to confirm the validity of Keynesian conceptions. The sharp increase in wages and especially minimum wages—the cornerstone of the Grenelle Agreements, which ended the huge strike wave—did not have the catastrophic results feared by business. Given the significant underutilization of capacity and involuntary unemployment (Keynesian in nature), consumption increased, generating more production, greater productivity, and higher levels of employment in such a manner that the inflationary pressure was more moderate than expected. The second semester of 1968 and 1969 turned out to be favorable both for wage earners, in more employment and improved real wages, and for businesses, in recovery of investment and real profits. Nevertheless, due to inflation and external disequilibrium, in 1969 the government decided to devalue the franc. This devaluation played a positive role in restoring the external competitiveness of French industry for three or four years.

In the economic context of 1983, these references sound somewhat strange, since the post–May 1981 policy seems to have had far less favorable consequences. It is thus necessary to present the evolution of economic policies (conceptions and practices) from 1969 to 1981.

The Seventies: Structural and External Limits to Traditional Keynesian Economic Policies

During the seventies, Keynesianism underwent the same type of crisis in France as in other advanced capitalist economies. But its use and general acceptance were such that its rejection seems not to have been as brutal or complete as in, for example, the United Kingdom and the United States. Nevertheless, various interdependent factors caused increasing doubts concerning the applicability of restrictive Keynesianism and a more critical appraisal of fine-tuning policies. Both the export-growth strategy promoted by the government and the inability of accelerating inflation to contain macroeconomic disequilibriums tended to eliminate two of the key underlying conditions of the Keynesian system. This destabilization was exacerbated by the spread of the international crisis after 1973 both in trade relations and financial and monetary flows. Let me briefly develop each of these themes.

The Thrust Toward Competitiveness in International Markets and Its Consequences. In large part, growth in key industries exhibited increasing returns to scale, so that the continuous extension of markets became increasingly a prerequisite for further productivity improvements.[46] At the same time, competition in mass-consumption markets was based on product differentiation, so that a country could both export and import the same category of product. These two characteristics are the direct consequences of the postwar pattern of development. Hence, it is not really surprising that almost every OECD country, once its home market was fully developed during the sixties, tried to extend growth by promoting through various measures exports of national industry. France was no exception.

The preparation of the Sixth Plan, covering the period 1971 to 1975, clearly expressed this new strategy of emphasizing, above all, improved international competitiveness, in order either to limit import penetration or to increase French world-market shares.[47] That orientation reflected an alliance between the larger industrial corporations and government officials. The unions were opposed to, or at least reluctant about, this development in the French economy because they feared a rise in unemployment, restraint on wages, and loss of autonomy in economic and social policy. Consequently there occurred a significant shift by workers away from unanimous support for French economic policies.

As far as economic analysis is concerned, the medium-term macromodel used for the Sixth Plan, was clearly non-Keynesian and was instead quite classical.[48] Assuming that the price of internationally traded goods was strictly fixed by foreign competitors, both in the home and world markets, their level of production was determined by the capacities that could be built by firms as a function of their cash flow and access to credit. In this way, the rate of growth was linked *positively* to productivity and available credit and *always negatively* to wages. This marked a first departure from the restricted Keynesianism for the French closed economy.[49] A second departure was, in the medium term at least, the assertion that an expansion of public spending would have no effect at all on production; this was at odds with the theory that the Keynesian multiplier was never less than 1. The new policies called for tax cuts and subsidies or selective credit for investment, provided they benefited companies confronting foreign competition and had a positive impact on growth.

So the emergence of the theory of competitive economies at the end of the sixties may be interpreted as the first challenge addressed to limited Keynesian orthodoxy.

To be sure, the underlying factors previously described and this new orientation of financial and economic policy toward competitiveness in world markets did increase significantly the part of French national production exported. Simultaneously, however, the share of domestic market gained by foreign producers grew.

This development proved to be rapid and almost without break from 1967 to 1980. In addition, during this period France's leading exporters had to specialize along very narrow product lines, at the same time abandoning many product lines to others. This phenomenon partially explains import penetration. By comparison with other developed countries, France possessed relatively few competitive industries. This feature constituted a second weakness as competition became harsher in the context of stagnating and even declining markets.[50]

At the end of the seventies, these structural changes had created an economy that was no longer amenable to the application of the traditional Keynesian system. In the French national economy, the circuit of production-income-consumption and financial flows could no longer be closed. The thrust toward competitiveness had become a reality and, given a variety of cumulative effects triggered by this process, a necessity.[51]

Two other major obstacles emerged, obstacles that called into question the Keynesian orthodoxy, if not Keynes's own analyses as well.

The Breakdown of the International Monetary System and the Problem of Inflation. This French strategy of export-led growth was undertaken rather late, but a few years before the international monetary system fashioned at Bretton Woods' manifested weaknesses and went into crisis. President Nixon's devaluation decision in 1971 and the defection from the fixed exchange-rates system after 1973 demonstrated the impossibility of the postwar financial institutions' accommodating the two diverging thrusts afoot among OECD countries, namely inflation and the degrees of competitiveness. Since then, in spite of many international conferences, no coherent system for exchange-rate stabilization has emerged. Under these circumstances, the same thrust toward competitiveness could have effects opposite to those obtained during the sixties. To take just one example, a permanent shift of a currency in a floating exchange-rate system may be largely different from a once-and-for-all devaluation supplemented by adequate national policies within a stabilized international context.

At first glance, Keynes's responsibility for the failure of the international monetary system is small since his proposals did not prevail during the Bretton Woods conference. Neverthless, some economists attribute to his theoretical work the world's tendency to permanent inflation. Hayek long ago claimed that worldwide inflation would have to end in a deep depression.[52] In France, Rueff warned politicians very early of the dangers of an international monetary system based on the dollar and argued in favor of a return to the gold standard which, in his opinion, was the only system with a mechanism governing national money creation.[53]

A Keynesian, of course, can point out the weakness of the pre-Keynesian conceptions of these authors or emphasize their misunderstanding of Keynes's writings. Nevertheless, their criticisms raise a real question regarding the Keynesian-reformist program: "Is it possible to manage money (effective demand) in order to prevent both hyperinflation and cumulative depression in an open system?" Many economists would agree on this central focus as the Achilles' heel of the Keynes legacy.[54]

One may find in Hicks's writings a stimulating analysis of the link between Keynesian national policy and the breakdown of the international monetary system.[55] In *The General Theory* and in the real world of advanced economies, a labor standard replaces the old gold standard. Accordingly, monetary policy had to adapt to a level of nominal wage, fixed by the social and institutional characteristics of each country.[56] In the Bretton Woods system, no built-in mechanism aligned the various national labor standards with the existing exchange rates, as seemed to occur under the gold standard.[57] For two decades the labor market in the United States limited money wage in creases. As long as this was true and America maintained its overwhelming hegemony, the consequences of U.S. monetary policy were positive and stabilizing for the rest of the world.

At the end of the sixties, however, the creeping crisis in North America manifested itself in declines in profit rates, productivity reductions, accelerating inflation, and massive capital outflows. The inflationary boom severely strained the international monetary system, since the dollar was now challenged by the German mark and the yen, the currencies of the two countries seeking industrial competitiveness, labor-market flexibility, and moderate inflation. The breakdown of the dollar standard that followed soon led to the general floating of exchange rates, initially presented as the best solution to deal with the world financial crisis. Based on classical liberal principles, would not the free market bring a new international stability and more autonomy in national economic policy choices?[58]

The experience during the period 1973–83 does not confirm these hopes. Exchange rates were more volatile than ever and their movements made forecasting difficult. Further, short-term international capital flows put major constraints on national monetary policy and reinforced the conflict between internal objectives; for example, keeping interest rates low to spur investment conflicted with the objective of raising interest rates to induce capital inflows. It is now more evident that the adoption of flexible exchange rates within a wrecked Bretton Woods system did not create a viable mechanism for the world of economy.

Paradoxically this failure of the laissez-faire strategy is the best argument in favor of a complete reform of the international monetary system using a Keynesian approach. This approach, using international cooperation, would try to create the minimal financial institutions that would allow money creation under regulatory mechanisms.[59] So as to create sufficient stability and allow for reliable expectations, successive French governments have advocated such reform, but without much success. The long tradition of Keynesian reformism and the intermediate position of France in international relations may explain these recurrent proposals. The pervading classical liberal approach explains their rebuttal and the present stagnation within an international economy in disrepair.

This disruptive influence of the international crisis has played havoc with the Keynesian economic policies in France as in all OECD countries. This is not to deny that the French economy had weaknesses of its own making. Crucial among them was the historical tendency to favor growth at the eventual cost of inflation. During the seventies this turned out to be a severe handicap.

As a matter of fact, the rather complete institutionalization of income and price formation and the tradition of accommodating monetary policies led to a more rapid inflation in France than in other advanced economies during the 1969–73 boom. This discrepancy with respect to trade partners widened during the 1974–75 recession. The more indexation and the quasi-guaranty of income increases were pushed independently of the economic environment, the more severe the inflation became.

In a sense, this stagflation process was the other side of the Keynesian built-in-stabilizer coin, one that hindered repetition of the cumulative depressions of the thirties. The slower adjustment of employment and wages, the automatic increases in social transfers, and the countercyclical utilization of public spending were basic to the success of Keynesian reformism. Finally, the Keynesian legacy manifests itself in the new role of the central bank. Contrary to its behavior during the interwar period, Banque de France now acted as a lender of last resort, granting distress credit and validating most of the refinancing of the commercial banks. So, in 1974–75 a massive financial bankruptcy, with devastating consequences, was avoided. But the cost of this very positive outcome was accelerating inflation associated with the most severe recession of the French economy since World War II.

This stagflation, without historical precedent,[60] illustrates quite well the contradictions that now characterize the economy. On one side, they do prevent repetition of the 1929 debacle. On the other side, their very success generates a new form of structural inflationary crisis, one that fine-tuning can no longer cure.

The economic policies pursued in France from 1973 to 1981 illustrate first the limits of Keynesian solutions. Second, they show how difficult it is to find an alternative to them. While the pure neoclassical approach has appeal, it is not a realistic substitute. Let me briefly explain these two points.

From the Disappointing 1975–76 Reflation to the Sway of More Classical Economic Policies. Act I of the French Keynesian drama began with a renewed statement by government officials of their belief in the effectiveness of the fine-tuning process. The recession triggered by the so-called oil shock was initially interpreted as resulting from an important but mainly sectoral crisis limited to energy and related financial problems. Its unwinding could be easily traced by a simple Keynesian model expressed first for the international system and then for each national economy. When it became clear in early 1975 that industrial production had rapidly declined since mid-1974, Prime Minister Jacques Chirac worked out a comprehensive series of countercyclical measures in the Keynesian tradition: subsidies to the housing and building sector, an increase in public investment, and a tax cut for private investment to stimulate productive capital, which was the more depressed component of demand and the key variable for medium-term growth. One notes that the public deficit accepted by the government had exactly the same magnitude as the deflationary impact of the oil shock and that the increase to public spending and the tax reductions were the principal tools of the expansionary policy. This approach derived clearly from modified Keynesianism, almost of the "Mainly Budget Matters" School.

The French economy experienced a fairly rapid recovery during the three quarters preceding the summer of 1976; then the expansion stopped. The moderate increase in profits was not sufficient to promote a self-sustained growth of investment. Foreign producers had taken a greater share of the internal market, however, for the recovery was stronger in France than elsewhere and sales were quite profitable. Imports ballooned; exports slowed. The inflation rate did not increase as increased productivity compensated for the pressures of demand, but its level remained high, so that the international competitiveness of French industry deteriorated. Accordingly, an external deficit soon appeared.[61] Under the floating exchange-rate mechanism, the franc weakened. In mid-1976 the government devalued the franc, which spurred a new round of internal inflation. So began a vicious cycle of inflation and devaluation. Expansionary policies were effectively blocked.

Recognizable here are all the limiting factors of a Keynesian reflation in a wide-open economy, such as France had become in the seventies. First, as a result of international competition, domestic production lagged behind growing internal demand. Second, the low growth of the world economy put strong limitations on national reflationary policies. Third, the rapid inflation persisted in countries where income and price formation were highly institutionalized. Fourth, a cumulative process combining inflation and devaluation evolved out of a flexible exchange-rate system.

Act II begins. This semifailure was related to Jacques Chirac's resignation and the formation in August 1976 of a new government, with Raymond Barre as prime minister. There followed a significant change in policy objectives and instruments employed. The primary aim was to control inflation in order to stabilize the exchange rate and to reduce the external trade deficit. The means used were a reduction in public deficit, a freezing of prices to moderate the growth of the money supply and to keep interest rates high.

The move away from previous Keynesian orthodoxy toward a soft monetarism and more classical views was clear enough. The continued reference to a balanced budget and the emphasis upon monetary stabilization coupled with ideas and proposals dominant in the interwar period seemed anachronistic after the Keynesian Revolution.

Similarly, unemployment was seen more and more as the *consequence* of inflation, so that the top priority for economic policy was to fight inflation, even at the cost of rising unemployment, which was supposed to be transitory. Consequently, short-term relief was expected from specific measures concerning youth employment, training and retraining of dismissed workers, and early retirement of older employees. More generally, the government aimed at a better functioning of the labor market, thanks to improved information about labor supply and demand. These policies were a far cry from the Keynesian orthodoxy, according to which full employment can always be reached by the state's insuring an adequate level of effective demand. Significantly, some economists and government officials came to wonder whether the notion of full employment made sense any longer for advanced economies. At the very moment when official statistics showed unprecedented levels of unemployment, old and young classical liberal economists[62] argued that the government should not worry about unemployment since most of it was the voluntary type.

While this analysis was neither adopted by the majority of economists working for the Treasury (Commissariat Général de Plan), nor explicitly put forward by Barre's government, it played some role in the political debate. Finally, the inflationary pressures and the external financial disequilibrium brought monetary policy to the forefront. After 1976, as in other OECD countries, France adopted monetary targets for M2, in order to reduce inflation rates and influence expectations. This shift was reflected in new objectives, too. Previously monetary policy was used to accommodate internal pressures at the cost of recurrent devaluations; after 1976 the objective was to pass onto the national economy the constraints exerted by international markets.[63]

These measures, applied from 1976 to 1978, were only partially successful. By mid-1978 the external deficit had been eradicated and the franc defended. But the rate of growth had slowed and unemployment had risen. Once the price freeze was removed, the same underlying structural causes generated more or less the same rate of inflation as before. Finally the dynamism of private investment was not restored; in industry, employment continued to fall and with it productivity.[64] End of Act II.

Opening of Act III. Conscious of these problems but following the same objectives, the government adopted in mid-1978 a more classical interpretation of the crisis. The reorientation of economic policy strayed even farther from orthodox Keynesianism.

First a new diagnosis of the crisis was adopted by the government. The interest in employment was limited mainly to concern about the high wage level; it was felt that the lack of investment derived from a too-low profit rate. Consequently, economic policy had to favor an income redistribution from wages to profits. This would serve as the basis for an expansion of productive capacities, productivity, external competitiveness, and the consequent increase in employment. According to a popular formula, called in France Aubert's theorem, "Wage moderation makes today's profit, tomorrow's investment and finally the job of the day after tomorrow."

Consequently, through the use of old and new tools, economic policy aimed at increasing profits and, in a longer perspective, at restoring market mechanisms and private initiatives. The system of price control that had prevailed almost without interruption since 1945 was abolished first for industry and later for most of the services. At the same time, the average wage was to increase no faster than consumer prices. This objective was enforced for government employees and served as a basis for the minimum-wage policy. It was expected that the depressed labor market would limit wage increases. The objective of profit restoration was pursued too by selective increases of contributions to social security.

There is doubt that these measures were consistent with the new interpretation of unemployment, less Keynesian, i.e., due to insufficient effective demand; more classical, i.e., corresponding to the lack of profitability. This was precisely the thesis advanced by various French theoreticians working on the microfoundations of macroeconomics.[65]

In a fixed-price model à la Barre-Grossman, Keynesian unemployment was only one of the three possibilities. According to the respective levels of autonomous demand and real wages, it was possible for classical unemployment or repressed inflation to prevail. Observing developments in France since 1974, an economist and official as influential as E. Malinvaud pointed out the likelihood of a classical component of unemployment.[66] So, what was called disequilibrium or neo-Keynesian theory had conclusions quite distinct from those of effective-demand Keynesianism.

The binding external constraint reinforced the view that full employment was not simply a question of aggregate demand. In France the important deficits in energy and raw materials in the face of a policy of maintaining a high exchange rate meant that the level of activity that maintained external equilibrium was well below full employment. Hence, after a decade, the theory of competitive economies did become relevant, or at least it presented a better approximation of the real world than the Keynesian theory of a closed economy.

Understandably French planning suffered an equivalent decline.[67] Existing Keynesian methods had difficulty coping with the radical uncertainty generated by the crisis. The sharpening of social and political opposition complicated the search for new social compromises. The problems raised by short-term economic policies were so acute that the formulation of a medium-term strategy was made much more difficult and was given less attention by the government. Moreover, most officials doubted the possibility and the efficacy of previous forms of planning, especially as they inclined toward greater laissez-faire.[68] Last but not least, the larger French firms were less interested in the domestic market and domestic social accord than in the conquest of foreign markets and the export of capital. So the decay of the planning institution was one consequence of the crisis of modernist-Keynesian reformism.

Finally, in France as in other countries, jettisoning Keynesianism during the seventies was part of a far-reaching economic and social process and not merely the outcome of an intellectual debate. The disappointment with Keynesian policies, reduced autonomy of the national economy with respect to a world system in crisis, the breaking off of post–World War II compromises, and the shift of political power to the right go far to explain the renewed interest in more classical views. But "prosperity was not necessarily waiting around the corner."

The Ambiguous Outcome of Conservative Policies: A Consequence of too Much . . . or too Little Keynesianism. The "new economics policy," implemented steadfastly during the years 1977 to 1980, produced some positive results but at high cost. While the end of the tunnel was always within sight, it was never reached. When Valéry Giscard d'Estaing was defeated in the presidential elections of May 1981, no way out of the crisis was at hand.[67]

On the one hand, the franc's exchange rate was maintained according to the rules of the European monetary system. The vicious cycle of accelerating inflation followed by consequent devaluation was stopped. The external exchanges were roughly balanced in 1979 before they deteriorated again after the second oil shock. The public budget, too, was balanced in 1980, quite an achievement by comparison with other OECD countries.

On the other hand, almost all other indexes of economic activity exhibited either no improvement or some deterioration. Inflation did not fall below 10 percent; this, however, was a better record than that of France's main foreign competitors. Thus the policy of nominal wage restraint was more difficult than expected. Finally, in 1980, for the first time in more than twenty years the real wage did not grow. Neither the profit nor the financial positions of businesses improved. In fact, the simultaneous slowing of growth and consumer demand made productivity increases more difficult. Social transfers and public expenditures proceeded to grow, forcing the state to raise taxes and the social contributions paid by firms. In the wake of the interest-rate surge, firms ran into debt. This acceleration of interest rates was the final factor that impeded the restoration of the profit share for the nonfinancial sector.

So the first part of Aubert's theorem was invalidated: in an underemployed equilibrium, lower wages may lead to lower profit. It comes as no surprise to find then that the second part of this theorem was not to be satisfied either: investment in the private sector stagnated at pre-1973 levels. Firms faced sluggish consumer demand, uncertain foreign markets, and high interest rates; they therefore expected low rates of return such as they had observed during the previous years. Investment in the nationalized sector was the only dynamic component, but it could not carry the private sector.[70] Finally after 1978, total employment growth stopped as productivity gains surpassed demand increases. Hence unemployment rose, in spite of various plans in favor of employment of the young and retraining and early retirement of older workers. In short, no part of Aubert's theorem was fulfilled.

The strategy introduced from 1976 to 1981 was not the success anticipated, but neither was it a complete failure. An economist, depending upon his economic persuasion—neoclassical or Keynesian—might consider the new strategy a partial success, one that needed more time and determination, or a partial failure, insofar as some parts of previous economic policies had been employed.

Raymond Barre, while prime minister, recognized the hybrid character of his economic policy, which combined the classical, the Keynesian, and the monetarist. Each contributed something to the solution of the problems that France faced. Barre clearly stated this eclectic approach in these words:

This policy draws from the classical school the idea that the control of production costs is the condition for price stability in the long run, for the basic competitiveness of an economy and soundness of its money. It borrows from Keynes the idea that economic equilibrium does not adjust automatically to a level ensuring a full utilization of resources; so that government action on aggregate demand is necessary to secure a given rate of growth. . . . During the last three years, the French government has steadily sustained economic activity by social expenditures in order to maintain a sufficient level for private consumption, by high public investment and by credit and tax measures in favor of private productive investment. French economic policy takes from the monetary school the idea that medium-term money growth has to be kept in check within the limits necessary to reach its anti-inflationary objective.[71]

After may 1982, Barre admitted that he had underrated the resistance of social groups to the new policies and the sluggishness of structures and of institutions in adjusting and that these factors had limited the success of his anti-inflationary policy. He suggested, too, that the characteristics of the political process had hindered his implementing tougher policies, which might have produced better results.[72]

One might counter here with the proposition that a more classical economic policy would have worsened the short-term problems without necessarily producing any medium-term positive effects. Let me explain why.

First, a severe fall in real wages could have reduced internal consumption and hence capital formation through an accelerator mechanism more than it would have stimulated net external balances. This is a likely result since the price elasticities of imports and exports are relatively low and the external market is smaller than the home market. Econometric studies and existing macromodels conclude that the relative price effects upon investment, production, and employment are outweighed by the influence of effective demand over the same variables.[73] Do not these results confirm that, in the past and even now, the Keynesian circuit may be a closer approximation to reality than the pure competitive model? Consequently, economic policies should not follow the pure classical liberal injunctions.

Second, the first estimations of a model with quantity rationing suggest that, in general, Keynesian, classical, and frictional employment do coexist but that their respective shares vary through time.[74] Classical unemployment seems to have been important during the years 1968, 1974–75, and 1977–78 and then to have decreased relatively to Keynesian unemployment. So, after 1980 a continuation of wage restraint could have had negative effects upon unemployment since it was perceived by businesses as mainly Keynesian.

Third, the resistance of social groups to classical policies is not necessarily to blame. For example, during the 1974–75 recession, the struggles for employment and against wage cuts played a positive role in preventing a cumulative depression as had happened in the thirties.[75] Of course, this defensive behavior, when maintained for long, can deepen the crisis.[76] One may argue that in England and in the United States, tougher conservative policies seem to have reduced the inflation rate. But the costs incurred are impressive in terms of mass unemployment, reduction in living standards, and reduced productivity and competitiveness leading to deindustrialization. More basically, no clear new pattern of development had emerged, and the problems of financial instability, reindustrialization, welfare, and unemployment remain to be solved. So the present recovery in the United States does not necessarily imply that classical liberal policies have found a way out of the crisis. Summarizing the seventies, in France as in other countries, the validity of traditional Keynesian effective-demand conceptions and fine-tuning policies was questioned by the very success of the modernist-Keynesian reformism. The problems concerning inflation, monetary policy, external imbalances, and the breakdown of the international monetary system gave many opportunities for a renewal of neoclassical and monetarist approaches. But in France, unlike other advanced economies, Keynes was not totally rejected; rather, his concepts were included in a new neoclassical-Keynesian synthesis.

The corresponding economic policies, when implemented from 1976 to 1981, turned out to be far from successful. Would another policy more closely linked to Keynesian reformism have achieved better results? In 1981 almost all the politicians of the Left and their economists thought the answer was yes. End of Act III.

French Economic Policy since 1981: A Crucial Test for Keynesianism

After June 1981, the new government founded its action on a two-part diagnosis. It combined a Keynesian analysis of the recession with a more structural interpretation of the present crisis. The deterioration of the economic and social situation during the years 1976–81 was blamed in part on wrong austerity policies and in part on the limits inherent in the postwar nature of economic development. A twofold program was derived from this analysis, comprising Act IV.

A short-term expansionary policy stimulated consumption and, in a second phase, investment. The objective—reduced unemployment—and the tools—public expenditure, social benefits, taxation of the wealthy—were undoubtedly inspired by Keynesian ideas.[77] But this program was not considered sufficiently strong to solve the crisis.

A program of far-reaching reforms was instituted to promote a new mode of development. On one side, welfare and fiscal reforms were introduced to reduce inequalities, in order to spur on both social justice and economic growth. The similarities with Keynesian reformism were quite clear. The nationalization of major industrial groups, holding companies, and commercial banks derived from the traditional proposals of the French Left. It aimed at socializing investment and removing the financial and speculative barriers to recovery. Even though Keynes explicitly rejected nationalization, it could be conceived of as a component of the Keynesian reformist program. Similarly, a reform of the planning process was instituted, aimed at giving it a new effectiveness through democratization, decentralization of decisions, and the use of new tools, such as planning agreements.

The rest of the reforms were somewhat eclectic. There were bills concerning the rights of the wage earners, aimed at reconciling more democracy in the workplace with the economic efficiency of firms. Similarly, the rapid reduction in the duration of work and the development of a "third sector" between private firms and public organizations defined far-reaching objectives outside the Keynesian tradition.[78]

This program started from the assumption that a Keynesian expansionary policy would succeed where previous attempts had failed. Next, its advocates foresaw that within a few years the structural reforms would yield positive effects and so strengthen the recovery. But it took only a short time before the new economic and social policy ran into major difficulties.

Limits of Keynesian Domestic Policies in a World Crisis. Act IV of the Keynesian drama seemed destined for a happy end. During the summer of 1981, the government proposed a modest raise in the minimum wage and more significant increases in some social benefits to families, unemployed workers, and retired people. There were plans to expand public employment. Industrial modernization was not neglected, since various public funding and tax cuts were supposed to raise investment. Essentially, the 1982 budget was projecting the favoring effects of a policy of Keynesian demand stimulus.[79]

Consumer expenditures were planned to expand so as to stimulate production and investment and hence productivity. A particularly rapid rate of productivity increase would make possible, it was hoped, a simultaneous increase in social benefits and wages, a reduction in the length of the workweek, and an improvement in the financial position of industrial firms. In many respects the government's 1982 strategy was comparable to the reflationary policies implicit to the Grenelle Accords of 1968, or explicit in 1975. But it was more limited as to the size of the expected expansionary effects.[80]

In fact, both the *national* and the *international* economic situations in 1982 were quite different from those of 1968 and 1975.

By the beginning of 1982, the sharp rise in transfer payments and public expenditures had stimulated household demand. But it led only to a reduced increase in production since half of it went to imports. At least three factors explain this accelerated penetration of the home market and simultaneously the first decline in French exports in a quarter of a century.[81]

The first factor was a faster growth in France than in other deeply depressed OECD countries. This was responsible for an increased deficit in the French external trade. To make matters worse, the international recovery expected at the end of 1981 failed to materialize, largely as a consequence of the failure of conservative policies in the United States and elsewhere to promote rapid recovery.

The second factor was the limited French recovery, which contributed to the perpetuation of inflationary pressures. There were reinforced increases in nominal income and the devaluation in October 1981. The inflation rate therefore remained at its former level, far above rates in the United States and in most European countries.[82] In these economies, continued recessions induced unions and workers to accept sizable wage cuts and reinforced price competition between firms, which contributed to a significant reduction in inflation. A loss in French competitiveness and an aggravation of the external deficit resulted from France's higher inflation rate.

Finally, the expansion of demand highlighted the weaknesses of French industry.[83] In fact it had been badly specialized and debilitated by the past overvaluation of the franc under the Barre government. The new equipment and consumer goods sectors were weak, while the main exporting sectors entered into maturity or decline. So, in a period of rapid technological change and acute international competition, French industry needed more appropriate specialization and more efficient methods of production in order to benefit from any increase in nominal income. The benign neglect of industrial organization and production by the Keynesian effective-demand policies was no longer appropriate. These developments brought forth a major source of external deficit.

There was no surprise when, in June 1982, the external crisis led to a second devaluation of the franc within the European monetary system. Yet other internal objectives were far from being met. The recovery had exhausted itself as industrial production declined and consumption stagnated. Growth in unemployment had been reduced but not halted. The share of profits had increased very slightly but not enough to induce a self-sustained rise in investment. In short, there was no ongoing cumulative process to extend the initial recovery. Consequently the public deficit surged more than expected and made urgent the question of its financing.[84]

The expansionary policy of June 1981 had led to much more favorable developments in France than in most of the other advanced economies, but it could not withstand world recession and the crisis in international relations. The failure was evident but not all-pervasive.

At this point we have the beginning of Act V. By mid-1982 the Socialist government faced a dilemma. The crisis was quite similar in nature to, but more acute than, that faced by Valéry Giscard d'Estaing in mid-1976. Would Act V repeat Act III? Not exactly, for time had elapsed and the crisis was deeper. Moreover, the relations among government, firms, and workers' unions were rather different.

This explains why the June 1982 devaluation was accompanied by an unprecedented price and wage freeze of four months and then prolonged by controls during the following year. The key objective was to reduce inflation to 10 percent in 1982 and 8 percent in 1983, as well as to keep nominal wage increases in line with expected inflation rather than past inflation. Once again a Keynesian policy had stumbled over the inflationary bias of income formation in France. The price and wage freeze, however necessary, was a poor substitute for either more flexible mechanisms or an accepted-incomes policy.

A reversal of fiscal policy was initiated with the 1983 budget. It limited the expansion in public expenditures and social transfers and raised taxes and contributions for welfare in order to check the public deficit. Within this restrictive policy, various measures promoted household savings and business investment in research and development. Simultaneously, important funding was devoted to young workers' training and to the reduction of the retirement age. In addition, the state fostered new agreements between firms and unions that linked early retirement or reduction in the duration of work to job creation. A very notable achievement of this policy was to stabilize unemployment while it was climbing sharply in most other countries. But inflation was only slightly contained, and consumption stagnated.

Moreover, the external trade deficit remained. The expectations of financial markets were such that, in March 1983, the government had to devalue for the third time. After a controversy between various factions in the main party, the authorities decided to maintain France within the European monetary system and to reduce drastically real income and effective demand. Canceling out the external deficit as soon as possible and reducing the public deficit were the two main objectives. The outcome of this new program is the paramount economic question in France at the end of 1983.[85]

Even though the government has been reluctant to recognize it publicly, this reversal reveals crudely the problems arising out of a Keynesian expansionary policy in one country. Paradoxically, at a time when international recovery is expected, or at least hoped for, France has had to adopt a very restrictive economic policy, possibly the most severe in its recent history.

In fact, the Socialist policy has been caught in a succession of vicious cycles—Keynesian fine-tuning policies could no longer eliminate them in the context of the global crisis of the post–World War II period. Is it possible that a more comprehensive program of institutional and structural reforms could have broken these linkages and reduced some of the economic constraints?

Is Keynesian Reformism Still a Way Out of Crisis?

The new government tried to implement its various reforms very quickly so that they could yield their expected positive effects as soon as possible. Yet three years later, the economic trends and linkages had not been significantly changed.

This apparently disappointing outcome is not really surprising. Since the reforms were far-reaching, they imply that basic transformation had to occur in a series of institutions, social relations, and individual and collective behaviors. Such a process takes a long time, one or two decades, at least.[86] Let us remember that in the United States the New Deal bore fruit only after World War II. This was true also for the Front Populaire and the Liberation of France. The modernist-Keynesian model became a social and economic reality only during the sixties. It is clear that the present project of the French government to promote a new economic milieu is not a matter of establishing a new economic interrelationship on the contemporary scene but rather of creating a new evolutionary process.

More basically, one may wonder whether these reforms can cope with the original form of the present crisis. Is it still sufficient for the state to intervene according to the Keynesian reformist tradition? The difficulties encountered in France since 1981 illustrate some key problems. Let us examine five of these.

The nationalization of the larger industrial groups was supposed to free investment decisions from shortsighted expectations and to reduce some financial constraints and the profit standard. In fact, two years after the change in industrial ownership, no clear new strategy has emerged; the task is not easy. What should be included in planning agreements? How does one combine the macroeconomic objectives of the state with the minimum degree of autonomy necessary for innovation and efficient management? Should the criteria and methods of management be different in the public sector from those in the private sector? These questions are still unresolved.

The deepening of the crisis created financial problems for most of the newly nationalized firms. Simultaneously, budgetary constraints have prevented the state from making massive investments in high technologies. Finally, the old nationalized sector, with its large deficits, has had to reduce its investment plans. Thus it has become more and more difficult for the public sector to be the engine of growth.

The nationalization of credit has run into similar difficulties. The banking sector has indeed benefited from the rise in interest rates and the increase of industrial debt. Profits are fairly high. But the puzzling matter is that the bankers have changed neither their methods nor their lending criteria. Particularly risk-averse, they prefer to lend to wealthy and well-known groups rather than to newly created and innovative small firms. Thus the banks do not encourage industrial modernization as much as it is desirable from a national point of view. But then, what should be the new criteria and financial procedures of the banks? How are they to avoid decisions that end up requiring massive refinancing by the Central Bank? Can inflationary pressures be checked by adequate rules enforced by the commercial banks and the lender of last resort? For the time being, few proposals have been forthcoming. At best, a recently proposed law promises only a modest reform of the banking system.

The definition and implementation of an industrial policy is another way for socializing investment decisions of firms according to longer-term views. The government has set its hope on an aggressive industrial policy in order to modernize the French economy and to reverse the negative evolution observed since 1973.[87] But the task has proved much harder than expected. First, the crisis has broken most of the past trends and patterns and has increased the uncertainty associated with economic and technological choices. The methods that had worked rather well during the forties and fifties, when the problem for France was to modernize industry according to a known mode of development, are no longer effective in the eighties. All over the world, there is a groping for new forms of industrial organization, but they remain largely unknown or at least very uncertain. Of course, adequate public intervention may reduce this uncertainty but cannot rule it out. In the eighties, adopting an industrial policy is riskier than ever. Second, technological and industrial choices are increasingly made more at the international level. Thus each country has less autonomy concerning its domestic industry, especially in high technology. A third difficulty has impeded the definition of a clear-cut industrial strategy. While the government particularly wants to promote new technologies, it has had to devote more and more funding to old or mature industries. In fact, as the reflation failed to restore a self-sustained growth, the situations of these industries have worsened and have called for more state intervention. Hence, the difficult choice between the socially preferred *defensive* industrial policy and the economic necessity of a more aggressive strategy.

Similarly, the institutional reforms of the French planning process have not yet proved sufficient to stop the economic decline of the last decade. The ambitious economic policy proposed by the intermediate plan for 1982–83—a growth rate of more than 3 percent expected—was difficult to implement and was thus unable to contribute to the recovery. During the preparation of the Ninth Plan, sophisticated technical studies analyzed the probable effects of various economic strategies. Differing from earlier studies, analysts suggested an original policy mix: perhaps active industrial modernization, a significant reduction in the length of the working life, and control of welfare costs could promote a sustained recovery. Later studies were less optimistic. Two of the traditional objectives of French planning were going to be difficult to achieve.

How does a single nation reduce uncertainty that derives largely from international crises?[88] The present uncertainty about possible developments in the world economy makes national choice riskier and more difficult than ever. Of course, the ideal would be to reduce uncertainty through international cooperation, but we are a long way from introducing indicative planning on a world level.

In France the breakdown of the postwar system has sharpened conflicts between social groups. Everyone had come to expect income increases as a matter of course. In a stagnating economy this is no longer possible. But the normal behavior of each group is to defend its advantages, even though ex post the outcome may be a deterioration of everyone's situation. During the preparation of the Ninth Plan, these tensions seem to have blocked any search for a new social accord. So a second and essential objective of French planning[89] could not be fulfilled at the very moment when an original compromise among unions, stockholders, and the state was needed.[90]

The last challenge to Keynesian reformism is the problem of the welfare state. In May 1981, the government thought that a significant reduction in distributional inequalities was both a social objective and a basis for economic recovery. So it decided to extend the welfare-state system, assuming economic growth would pay for it. But developments were worse than expected. For all the reasons that have been analyzed, the recovery was short-lived. It soon became clear that social expenditures had created more demand but no equivalent increase in production. The situation was different from that of the fifties and sixties. During those periods the improvement of the welfare state had been financed by very rapid economic growth and had fostered industrial modernization. So social security had been an ingredient, not the cause, of the "French miracle."

Consequently, when the recovery ended in 1982, increasing public and social deficits had to be financed by taxing wealthier households and businesses. But the problem was not so simply solved. On one side, within the French tax system, there was mainly a redistribution of income among wage earners, with white-collar workers and salaried managers bearing most of the burden. These were precisely the groups whose cooperation the government needed in order to modernize the French economy. On the other side, business, with its profits at an unprecedented low, reacted negatively to a tax increase. Is it possible to stimulate investment and employment if businesses consider themselves overtaxed? The government has become more and more sensitive to this problem. But then, how does the government reduce the public debt?

In order to solve this dilemma, reforms of the tax system and of the welfare state have been recurrently announced. But up to now, every proposal has been blocked by whatever social group that would have to pay for the reform.

Clearly, the breakdown of growth has led to a fiscal crisis—a crisis that seems unamenable to a traditional Keynesian solution. Hence the vicious cycles we have observed for a decade.

Does this crisis in Keynesian economic policy legitimate a return to laissez-faire? We propose to argue now that, on the contrary, the present difficulties call for a renewal of Keynesian fundamentalism and reformism.

Conclusion: Keynesians Have to Propose Original Solutions to New (And Old) Problems

So this review of Keynesianism in France clearly shows, first, a fascinating achievement for the new economic policies, then a progressive decline in their effectiveness, and finally an open-economy crisis, which calls for an innovative revival of Keynesian fundamentalism and reformism. Let me examine these points briefly.

1. After World War II, French society underwent a major change. A fusion of a new social alliance, a modernist drive, and Keynesian reformism induced unprecedented economic growth. Most politicians and economists adopted the core of Keynes's message, that pure market mechanisms are unable to promote and maintain full employment, growth, and stability. Consequently, the state implemented a series of far-reaching reforms in order to oppose this alleged instability of accumulation inherent in a free-market economy. Among these reforms were nationalization, indicative planning, tax reform, welfare measures, and control of money.

2. The history of Keynesianism in France illustrates three other points. First, the countercyclical use of taxes and public expenditures

has been the crowning achievement of the Keynesian-modernist program, not the basis of the so-called "French miracle." It is erroneous to define Keynesianism in terms of the effectiveness of fine-tuning policies. Second, it took more than a decade to build all the institutions, social behaviors, and economic mechanisms that were necessary to promote the process of development associated with Keynesian-modernist policies. Third, as in many other advanced economies, the mid-sixties represented the heyday of Keynesian ideas and economic policies.

3. The very success of this strategy led, during the seventies, to structural developments that undermined the stability of post–World War II growth. Inflationary pressures have become permanent since they are a means for resolving struggles over income distribution. Managed money allows the solutions to be validated. This has introduced a major instability in the *international* monetary system. The internationalization of trade and production has destabilized the internal Keynesian circuit. More basically, the joint increases in real wages, profits, and social benefits were made possible by productivity gains. So the slowing down of productivity in the United States and then the rupture of the Bretton Woods system were the key elements in the beginning of the present crisis. Therefore, profitable production has become as important as effective demand, and money matters have become as important as budget matters.

4. There are, in addition, underlying factors that, after 1973, may explain the progressive disappointment with Keynesian stabilization policies. Whatever their political orientations, all French governments were compelled to change their economic strategies. The very strong Keynesian expansionary policy rapidly faltered in 1976 under the pressures of inflation, the external deficit, and devaluation. Consequently, later governments had to reverse completely the expansionist policy. More significantly, a new classical Keynesian synthesis arose to replace the older, deeply rooted Keynesian tradition in France. The same process took place when François Mitterand replaced Valéry Giscard d'Estaing as president. The quasi-failure of the reflation undertaken by the left-wing government obliged it to change drastically the objectives of, and means to, its short-term economic policy. Few officials and politicians today consider orthodox Keynesianism an adequate answer to the present crisis. Thus, doubts about Keynesianism are not a simple matter of political alliance ideology or propaganda. Monetarists, supply-siders, and the rational-expectations school, however, may have the wrong answers to very real problems.

5. The experience of France since May 1981 illustrates, too, the many difficulties that a left-wing variant of the Keynesian reformist program may encounter. First, far-reaching institutional transformations cannot be made effective rapidly enough to break the vicious cycles related to the structural character of the present crisis. Second, neither

nationalizations nor tentative industrial policies have restored the required investment dynamism. The medium- and long-term views of
businesses are as blurred as ever, and the search for a new social accord
among firms, unions, and state goes on. It is disappointing because
reducing the uncertainty and promoting compromises between social
groups have been two of the main functions of the French planning,
which recent reforms should have reinforced. Third, the extension of the
welfare state seems no longer to have massive stimulating economic
effects. Hence, to the extent that a zero-sum society prevails, new taxes
or welfare-state reforms necessarily encounter opposition from the social groups that will have to pay for them. In conclusion, the very
program that showed the way out of the Great Depression seems inadequate in the present crisis.

    6. This is not to say that a return to a free-market economy will
solve the ongoing social and economic problems. On the contrary,
Keynes's critique of laissez-faire is as relevant as ever. Classical liberal
policies have been trying to reduce the public deficit and intervention
and, in some cases, to do away with some key institutions introduced by
the Keynesian reformers. The outcome has been an unprecedented and
massive public deficit. The cost of disinflation has been frightening. To
most economists the experience is clear enough: market mechanisms, in
themselves, do not lead automatically to full employment. On the contrary, under deregulation, investment and financial decisions are as
unstable as ever and induce erratic economic activity. What is needed
are some new institutions and adequate forms of public intervention to
socialize expectations and to move toward full employment. The failure
of flexible exchange rates to promote an alternative to the wrecked
Bretton Woods system is another argument for a Keynesian approach to
international monetary reform. What are the international institutions
that would lead to global stability of the world economy while restoring
the effectivenesss of market mechanisms? The answer is not at hand.

    7. Finally, Keynesians are now facing a major challenge. Will
they be able to elaborate an adequate theory of present crisis and then
design unique reforms and new economic policies? Both *The General
Theory* and the New Deal reflected a particular structural crisis. The
Great Depression derived largely from a structurally insufficient effective demand, when there were high productivity gains and good pro-
spective profits. In the seventies a sustained effective demand stumbled
over sluggish productivity and low profits. Therefore, a stagflationary
stop-and-go has replaced the drastic cumulative deflation of the thirties.
This means that Keynesians have to build a theoretical model to explain
these new characteristics.

    Let us propose some agenda headings for such an examination. First, a
better theory of production and technical change seems essential in order to
round out effective-demand analysis. Second, the internationalization of pro-

duction, trade, and finance has to be included in any national model. Third, in order to understand the present inflation and economic instability, a theory of managed money and modern financial markets is fundamental to Keynesians. Then, unique economic policies and reforms could probably be derived from such a theory. For example, what kinds of institutions would best promote technological changes that lead to positive economic and social effects? What are the minimum rules of a new international system that would stop beggar-my-neighbor policies and bring some stability and cohesion to a distressed and chaotic world economy? Is there any built-in mechanism or monetary policy that would eradicate the inflationary effects of modern managed money? Of course, the solutions are not likely to be simple, but Keynesians do have some proposals along these lines. They remain to be built into a coherent and simple model.

After all, such a program is not inconsistent with the very pragmatic approach that John Maynard Keynes utilized all his life. Would not the Cambridge economist urge his followers to make path-breaking contributions and not to worship his own past achievement?

"Innovate or decline and perish." This is the key challenge addressed to Keynesians in the eighties.

Notes

1. John Maynard Keynes, *The General Theory of Employment, Interest, and Money*, (Papermac edition, 1970), pp. 383–84.
2. The works of Hayek and Friedman support these views.
3. Keynes, op. cit., p. 376.
4. Ibid., p. 378.
5. J. M. Keynes, *Essays in Persuasion*, p. 317. Estrin and Holmes (1983) emphasize this intellectual connection between Keynes and French planners.
6. The ZOGOL model built by Herzog and Olive in 1966 was Keynesian in this respect.
7. In France, Benassy (1982) and Malinvaud (1977, 1980) recognized that demand deficiency is not the only factor limiting employment.
8. See A. Sauvy (1967), pp. 188–91.
9. Portions of Keynes's analysis were foreshadowed independently by Kalecki (1933, 1935) in Poland, Grunig (1933) in Germany, and Benassy and Malinvaud in France. See Endnote 7 above and G. R. Feiwel (1975).
10. See article by T. de Montrial in *X-Crise* (1931–1939), p. 290.
11. A. Sauvy (1967), pp. 67 and 352.
12. Direct influence may be traced through the persons of Georges Boris and P. Mendès-France.
13. There were exceptions, i.e., John Nicoletis, Georges Boris, and Pierre Mendès-France. See *X-Crise*, selected papers, *Economica*, 1982, pp. 172–86.
14. See P. Mendès-France with Gabriel Ardant (1973) or *Choisir*, Stock (1974).
15. F. Fourquet (1980), pp. 312–19.
16. On the Left, for example, there were Jacques Delors and Philippe Herzog.
17. Perhaps this is more apparent than real. See A. R. Sweezy (1972) and L. H. Keyserling's reply.
18. See Raymond Barre (1956), Vol. 2. This is a popular French text in which the Keynesian model is treated as part of the neoclassical mainstream.
19. Of the Von Neumann type. See R. Boyer (1976), pp. 887–92.
20. See Claude Gruson (1968) for comprehensive analysis of this rupture.
21. See Claude Gruson (1969) for a description of the model.

22. See J. Denizet (1967).

23. Carre, Dubois, and Malinvaud (1972) are cautious in their appraisal; Kindleberger (1963), Masse (1965), Gruson (1968), Fourquet (1980), and Estrin and Holmes (1983) are more positive in assessing the role of indicative planning in the 1950s and 1960s.

24. See Mendès-France (1974), Gruson (1968), and Bouvier (1974).

25. For a historical review of Taylorism, see various articles in *La Dècouvert/Maspero* 1984; and for a view of the 1968–82 crisis, see R. Boyer's article in *Tocqueville Review*, Spring–Summer, 1983, pp. 138–40.

26. See M. Aglietta (1982) for one analysis of the American problem; a similar model for France may be found in H. Bertrand (1983), pp. 305–443.

27. Carre, DuBois, and Malinvaud, *La çroissance française* (1972), pp. 25–40.

28. For an econometric analysis of wage formation in the French economy, see R. Boyer (1979), pp. 99–118.

29. See J. R. Hicks (1955).

30. For an analysis of transfer payments, see André and Delorme (1983).

31. European analyses include Negri (1978), Coriat (1979), and B. Kundig (1984).

32. See L. Boltanski (1982).

33. See statistical appendix in Andrè and Delorme (1983), and Andrè (1984).

34. Econometric analysis shows the marginal propensity to consume for transfer payments to be nearly equal to one, according to R. Boyer (1976). The stabilizing effect of investment in nationalized industry has been substantiated by Artus and Muet (1982).

35. J. P. Rioux, *La France de la Quatrième République, Vol. 2, 1952–1958* (1983). Also C. P. Kindelberger, "La renaissance de l'économie française après la guerre" in S. Hoffman, *A la recherche de la France* (1963).

36. André and Delorme (1983), pp. 681–89 and R. Delorme (1984).

37. See Gruson (1968) and Boyer (1979).

38. W. V. Heller, (Ed.) (1968) and James Tobin (1966).

39. See Masse (1963–64) and Masse and Bernard (1969).

40. See H. Guillaume (1972) and Guillaume and Rochard (1973).

41. Originated by P. Masse; for a recent example see Cremieux, Guesnerie, and Milleron (1979).

42. INSEE-DP (1966) and Herzog and Olive (1968).

43. Gruson (1971), Fourquet (1980), and Estrin and Holmes (1983).

44. Malinvaud's early syllabus for a course in macroeconomics was revised and published. See Malinvaud (1981–82).

45. Published in English by North Holland in 1975 as *Economic Equilibrium and Growth*. See Stoleru (1967).

46. See Kaldor (1966), and for Europe, Boyer and Petit (1981) and Bertrand (1983).

47. For an analysis in English, see Estrin and Holmes (1983).

48. Aglietta and Courbis (1969) and Edgren, Faxen, and Odhner (1963).

49. Treated more fully in Boyer (1976).

50. C.E.P.I.I. (1982) and Ministère de la Recherche et de L'Industrie (1983).

51. The political economy of Keynesianism is analyzed in Boyer (1983).

52. Hayek (1983), p. 45.

53. Rueff (1963), (1965), and American translation (1967), (1975), and (1976).

54. There is general agreement that Keynes underestimated the inflationary effects of deficits. See *The Economist* for Friedman's views (June 4, 1983), Hayek's (June 11, 1983), Hicks's (June 18, 1983), and Samuelson's (June 25, 1983).

55. See Hicks (1955) and (1983).

56. The effects of legal and institutional changes in the labor market have been analyzed by many; e.g., Boyer (1979), Gordon (1977), Sachs (1980), and Artus (1983).

57. Gelpi (1983).

58. The experience of the 1970s has reduced the number of those believing this.

59. This position is espoused by the Washington-based Institute for International Economics. See Bergsten (1982) and Williamson (1984) and Williamson's paper in this collection. Banker F. Rohatyn shares the position according to an article in *Business Week*, February 28, 1982, pp. 15–18.

60. For analyses of the French case, see CEPREMAP—CORDES (1978) and Benassy, Boyer, and Gelpi (1979).

61. The external debt rose from 7.5 billion francs in 1973 to 41.8 billion francs in 1976.

62. For example, J. Rueff and M. Allais, *Le Monde*, January 27, 1976 and February 19 and 20, 1976. See also A. Fourcans and J. J. Rosa (1977).

63. See OECD (1980) and (1981).

64. Details are found in *Ministère des finances, Comptes de la nation*, especially C 72-3 and C 101-2.

65. Y. Younes (1970), J. P. Benassy (1976 and 1982), J. M. Grandmont (1976), and E. Malinvaud (Blackwell, 1979).

66. E. Malinvaud (Blackwell, 1979). Later works include Artus, LaRoque, and Michel (1982).

67. See Fourquet (1980), Gruson (1971), Estrin and Holmes (1983), and Delors (1982).

68. Fourquet (1980), pp. 291 ff.

69. For statistical review, see Boyer and Petit (September 1981). An analysis of the French economy before the election of Mitterand is found in F. Bloch-Laine (1982).

70. Statistics found in Artus and Muet (1982), p. 63.

71. R. Barre (1981), pp. 122–23.

72. R. Barre (1980).

73. The relative importance of the price effect is demonstrated in Muet (1979), pp. 85–133.

74. Macro aspects are found in Artus, LaRoque, and Michel (1982) and micro aspects in Boissou, LaFont, and Wong (1983).

75. Boyer and Mistral (1983), Appendix, Table A 25.

76. Boyer and Mistral (1983).

77. M. Beaud (1983) and A. Liepietz (1983). In Liepietz, see also papers on left-wing economic policies.

78. Commissariat Général du Plan (1982).

79. M. Beaud (1983).

80. INSEE (C 108-9, Vol. 1, 1983).

81. INSEE (1982), also Aglietta and Boyer (1983).

82. Artus (1983).

83. CEPII (1982) and note # 50 above.

84. INSEE (C 108-9, Vol. 1, 1981), p. 121.

85. The external deficit by January 1984 had been reduced to 42 billion francs. The national deficit was about 3 percent of GNP, inflation was above 9 percent, and unemployment was higher than planned.

86. CEPREMAP-CORDES (1977) and André and Delorme (1983).

87. Ministère de la Recherche et de L'Industrie (1983). See Chevenement (1983).

88. Earlier this goal was to reduce uncertainty by dampening fluctuations. See Masse (1965) and DeLeau, Guesnerie and Malgrande (1973).

89. See article by Delors in Stuart Holland, Ed. (1978).

90. See concluding paper in Boyer and Mistral (1983) and their article in *Futuribles* (October 1983).

References

Aglietta, M. (1982) *Regulation and crisis of capitalism*, Monthly Review Press.

Aglietta, M., and Boyer, R. (1983) *Pôles de compétitive, stratégie industrielle et politiques macroéconomique*. Mimeograph CEPREMAP no. 8223. Reprinted in *Une politique industrielle pour la France*. Paris: La Documentation Française (1983).

Aglietta, M., and Courbis, R. (1969) "Un outil pour le Plan: Le modèle FIFI." *Economie et Statistique*, no. 1, May.

André, C. (1984) "Les evolutions specifiques des diverses composantes du salaire indirect à travers la crise." *Critiques de L'Economic Politique*, no. 26–27, January–June.

André, C., and Delorme, R. (1983) *L'état et l'économie*. Seuil, Paris.

Ardant, G., and Mendès-France, P. (1973) *Science économique et lucidité politique*. Paris: Gallimard.

Artus, P., La Roque, G., and Michel, G. (1982) "Estimation of a quarterly macroeconomic model with quantity rationing." Paper for the "Colloque sur les développements recents de la modelisation macroéconomique," Paris, September.

Artus, P., and Muet, P. A. (1982) "Politique conjoncturelle et investissement dans les années 70." *Observations et Diagnostics Economiques*, no. 1, June.

Attali, J. (1981) *Les trois mondes*. Paris: Fayard.

Barre, R. (1956) *Economique politique*. Vol. 2, Paris, Presses Universitaires de France. Réedité regulièrement.

Barre, R. (1980) "L'économie française quatre ans après (1976-1980)." *Revue des Deux Mondes*, September.

Barre, R. (1981) *Une politique pour l'avenir*. Paris: Plon. In particular "De la théorie à la politique économique: les leçons d'une expérience."

Barrère, A. (1952) *Théorie economique et impulsion Keynesienne*. Paris: Dalloz.

Barrère, A. (1981) "La crise n'est pas ce que l'on croit." *Economica*, Paris.

Beaud, M. (1983) *Le mirage de la croissance. La politique économique de la Gauche*. Syros.

Benassy, J. P. (1976) "Théorie du déséquilibre et fondements microéconomiques de la macroéconomie." *Revue Economique*, September.

Benassy, J. P. (1982) *The Economics of Market Disequilibrium*. New York: Academic Press.

Benassy, J. P., Boyer, R., and Gelpi, R. M. (1979) "Regulation des économies capitalistes et inflation." *Revue Economique*, May.

Bergsten, F. (1982) *Preventing a World Economic Crisis: What Must the United States Do Now?* Washington, D.C.: Institute for International Economics.

Bertrand, H. (1983) "Accumulation, regulation, crise: Un modèle sectionnel théorique et appliqué." *Revue Economique*, Vol. 34, no. 2, March, pp. 305-443.

Bloch-Laine, F. (1964) *A la recherche d'une économie concertée*. Editions de l'epargne.

Bloch-Laine, F. (Ed.) (1982) *Commission du bilan: La France en Mai 1981*. (4 volumes) Paris: Documentation Française.

Boissieu, C. de (1980) "Analyse macroéconomique et politiques économiques." *Encyclopedia Universalis*, Vol. 17, pp. 612-14.

Boltanski, L. (1982) *Les Cadres. La formation d'un groupe social*. Paris: Editions de Minuit.

Boris, G. (1934) "L'éxperience Roosevelt. Conference 20 Avril." Repris in X-Crise, *Economica* (1982).

Bouissou, M. B., Laffont, J. J., and Wong, A. H. (1983) Econométrie du déséquilibre sur données microéconomiques. Working Paper GREMAQ, University of Toulouse I, March.

Bouvier, J. (1974) "Sur la politique économique en 1944-1946." In Comité d'histoire de la seconde guerre mondiale. Actes du colloque du 28 au 31 Octobre. C.N.R.S.

Bouvier, J., and Caron, F. (1980) "Structures des firmes, emprise de l'Etat: 1914-1950." In Braudel, F., Labrousse, E. *Histoire économique et sociale de la France*. Paris: Presses Universitaires de France.

Boyer, R. (1976) "La croissance française de l'après guerre et les modèles macroéconomiques." *Revue Economique*. September.

Boyer, R. (1979) "Wage Formation in Historical Perspective: The French Experience." *Cambridge Journal of Economics*, no. 3, pp. 99-118.

Boyer, R. (1981) Les modeles macroéconomiques globaux et la comptabilité nationale. Working Paper CEPREMAP no. 8108, May.

Boyer, R. (1982) "Origine, originalité et enjeux de la crise actuelle en France: Une comparaison avec les années trente." In G. Dostaler, *La crise économique et sa gestion*. Boreal Express.

Boyer, R. (1983) "Wage Labor, Capital Accumulation and the Crisis 1968-1982." *The Tocqueville Review*, Spring-Summer.

Boyer, R. (1983) "Formes d'organisation implicites à la Théorie Générale." *In Keynes Aujourd'hui: Théories et politiques*.

Boyer, R., and Lepas, A. (1984) "Debate About the Present Economic Policy in France." *The Tocqueville Review*.

Boyer, R., and Mistral, J. (1983) *Accumulation, inflation, crises*. 2d. Ed. Paris: Presses Universitaires de France.

Boyer, R., and Mistral, J. (1983) "Politiques économiques et sortie de crise. Du carre infernal à un nouveau New Deal." *Futuribles*, October.

Boyer, R., and Petit, P. (1981) "Progrès technique, croissance et emploi: Un modèle d'inspiration kaldorienne pour six industries européennes." *Revue Economique*, Vol. 32, no. 6, November, pp. 1113-53.

Boyer, R., and Petit, P. (1981) "Crisis y politicas economicas en la communidad economica europea: el caso de Francia." Informacion Comercial Espanola (Ministerio de Economica y Comercio). *Revista de Economia*, September.

Brandt, W. (Ed.) (1980) *North–South: A Program for Survival.* Independent Commission on International Development Issues. French Edition, Paris: Gallimard.

Braudel, F., and Labrousse, E. (1980) *Histoire économique et sociale de la France.* Vol. IV. De 1880 à nos jours. Paris: Presses Universitaires de France.

Buckingham, W. S. (1958) *Theoretical Economic Systems.* New York: Ronald Press.

Carre, J. J., Dubois, P., and Malinvaud, E. (1972) *La croissance française.* Paris: Seuil.

C.E.P.I.I. (1982) *L'économie mondiale 1970–1990, La troisième revolution industrielle.* Editions Economica.

CEPREMAP-CORDES (1977) *Approches de l'inflation: l'exemple français.* 5 vols. Convention de recherche no. 22, December.

CEPREMAP-CORDES (1978) *Approches de l'inflation: l'exemple français.* Recherches Economiques et Sociales no. 12, October.

Chadeau, E. (1982) *Les modernisateurs de la France et de l'économie du vingtième siècle.* Bulletin de l'Institut d'Histoire du Temps Présent, no. 9, September.

Chevenement, J. P. (1983) ''Allocution d'ouverture des journées de travail des 16 Novembres 1982,'' *Une politique industrielle pour la France.* Paris: La Documentation Française.

Coddington, A. (1976) ''Keynesian Economics: The Search for First Principles.'' *Journal of Economic Literature,* December.

Cohen, Y. (1983) *Un Taylorien chez Peugeot, Ernest Mattern, 1906–1918.* Actes du colloque sur le taylorisme. Paris: La Découverte/Maspero.

Commissariat Général du Plan (1970) *Cinquième Plan (Options).* Paris: La Documentation Française.

Commissariat Général du Plan (1979) *Huitième Plan (Options).* Paris: La Documentation Française.

Commissariat Général du Plan (1981) *Stratégie pour deux ans, 1982–1983. Project de loi.* Publication des Journaux Officiels. November.

Commissariat Général du Plan (1983) *Rapport sur le IXeme Plan de Développement économique, social et culturel (1984–1988).* J. O. July 17.

Coriat, B. (1979) *L'atelier et le chronometre.* Paris: C. Bourgois.

Cremieux, M., Guesnerie, R., and Milleron, J. C. (1979) *Calcul économique et decisions publiques.* Paris: La Documentation Française.

Dahrendorf, R. (1982) *La Crise en Europe.* Paris: Edition Française Fayard.

Deleau, M., Guesnerie, R., and Malgrange, P. (1973) ''Planification, incertitude et politique économique. L'étude Optimix, une approche de la liaison court terme-moyen terme dans le cas de la France.'' *Revue Economique.*

Deleau, M., and Malgrange, P. (1977) ''Recent trends in French Planning.'' In *Frontiers in Quantitative Economies,* Vol. III, edited by M. Intriligalor. Amsterdam: North Holland.

Delorme, R. (1984) ''Compromis institutionalisé, Etat inseré et crise de l'Etat inseré.'' *Critiques de l'Economie Politique,* no. 26–27, January–June.

Delors, J. (1980) *La social-democratie en Quête d'une nouvelle frontière.* Echange et Projets. December.

Delors, J. (1981) ''Le double compromis.'' In I.S.E.R. *La social-democratie en questions.* Editions de la R.P.P.

Delors, J. (1982) ''L'économie française: Une modernisation entravée, une dynamique à retrouver.'' In *La crise en Europe.* Dahrendorf, R., Ed.

Delors, J. (1983) Allocution au colloque ''Keynes aujourd'hui.'' (forthcoming)

Denizet, J. (1967) *Monnaie et financement dans les années 80.* Rev. ed. 1982. Paris: Dunod.

Edgren, G., Faxen, F. O., and Odhner, C. E. (1963) ''Wages Growth and the Distribution of Income.'' *Swedish Journal of Economics.*

Eichner, A. S., and Kregel, J. A. (1978) ''An Essay on Post-Keynesian Theory: A New Paradigm in Economics.'' *Journal of Economic Literature,* pp. 1293–1314.

Estrin, S., and Holmes, P. (1983) *French Planning in Theory and Practice.* London: Allen and Unwin.

Feiwel, G. R. (1975) *The Intellectual Capital of Michael Kalecki.* Knoxville: University of Tennessee Press.

Fonteneau, A., and Muet, P. A. (1983) ''La politique économique depuis mai 1981: Un premier bilan.'' *Observations et Diagnostics Economiques,* no. 4, June, pp. 53–90.

Forum des Economistes (1983) *Les competes de la puissance. Histoire de la compatabilité nationale et du Plan.* Editions Recherches.

Fourcans A., and Rosa, J. J. (1977) ''Le mirage du plein-emploi.'' *Banque,* no. 366, October, pp. 1039–1045.

Fourquet, F. (1980) *Les comptes de la puissance. Histoire de la comptabilité nationale et du Plan*. Editions Recherches.

Friedman, M. (1983) "The Keynes Centenary." *The Economist*, June 4.

Gelpi, R. M. (1983) *Mecanismes de la création monetaire et regulations économiques*. These Université Paris IX-Dauphine.

Giscard d'Estaing, V. (1965) "Preface" à l'ouvrage de J. Denizet, *Monnaie et financement*. Paris: Dunod.

Gordon, R. J. (1977) *World Inflation and Monetary Accumulation in Eight Countries*. Brookings on Economic Activity, no. 2, pp. 409–477.

Grandmont, J. M. (1976) "Théorie de l'équilibre temporaire général." *Revue Economique*, September.

Grunig, F. (1933) *Le circuit économique*. German edition. French translation. Paris: Payot 1937. See abstracts in F. Fourquet (1980). Appendix 5, pp. 392–94.

Gruson, D. (1949) *Esquisse d'une théorie générale de l'equilibre économique*. Paris: Presses Universitaires de France.

Gruson, C. (1950) *Note sur les conditions d'etablissement d'une comptabilité nationale et d'un budget économique national*. Statistiques et Etudes Financières, no. 19, July.

Gruson, C. (1968) *Origine et espoirs de la Planification française*. Paris: Dunod.

Gruson, C. (1971) *Renaissance du Plan*. Paris: Seuil.

Guillaume, H. (1972) *Prix fictifs et decentralisation des décisions publiques*. Thesis, Université Paris I.

Guillaume, H., and Rochard, P. (1973) *Compatibilité entre approches sectorielle et globale*. Statistiques et Etudes Financières, first trimester.

Hansen, A. H. (1953) *A Guide to Keynes*. New York: McGraw-Hill. French Edition, Paris: Dunod, 1967.

Hayek, F. A. (1983) "The Keynes Centenary." *The Economist*, June 11.

Heller, W. (Ed.) (1968) *Perspectives on Economic Growth*. New York: Vintage Books.

Henin, P. Y. (1982) Controversés macroéconomiques et fondements des politiques de l'emploi. Cahiers de l'I.S.M.E.A.

Herzog, P. (1968) *Previsions économiques et comptabilité nationale*. Paris: Presses Universitaires de France.

Herzog, P. (1982) *L'économie à bras le corps*. Editions Sociales.

Herzog, P., and Olive, G. (1966) *Le Modèle de projection à court-terme ZOGOL I*. Internal Note. INSEE-DP Treasury.

Herzog, P., and Olive, G. (1968) *L'elaboration des budgets économiques*. Etudes de comptabilité nationale no. 8.

Hicks, J. (1955) "Economic Foundation of Wage Policy." *Economic Journal*, September.

Hicks, J. (1983) "The Keynes Centenary." *The Economist*, June 18.

Hoffman, S. (1963) *A la Recherche de la France*. Paris: Seuil.

Holland, S. (1978) *Beyond Capitalist Planning*. Oxford: Basil Blackwell.

Holland, S. (Ed.) (1983) "Out of the Crisis: A Projection for European Recovery." *London Spokesman*.

INSEE (1975–1983) *Rapport sur les comptes de la nation*. Collections de l'INSEE, annual issues, C 49 (1975), C 52-53 (1976), C 72-73 (1978), C 101-102 (1982) (The last one C 108-109, June, 1983).

INSEE *Tendances de la conjoncture*, various issues.

INSEE (1981) *Le movement économique de la France 1969-1979*. May.

INSEE (1982) *Le commerce exterieur de la France 1981-1982*. Mimeographed Service de la Conjoncture, September.

INSEE-DP (1966) *Le modèle de projection à court terme ZOGOL I*. Mimeographed Ministère des Finances, May.

Jones, B. L. (1972) "The Role of Keynesians in Wartime Policy and Postwar Planning 1940–1946." *American Economic Review*, May.

Kaldor, N. (1957) "Capitalist Evolution in the Light of Keynesian Economics." Reprinted in *Essays on Economic Stability and Growth*, Duckworth 1960.

Kaldor, N. (1966) *Causes of the Slow Rate of Growth of the United Kingdom*. Cambridge University Press.

Kaldor, N. (1971) "Conflicts in National Economic Objectives." *Economic Journal*, March.

Kalecki, M. (1933) "Proba teorii Koniunktury." *Essays on Business Cycle Theory*. Warsaw Instytut. Badania Koniunktur Gospodarczychi Cen. (quoted by Feiwel, G. 1975).

Kalecki, M. (1935) "Essai d'une théorie du mouvement cyclique des affaires." *Revue*

D'Economie Politique, no. 2, pp. 285–305.

Kalecki, M. (1935) "A Macrodynamic Theory of Business Cycles." *Econometrica*. July.

Keynes, J. M. (1919) *The Economic Consequences of the Peace*. Collected Writings of John Maynard Keynes Vol. IX. Macmillan.

Keynes, J. M. (1931) *Essays in Persuasion*. London: Rupert Hart-Davis.

Keynes, J. M. (1936) *The General Theory of Employment, Interest and Money*. Macmillan. Reprinted 1970.

Keyserling, L. H. (1972) "Keynesian revolution. Discussion." *American Economic Review*. May.

Kindleberger, C. P. (1963) "La renaissance de l'économie française après la guerre." In S. Hoffman *A la recherche de la France*. Paris: Seuil.

Klein, L. R. (1949) *The Keynesian Revolution*. London: Macmillan.

Klein, L. R. (1954) "The Empirical Foundations of Keynesian Economics." In *Post-Keynesian Economics*, edited by Kurihara. New Brunswick, N. J.: Rutgers University Press.

Kundig, B. (1984) "Du taylorisme classique à la 'flexibilisation' du système productif: l'impact macroéconomique des differents types d'organisation du travail." *Critiques de l'économie politique*, no. 26–27, January–June.

Le Monde (1976) January 27–February 19–20.

Levy-Garboua, V., and Weymuller, B. (1979) *Macroéconomie contemporaine*. Paris: Economica.

Liepietz, A. (1983) "L'echec de la première phase." *Les Temps Modernes*, special issue 441 Bis, April.

Lorenzi, H., Pastre, O., and Toledano, J. (1980) *La crise du XXème siecle*. Paris: Economica.

Malinvaud, E. (1977) *The Theory of Unemployment Reconsidered*. Oxford: Basil Blackwell.

Malinvaud, E. (1978) "Nouveaux développements sur la théorie macroéconomique du chômage." *Revue Economique*, January.

Malinvaud, E. (1979) *The Theory of Unemployment Reconsidered*. Mimeographed INSEE, September.

Malinvaud, E. (1979) *The Theory of Unemployment Reconsidered*. Oxford: Blackwell.

Malinvaud, E. (1980) *Profitability and Unemployment*. Cambridge University Press.

Malinvaud, E. (1981–1982) *Théorie macroéconomique. Vol. 1. Vol. 2 (1982)*. Paris: Dunod.

Masse, P. (1963–1964) *Rapport sur la politique des revenus établi à la suite de la Conference Des Revenus*. Recueils et Monographies no. 47, October–January 1964. Paris: La Documentation Française.

Masse, P. (1965) *Le Plan ou l'anti-hasard*. Paris: Gallimard.

Masse, P., and Bernard, P. (1969) *Les dividendes du progres*. Paris: Seuil.

Massenet, M. (1983) *La France socialiste*. Paris: Hachette.

Mauroy, P. (1982) *C'est ici le chemin*. Paris: Flammarion.

Mendès-France, P. (1974) *Choisir*. Paris: Stock.

Ministère des Finances *Comptes previsionnels de la nation et hypotheses économique*. Rapport économique et financier au projet de loi de Finances (annual publication). Paris: Imprimerie Nationale.

Ministère de la Recherche et de L'Industrie (1983) *Une politique industrielle pour la France*. J. P. Chevenement. Paris: La Documentation Française.

Minsky, H. P. (1975) *John Maynard Keynes*. New York: Columbia University Press.

Minsky, H. P. (1983) *The Legacy of Keynes*. Working Paper no. 49, April, Department of Economics. Washington University.

Monthly Review Editors (1977) "Keynesianism: Illusions and Delusions." *Monthly Review*, April.

Monthly Review Editors (1983) "Listen, Keynesians!" *Monthly Review*, January.

Mosse, R. (1937) "L'experience Blum." In A. Sauvy, *Histoire économique de la France 1931–1935*. Paris: Seuil.

Moutet, A. (1983) "La première guerre mondiale et le taylorisme." *Actes du colloque sur le Taylorisme*. Paris: La Découverte/Maspero.

Muet, P. A. (1979) "Modèles économétriques de l'investissement: une etude comparative sur données annuelles." *Annales De L'INSEE*, no. 35, pp. 85–133.

Negri, A. (1978) "John M. Keynes et la théorie capitaliste de l'Etat en 1929." In *La classe ouvrière contre L'Etat*, Edition Française Galilee.

OECD (1980) (1981) *Perspective économiques*.

Parti Socialiste (1980) *Projet Socialiste*. Paris: Flammarion.

Perroux, F. (1949) *Les comptes de la Nation*. Paris: Presses Universitaires de France.

Petit, P. (1983) *Origine et originalité de la Planification française*. Note roneotypee CEPREMAP, Juillet.
Pietre, A. (1980) "Interventionnisme," In *Encyclopedia Universalis*, Vol. 9.
Polanyi, K. (1944) *The Great Transformation*. French translation, Paris: Gallimard (1983).
Prou, C. (1976) *Leçons Introductives D'Economie*. Lessons 16 and 17. Paris: Masson.
Ribeill, G. (1983) "Les organisations du mouvement ouvrier en France face à la nationalism (1926–1932)." *Actes du colloque sur le taylorisme*. Paris: La Decouverte/Maspero.
Rigaudiat, J. (1983) *Tendances et politiques de l'emploi et du chômage*. Working Paper IRES, April, Paris.
Rioux, J. P. (1983) *La France de la Quatrième République*. Vol. *1: 1944–1952*. Vol. *2: 1952–1958*. Paris: Seuil (1982).
Robinson, J. (1971) "Michael Kalecki." *Cambridge Review*, October.
Robinson, J. (1973) "The Second Crisis of Economic Theory." In *Collected Economic Papers*, Vol. IV. Oxford: Basil Blackwell.
Rougier, L. (1938) "Les mystiques économiques." In A. Sauvy, *Histoire économique de la France*. Paris: Seuil.
Rowley, A. (1983) "Taylorisme et missions de productivité." *Actes du colloque sur le Taylorisme*. Paris: La Découverte/Maspero.
Rueff, J. (1963) *L'Age de l'inflation*. Paris: Payot.
Rueff, J. (1965) *Le lançinant problème des Balances de Paiement*. Paris: Payot. English translation. New York: Macmillan (1967).
Rueff, J. (1975) "Pourquoi la crise?" *Le Monde*, June 17–18.
Rueff, J. (1976) "La fin de l'aire Keynesienne." *Le Monde*, February 19–20.
Samuelson, P. A. (1983) "The Keynes Centenary." *The Economist*, June 25.
Sauvy, A. (1967) *Histoire économique de la France 1931–1935*. Paris: Seuil.
Shonfield, A. (1965) *Modern Capitalism*. Oxford University Press.
Stoleru, L. (1967) *L'equilibre et la croissance économique*. Paris: Dunod. English translation *Economic Equilibrium and Growth*. Amsterdam: North Holland.
Sweezy, A. R. "The Keynesians and Government Policy, 1933–1939." *American Economic Review*, May 1972.
The Economist (1983) June 11.
Thibault, P. (1971) *L'age des dictatures 1918–1947*. Paris: Larousse.
Thibault, P. (1971) *Le Temps de la contestation 1947–1969*. Paris: Larousse.
Thomas, J. G. (1981) *Politique monetaire et autodestruction du Capital*. Paris: Economica.
Tobin, J. (1966) *National Economic Policy*. New Haven, Conn.: Yale University Press.
Vogel, F. E. (1979) *Japan as Number One*. Cambridge, Mass.: Harvard University Press.
Wallich, H., and Weintraub, S. (1971) "A Tax Based Incomes Policy." *Journal of Economic Issues*, June.
Williamson, J. (1984) *Financial Intermediation Beyond the Debt Crisis*. Institute for International Economics. Washington, D.C.
X-CRISE (1931 to 1939) *Les crises économiques et leur recurrence*. Paris: Economica, reedition 1982.
Younes, Y. (1970) *Sur les notions d'équilibre et de déséquilibre utilisées dans les modèles décrivant l'évolution d'une économie capitaliste*. Mimeograph CEPREMAP, Paris.

9

The Influence of Keynesian Thought on German Economic Policy

Dudley Dillard

From World War I Through World War II

John Maynard Keynes had a special relation with Germany dating from his participation in the Versailles peace conference as a member of the British delegation in 1919. Between January and June of that year, he participated actively in negotiations for a peace treaty in what he later described as "One of the greatest errors of international statesmanship ever committed" (Keynes, XXI:45). In June 1919 Keynes resigned from the British delegation and returned to Cambridge University, where he wrote *The Economic Consequences of the Peace* (1919) and two years later *A Revision of the Treaty* (1922). These experiences immersed him in the economic and political affairs of Germany for the remainder of his life.

Keynes's denunciation of the peace treaty, and of reparations in particular, won him the sympathy of Germans and the enmity of the French. Throughout the 1920s he was a frequent visitor to Germany in the role of adviser, lecturer, and observer of the German scene.

In *The Economic Consequences of the Peace*, Keynes's main contentions were: (1) the reparations being contemplated were impossible for Germany to pay, and (2) any attempt to enforce these claims would probably be ruinous to Europe as a whole (III:68–69). Inclusion of pensions for allied veterans as part of the reparations against Germany was unreasonable and a breach of faith with President Woodrow Wilson's Fourteen Points. In *A Revision of the Treaty*, Keynes argued that the actual physical damages to France and Belgium were grossly exaggerated. If accurately assessed, Keynes said, these damages were within the ability of Germany to pay. He warned that

For assistance in the preparation of this paper, I wish to thank the following individuals: Richard Freeman, Head, Country Studies II (German Desk), OECD; Professor Allan G. Gruchy, University of Maryland; Professor Helmut Hesse, Visiting Professor, Georgetown University; Dr. Friedrich Klau, Head, Growth Studies Division, OECD; Professor Henry W. Spiegel, Catholic University of America; Axel Senftleben, First Minister of Economic and Industrial Affairs of the German Delegation to OECD; and, as always, Louisa Gardner Dillard, my wife and colleague.

116

France was much more likely to get what she deserved if the claims were reasonable. Keynes's own preference was to cancel all reparations and interallied war debts, but his actual proposal was to reduce greatly the amounts to be paid by Germany to France and Belgium to sums that could be met without great strain to Germany.

Although Keynes's proposals were not accepted, his two books about the peace treaty and numerous other writings on reparations were powerful and persuasive arguments that gained worldwide attention and made Keynes famous. With the passage of time, the correctness of his judgments led to wide acceptance of his position. The French were least convinced of the oppression and injustice of the treaty. The Germans needed no Keynes to persuade them of the villainy of the treaty, but Keynes, as an outsider and a leading publicist, aided them in the fight to end reparations. In his brilliant essay ''Dr. Melchior: The Defeated Enemy,'' Keynes wrote:

> . . . the insincere acceptance . . . of impossible conditions which it was not intended to carry out [made] Germany almost as guilty to accept what she could not fulfill as the Allies to impose what they were not entitled to exact . . . .(X:428)

As much as any other single person, except possibly President Franklin D. Roosevelt, Keynes was to be responsible for the absence of reparations and intergovernmental war debts after World War II.

During World War II, Keynes, from the British Treasury, spearheaded the United Kingdom's lend-lease financing. He visited Washington to negotiate lend-lease arrangements. On several occasions he met with President Roosevelt (See Keynes, XXIII). In the transition to peace toward the end of World

end-of-war plans with the United States, Keynes not only used his influence to oppose reparations and war debts, but he helped rout the Morgenthau Plan. Morgenthau once said to Keynes, ''It is a question of a strong Britain or a strong Germany, and I am for a strong Britain'' (XXIV:135). Referring to Morgenthau's plan to deindustrialize Germany and convert it to a pastoral economy, Keynes wrote satirically, ''So whilst the hills are being turned into a sheeprun, the valleys will be filled for some years to come with a closely packed bread line on a very low level of subsistence at American expense'' (XXIV:134).

Between the wars, Keynes followed, and participated in, efforts to stabilize and rebuild the German economy. He served as an unofficial adviser to the German government during the middle stages of the hyperinflation. In November 1922 he had a bold plan for saving the mark. A prerequisite was an agreement to a moratorium on reparations. He would then announce an exchange rate of 1500 to 1 with the British pound sterling and stick with this exchange ratio, using Germany's not inconsiderable supply of gold to sustain the ratio until confidence was restored.

Keynes had an hour-long interview with Chancellor Heinrich Brüning in Berlin on January 11, 1933 (XXI:48, XVIII:366–69). That same day Brüning announced that Germany would not be able to resume reparations payment at the end of the one-year Hoover moratorium. Apparently Keynes tried to persuade Brüning to reverse a deflationary policy of cutting wages and expenditures, the kind of policy Keynes always opposed with all his intellectual powers. Deflation and the gold standard, which Germany still retained, were killing German exports—exports needed to pay debts and reparations. Keynes reported that the psychological, political, and economic atmosphere in Germany was the most depressed he had ever seen.

In April 1933, three months after Hitler became chancellor, Keynes gave an appraisal of Germany as a market for foreign investment. His conclusions were negative.

My general conclusion is to the effect that the position of the foreign investor in Germany is even worse than is commonly supposed. In the present national mood there will be no inclination to treat the foreign capitalist well . . . A bold and blustering policy towards the foreign investor will be popular. (XXI:250–51)

Much depends, Keynes added, on Dr. Hjalmar Schacht, who had again become president of the Reichsbank, because he was strong-willed and the only one of the new German leaders with any experience or knowledge about international finance (XXI:247).

Hjalmar Horace Greeley Schacht (1877–1970) wrote a doctoral dissertation on *The Theoretical Content of English Mercantilism* (Kiel, 1900). He was, to say the least, an enigmatic figure who held high offices in both the Weimar Republic and the Hitler Reich until 1939. He led the fight against reparations; was a central figure in the stabilization of the mark in 1924; was twice president of the Reichsbank, first under the Weimar Republic and later under Hitler; and was a central figure in eliminating unemployment in Germany during the Great Depression. On at least three points Schacht's activities paralleled Keynes's interests: he opposed German reparations to the Allies, he favored central bank management, and he urged national government initiatives to reduce unemployment.

As president of the Reichsbank during the 1930s, Schacht provided financing for work-creation programs which, in combination with rearmament, eliminated German unemployment. Schacht's methods of financing the work-creation program were ingenious. He used special notes called Mefo bills, which were a direct obligation of neither the government nor the central bank. Thus Schacht achieved the general purpose of putting the unemployed to work while avoiding the appearance of increasing the national debt. From the beginning he seems to have recognized that once full employment was achieved, Mefo bills would become inflationary. When full employment was attained in 1938, with measured unemployment at 0.01 percent, Schacht called for a halt to deficit financing, including Mefo bills. He recommended tax increases if there was to be continued spending on rearmament. A member of the Reichsbank directory, Emil Puhl, testified: "It was understood at the beginning that Mefo-financing could be used only to the point where full employment and full production were achieved" (Peterson, p. 175). In a courageous letter to Hitler on January 7, 1939, Schacht wrote that the Reichsbank would no longer use Mefo bills or other forms of deficit spending to finance armament or other public expenditures. Legend has it that as Hitler read Schacht's letter, he muttered, "This is treason" (Peterson, p. 179). Thereupon Hitler dismissed Schacht as president of the Reichsbank. Schacht later participated in an attempted coup against Hitler; he was imprisoned by the Gestapo, held in custody after the war by the British and Americans, tried and found not guilty at Nuremburg, and freed from internment in September 1948.

Were Schacht's policies for eliminating unemployment influenced by Keynes? Probably not. Keynes and Schacht were personally acquainted, and Schacht undoubtedly knew about Keynes's writings and recommendations for combating unemployment with deficit-financed public works. Keynes was aware of Schacht's work-creation programs of the 1930s and probably had Germany in mind when he wrote in the London *Times* in 1938 "How can we hope to keep pace with a form of government which has devised a means of producing and maintaining full employment?" (XXI:482). There is nothing unusual about the idea of using public works to reduce unemployment. What was unusual about Keynes in this connection was that he erected a theoretical structure to analyze unemployment and to demonstrate the necessity and desirability of such a policy. What was unusual about Schacht was that he had the power to finance public works with full command of a central bank. Only infrequently has the head of a central bank believed in the efficacy of putting the unemployed to work through increasing the supply of money. An exception was Marriner Eccles, chairman of the Federal Reserve system from 1936 to 1948. Eccles got his ideas about deficit spending as a Utah banker observing unemployment during the Great Depression. Thus there is no reason to assume that Schacht's ideas and actions were inspired by Keynes's theories.

Keynes's Preface to the German Edition of *The General Theory*

In the special preface to the German edition of *The General Theory*, dated September 1936, Keynes expressed the hope that German readers would take to his theory even though it was written mainly with conditions in English-speaking countries in mind. Then he wrote a sentence that needs to be read with care:

> Nevertheless the theory of output as a whole, which is what the following book purports to provide, is much more easily adapted to the condition of a totalitarian state, than is the theory of the production and distribution of a given output produced under conditions

of free competition and a large measure of laissez-faire (VII:xxvi).

In this statement Keynes does *not* say that his theory is more applicable to a totalitarian state than to a democratic state. What Keynes says is that his macroeconomic theory of output as a whole is more easily adapted to a totalitarian state than is classical microeconomic theory of the production and distribution of a *given* output produced under conditions of competition and a large measure of laissez-faire. The distinction is an important one. Keynes is comparing the usefulness of micro and macro theory in a totalitarian state. He is not comparing the usefulness of his macro theory in a totalitarian state with its usefulness in a democratic state. One can argue that Keynes's statement lends itself to misinterpretation, especially for those critics inclined to misinterpret it, as, for example, Hayek does in his centennial essay on Keynes in *The Economist* (p. 41).

The Schacht experience in Germany during the 1930s perhaps illustrates the point that, under assumptions of pure competition and a given total output, a theory such as Keynes's would be more useful for policy than a theory of the firm. Keynes's theory would also probably be more useful in a democratic society. In the United Kingdom during the late 1930s, virtually full employment was achieved with large public expenditures on armaments. Keynes viewed this British experience of the late 1930s as a vindication and confirmation of his theory and policy (XXI:528). He referred to it as "the grand experiment." Certainly some of Keynes's policies are less applicable in a totalitarian state than in a democratic one. In Chapter 19 of *The General Theory*, he compares a flexible wage policy with a flexible monetary policy and concludes that analytically they may come to the same thing "inasmuch as they are alternative means of changing the quantity of money in terms of wage-units" (VII: 267). As alternative policies, however, there is a world of difference between them. Concerning the feasibility of a flexible wage policy, Keynes wrote in 1936: "One can imagine it in practice in Italy, Germany or Russia, but not in France, the United States or Great Britain" (VII:269).

Policy in the Social Market Economy

A transformation in German academic economics after World War II included wide acceptance of Keynes's *General Theory* as well as other aspects of Anglo-American economics. The long-dominant Historical School of economics occupied a decreasing share of attention from German academics. German acceptance of Keynes was part of a worldwide movement toward the acceptance of macroeconomics as one of the two major branches of economic theory. Keynes, much more than anyone else, was the father of modern macroeconomics.

A German translation of *The General Theory* was published a few months after its initial publication in English in 1936. After World War II Erich Schneider's popular text, *Geld, Kredit, Volkseinkommein, und Beschäft-*

gung (Tübingen: J. C. Mohr, 1st ed., 1952) seems to have been widely influential in spreading Keynes's type of macroeconomics in Germany. This macroeconomics book by Schneider was Volume III of a work on economic theory, *Einführung in die Wirtschaftstheorie*. Volume III has been translated into English as *Money, Income and Employment* (London: George Allen & Unwin, 1962).

Among the academic Keynesians who became policymakers in government, probably the most influential was Karl Schiller. Born in 1911, Schiller studied at several German universities and completed his training for university teaching at Kiel. In 1947 he became a professor of political economy at Hamburg University, where he served as vice-chancellor from 1956 to 1958. One of his students in economics at Hamburg was Helmut Schmidt. Schiller joined the Social Democratic party and held governmental posts in Hamburg and Berlin before becoming minister of economics in the coalition government in Bonn in 1966. After the national election of 1969, when Willy Brandt became chancellor, Schiller continued as minister of economics and also became minister of finance. When he resigned from the government in 1972, he was succeeded as minister of finance by his former student Helmut Schmidt, who became chancellor two years later and remained head of the West German government unil 1982.

The acceptance of Keynes's *General Theory* as a way of analyzing problems of national income, investment, savings, consumption, and money did not carry with it, in many cases, an acceptance of the policies recommended by Keynes. This has certainly been true in Germany, where the social market economy is quite un-Keynesian in its emphasis on the unregulated market as the focus of economic policy. Postwar Germany has not presented a Keynesian-type situation, by which is meant high levels of chronic unemployment associated with a deficiency of investment outlets. Until quite recently, the West German economy has enjoyed remarkable success, with rapid growth, stable prices, and low levels of unemployment.

During the Adenauer-Erhard era, German economic policy was little affected by Keynesian thought. Beginning in the mid-1960s, changing economic conditions led to some new policies of a macroeconomic type of demand management, which can be described as Keynesian. These changes were, however, accommodated within the framework of the social market economy.

In relating Keynes's ideas to German economic policy, account should be taken of changes in Keynes's theories and policies over his lifetime. At the time he wrote *A Tract on Monetary Reform* (1923), he emphasized the importance of a stable price level. By "Keynesian thought" we shall have primarily in mind the ideas associated with Keynes's later work, *The General Theory of Employment, Interest and Money* (1936).

The Adenauer-Erhard Era, 1949–65

At the end of the war in 1945, the battered German economy almost completely collapsed. The Allied occupation authorities continued controls over prices, wages, and administrative rationing, but the quantity of money in circulation was so great that these controls could not be enforced. The first major step back toward a genuine peacetime economy was the currency reform of 1948. Money supply was reduced by more than 90 percent. All debts were devalued in money terms by a ratio of ten to one. Germany was thus spared the traumatic inflation experienced after World War I. These deflationary reforms were promulgated primarily by Germans and carried out by the occupation authorities. They involved major inequities that would have been very difficult for a democratically elected government to administer. The currency reform succeeded beyond expectations. Goods came out of hiding, and incentives to work, save, and invest were rapidly restored.

Some price and rationing controls continued after the currency reform but, in general, decontrol became the order of the day. Economist Ludwig Erhard emerged as the strong voice for complete market decontrol. He laid the groundwork for the new social market economy, which has remained the dominant form of economic policy in West Germany. Erhard was no Keynesian, and economic policy in West Germany was very little influenced by Keynesian thought during the Adenauer-Erhard period. Priority was given to a stable domestic price level as the primary condition for successful functioning of the free market. Although a stable domestic price level was the monetary reform Keynes recommended in his *Tract*, Keynes was more antideflation than anti-inflation.

In another respect the Erhard policy was consistent with Keynes's thought although not derived from it. This is the emphasis on a high rate of investment. Erhard favored high investment as the road to a high rate of economic growth in output. He was not particularly sensitive to the high rate of unemployment during the early 1950s. On the other hand, Keynes, in *The General Theory*, favored a high rate of investment primarily as a way to bring down unemployment. In brief, Erhard gave a supply-side and Keynes a demand-side emphasis to investment.

Keynes's *General Theory* is a theory of mature capitalism in which the accumulation of durable capital assets over a long period has brought down the rate of return to levels that weaken the inducement to invest. Germany's economy in the early postwar period did not fit this description. Physical destruction of plant, equipment, transportation, and infrastructure, along with delayed maintenance of capital assets, was so great that the marginal efficiency of investment remained high throughout the 1950s. Even a victorious capitalist economy in its first postwar decade, such as the United States in the 1920s and the 1950s, had such a backlog of demand accumulated from war years that it could sustain prosperity without any such special stimulus as Keynes's compensatory fiscal policy. Nations such as Germany and Japan, which suffered great destruction in war, had no difficulty maintaining prosperity for a decade following the war. Germany's "economic miracle" of the 1950s was no miracle in Keynesian terms. The high level of demand for durable capital assets was a normal outcome of the wartime experience. Germany enjoyed the additional advantage of a large supply of labor from East Germany. This abundant labor supply prevented wages from rising more than productivity. After the initial decontrol period ended, the consumer price index rose at the modest rates of 1 to 2 percent annually. Wholesale prices rose even less. With low labor costs, Germany enjoyed an advantage in the export markets that helped to maintain vigorous economic activity. Trade unions were relatively undemanding as a result of historic tradition and the abundance of labor available to the West German economy. Investment was further aided in these conditions of rapid growth by a relatively unequal distribution of income after taxes.

The Erhard regime had an active monetary policy, as every modern economy must, but it lacked the Keynesian emphasis on pushing down interest rates and keeping them there in order to stimulate investment. Keynesian fiscal policy to offset deficiencies of demand in the private sector was not needed.

As a member of the European Economic Community, West German officials encountered representatives with different economic philosophies. In his final year as minister of economic affairs (1962), Ludwig Erhard confronted Walter Hallstein, president of the EEC Commission, on the desirability of macroeconomic projections and programs. Two German economists have described Erhard's behavior as follows: "Erhard decisively opposed the Brussels conception of medium-range forecasts and medium-term programming which, in the final analysis, represented the Keynesianism which he rejected uncompromisingly . . . '' (Kloten and Vollmer, p. 98). But this may be an exaggeration of Erhard's views in the light of his subsequent actions. The West German advocates of the social market economy opposed most strongly the French form of economic planning. Keynesian monetary and fiscal policies are quite consistent with a free-market economy, whereas general economic planning is not.

Erhard succeeded Adenauer as chancellor in 1963. Subsequent difficulties in the West German economy gave rise to new policies that may be termed Keynesian. Chancellor Erhard took cautious steps toward an anticyclical policy by the federal government. A council of economic experts was created in 1964 as an advisory group of "Five Wise Men" to make macroeconomic projections and to issue annual reports analyzing national economic trends and problems. The council, however, is not charged with making specific recommendations concerning policies. It operates outside the formal channels of government in order to encourage independent nonpolitical judgments.

In order to curb an incipient boom in 1965–66, monetary and fiscal tools were applied, but they overshot the mark and led in 1967 to no growth in gross national product for the first time in the postwar period.

The Schiller (Keynesian) Period, 1966–72

In 1967, with Karl Schiller as minister of economics, the most Keynesian legislation of the postwar era, the Stability and Growth Act, was passed. It charges the government with four macroeconomic goals: a stable price level, high employment, stable growth, and equilibrium in West Germany's international balance of payments. The most Keynesian of these is, of course, the high-employment goal, which has its American counterpart in the Employment Act of 1946. Notable is the absence of an annually balanced budget among the legislated aims of macro policy. Such a provision would render the legislation anti-Keynesian, or at least non-Keynesian, because Keynes's policies rely so heavily on loan financing in periods of low employment.

The consistency of the four legislative goals has been subject to controversy. High employment is fully consistent with growth in the gross national product but not necessarily with stable price levels. The Phillips curve tradeoff between unemployment and prices (wages) is in the German literature. Although high employment, stable prices, and stable growth are not inherently inconsistent, yet, given the history of business cycles during the past two hundred years since the Industrial Revolution, a policy that would successfully induce these goals simultaneously would score the greatest breakthrough in policymaking in the history of capitalism.

Debates concerning the consistency of the Stability and Growth law have turned on demand management, that is, attempts to control the volume of effecive demand—a Keynesian concept—through governmental policies as stipulated in the 1967 law. One writer maintains that after the Adenauer-Erhard era (1949–65), there was '' . . . initially a decay in the concept of the Social Market Economy and finally its replacement by the new experiment of Demand Management'' (Tuchtfeldt, p. 113). The same author continues, ''As far as the ideological background is concerned, Demand Management developed from the 'Keynesian Revolution' '' (p. 122). He contends there is no continuity between the two ''experiments,'' that is, that the Keynesian Revolution represents a clean break from the social market economy. This seems to exaggerate the degree of change. What happened in the mid-1960s was a shift of emphasis and not a reversal of the social market philosophy. The 1967 law specifically states that demand management shall take place ''within the framework of the market economy order.'' The Social Democrats, who followed in office beginning in 1969, accepted the social market economy, perhaps out of political expediency rather than ideological conviction, since both Willy Brandt and Helmut Schmidt were basically socialists operating in coalition governments. Schmidt, who was trained in economics and who was minister of finance before becoming chancellor in 1974, probably placed a higher priority on employment than on price stability, but he did not repudiate the social market philosophy (Schmidt, p. 232).

How successful was the Stability and Growth Act of 1967? No simple answer is possible. It attained some but not all of its stated goals. Even if all the data were available for making a judgment, one could not be certain whether the results represented inherent defects in the law or a change of circumstances or some combination of the two. During the early 1970s, economic growth slowed, inflation increased, and there were balance-of-payments surpluses. Unemployment rates remained low for some time after 1967. Consumer prices increased more than twice as much on the average in the three years 1971 through 1973 as in the three preceding years (6.0 percent vs. 2.7 percent). In these same years the average growth rate in gross national product fell to one-half the earlier three-year period (3.6 percent in 1971, 1972, and 1973 compared with 7.2 percent in 1967, 1968, and 1969. Kloten and Vollmer, p. 103). By the standards of most other capitalist economies, this performance was still above average. By the chief Keynesian criterion of unemployment, the experience was highly successful. Unemployment remained approximately 1 percent of the labor force. Only in the early 1980s did rates exceed 7 percent.

With the shift in government leadership to the Social Democrats (1969), wages increased more rapidly than in earlier years. The average hourly wage rate in manufacturing increased from 5.7 percent in the final three years of the 1960s to 12.3 percent in the first three years of the 1970s (Gruchy, p. 156). Since wage rates increased more than productivity during this period, labor costs per unit of output rose and helped to push up prices. One result of higher costs and prices was a relative cutback in German exports. This, however, hardly shows up in the foreign-trade data, partly because wage rates relative to productivity were rising even more rapidly among most of Germany's competitors in international markets. The distribution of income, which had shifted against wages and salaries in the earlier years, now shifted toward a larger share to wages and salaries as compared to nonwage income.

Fiscal policy. The chief instruments of Keynesian policy are fiscal and monetary policy. As compared with other forms of governmental intervention, these policies are consistent with a free-market economy such as that of West Germany. Fiscal and monetary policies operate at the aggregate level and leave, for the most part, the micro sector free of controls. Consumers and firms are affected by the taxes they pay and the services they receive under fiscal policy, but wages are left to collective bargaining and prices to the market. A peculiarity of Germany, as a heritage from its distant past, is the large size of the public sector. In recent times the share of federal, provincial, and local governments has been just under two-fifths of total national income, which is exceeded by Sweden and Norway but is considerably higher than the United States, where it is about 30 percent. Since the days of Bismarck, social-security payments in Germany have been high by international standards. High payments for social security and for social equity are an accepted part of the philosophy of social market economy. Although personal income tax rates are not low in West Germany, two-thirds or more of total revenue is derived from indirect taxes, including the value-added tax.

The Stability and Growth Act of 1967 changed fiscal policy to correspond more with Keynesian principles. Fiscal policy became part of anticyclical policy. Under the 1967 law the federal government was authorized to raise or lower income taxes by as much as 10 percent of the tax. Repayable sur-

charges on personal and business income taxes could be assessed in boom
years to dampen effective demand. These surcharges would be refunded when
needed to stimulate the economy with more spending. Unbalanced budgets
came to be acknowledged as devices to stimulate a lagging economy. Although
German economists probably never really accepted classical economics, this
new fiscal policy rejects Say's Law that supply creates its own demand,
substituting Keynes's proposition that expenditure creates its own income.
Thus, fiscal policy in West Germany under Social Democrats Brandt and
Schmidt moved in a Keynesian direction.

  Monetary policy. Keynes's *General Theory* suffers from the limitation
that it is the theory of a closed economy. Consequently it does not directly
address Germany's concern with domestic inflation resulting from the inflow
of funds derived from an export surplus. Keynes was, of course, one of the
world's leading authorities on international finance, but he does not discuss
the international sector in *The General Theory.* These problems were handled
skillfully through the German banking system. Although fiscal policy became
more important after the Stability and Growth Act of 1967, monetary policy
has borne the chief burden of stabilizing Germany's economy.

  Keynes's concern with monetary policy as an instrument for maintaining
low interest rates in order to stimulate investment has not related to an important problem in the post–World War II German economy. An OECD study,
Monetary Policy in Germany, makes this point in its conclusion:

> While the evidence indicates that monetary policy can have an
> important influence on business investment through changing interest
> rates, the policy contribution to the stabilization of this demand
> component seems to have been small in most of the period under re-
> view. (OECD, p. 96)

Summary and Conclusion

From the time of Keynes's participation in the Versailles peace conference, he
had an abiding interest in German economic policy. As the world's best-
known opponent of German reparations, Keynes probably influenced the
Dawes Plan, the Young Plan, and the ultimate end of German reparations. As
an adviser to the German government on the stabilization of the mark midway
through the hyperinflation, Keynes offered a plan that was not accepted. In
early 1932 Keynes tried unsuccessfully to persuade German Chancellor Heinrich Brüning to reverse the deflationary policies that hastened the breakdown
of Germany's economy on the eve of Hitler's ascension to power. Hjalmar
Schacht's work-creation projects during the 1930s bore similarities to policies
recommended by Keynes, but Keynes seems to have had no direct influence on
the projects to eliminate unemployment in Germany.

  In the transition to peace after World War II, Keynes was in a strong
position to influence both American and British policies toward Germany. As
the author of *The Economic Consequences of the Peace* and the chief architect

of the lend-lease program, he was a force against reparations and interallied debts.

In the early postwar decades, Keynes's New Economics penetrated academic circles worldwide. In West Germany the coming of Keynesian economics coincided with a fundamental shift to a more formal type of economic theory and ended the long dominance of the Historical School.

In German policy since World War II, Keynesian thought has had relatively little direct influence, especially as compared with its impact in the United States and the United Kingdom. This lack of influence on policy can be explained by the fact that Keynes's policies are oriented to a stagnating capitalism and therefore have not been applicable to Germany's dynamic postwar economy. Following the Stability and Growth Act of 1967, Keynesian thought played a role in the formulation of stabilization programs. Some of the German fiscal policies arising from that law may appropriately be described as Keynesian. On monetary policy, low interest rates stressed by Keynes as a stimulus to private investment and high employment have not coincided with the need. Hence, even since 1967, Keynesian monetary policy has had little impact on the West German economy.

References

Gruchy, Allan G. *Comparative Economic Systems*, 2nd ed. (Boston: Houghton-Mifflin, 1977).
Hayek, F. A. "The Keynes Centenary: The Austrian Critique." *The Economist* (June 11, 1983), pp. 39-41.
Keynes, John Maynard. *The Collected Writings of John Maynard Keynes*. 30 vols. (London: Macmillan for the Royal Economic Society, 1971-).
Kloten, Norbert, and Rainer Vollmer. "Stability, Growth and Economic Policy." *German Economic Review* (1975), pp. 105-16. Organization for Economic Cooperation and Development (OECD) *Economic Surveys: Germany*. (Paris: OECD, Annual Edition)
Organization for Economic Cooperation and Development (OECD). *Monetary Policy in Germany*. (Monetary Study Series. Paris: OECD, 1973)
Peterson, Edward Norman. *Hjalmar Schacht: For and Against Hitler*. (Boston: Christopher Publishing House, 1954)
Schacht, Hjalmar Horace Greeley. *Confessions of "The Old Wizard": An Autobiography*. (Westport, Conn.: Greenwood Press, 1974)
Schmidt, Helmut. *Helmut Schmidt: Perspectives and Politics*. Edited by Wolfram F. Hanrieder. (Boulder, Colo.: Westview Press, 1982)
Schneider, Erich. *Einführung in die Wirtschaftstheorie*. 4 vols. (Tübingen: J. C. Mohr, 1947)
Schneider, Erich. *Money, Income and Employment*. (London: George Allen and Unwin, 1962)
Tuchtfeldt, Egon. "Social Market Economy and Demand Management: Two Experiments in Social Policy." *German Economic Review* (1974), pp. 111-33.
Wallich, Henry C. *Mainsprings of German Revival*. (New Haven: Yale University Press, 1955)

10

Relevance of Keynes for Developing Countries

H. W. Singer

I wish to dedicate this paper to Dudley Seers, whose essay "The Limitations of the Special Case"[1] has been one of my chief sources of guidance. His death a few months ago was a great loss. I also wish to acknowledge my indebtedness to Albert Hirschman,[2] whose essay on "The Rise and Decline of Development Economics" has provided me with the starting point, and much more, for my own paper. Thirdly, I have of course learned a great deal from the 1952 pioneer paper by V. K. R. V. Rao in the *Indian Economic Review* on "Investment, Income and the Multiplier in an Underdeveloped Economy"[3] and from many discussions with him on this subject.

Albert Hirschman credits Keynes with the major methodological step in establishing the analysis of problems of developing countries on a firm scientific footing, which he dates from some thirty-five years ago. That step was, in his own terminology, to move away from monoeconomics to the proposition that different laws and rules apply to economics that find themselves in different situations. In the case of Keynes, the distinction was of course between an economy in full employment and an economy with unemployment, for which he described the laws and rules in 1936 in *The General Theory of Interest and Money*. By contrast, the preceding classical and neoclassical economists assumed that the laws and rules of economics had universal validity comparable to physical laws such as the law of gravity. The question immediately arose whether the Keynesian model of *The General Theory* was more relevant than the classical model for analyzing problems of developing countries. A number of fairly obvious features made a positive answer to this question at least superficially plausible. These included:

1. The assumption of unemployed resources seems to correspond directly to the existence of surplus labor, unemployment, disguised unemployment, underemployment, low-productivity employment, the informal sectors, and the like in developing countries. However, this superficially attractive feature of the Keynesian model soon turned out to be doubtful. Of this more later.

2. *The General Theory* established a situation of low-level equi-

librium in which market forces left to themselves would be unable to break the vicious circle. This market-failure situation required some external agency to intervene and change the situation so that forces moving to a higher-level equilibrium could be set in motion. Moreover *The General Theory* showed that such intervention could be self-financing and that it would in fact constitute a positive-sum game for the economy as a whole. This again seemed to correspond to conditions in developing countries, where market failures, interventionist policies, and government planning rapidly became familiar and almost universally accepted concepts.

3. A related feature of *The General Theory* model, as distinct from the classical model which also seemed to make it directly more relevant to developing countries, is that the emphasis is on the *mobilization*, as well as the *allocation*, of resources. Moreover, the mobilization of resources in the Keynesian model takes place mainly through additional investment, with its associated multiplier and accelerator effects; this is most clearly expressed in the Harrod-Domar model derived from Keynesian analysis. The Harrod-Domar model soon became the cornerstone of much of the policies and development planning of developing countries in the early postwar years.

4. Just as in the developing countries, so also in the Keynesian system, the objective of the analysis is how to *change* an unsatisfactory initial condition, whereas in the classical system the emphasis was on *understanding* the system. This is related to a feature of Keynes's thinking and reasoning on which all commentators and biographers agree: that his main interest was in policies rather than theories. Hayek, Friedman, and Samuelson, for example, take up this point in their respective contributions on the Keynes Centenary in the series recently published in *The Economist*.[4] Hayek mentions it reproachfully and critically, saying that Keynes did not "think much of economics as a science" and used his interest in policies in a Machiavellian way to bend "science" to his own policy preferences ("tending to regard his superior capacity for providing theoretical justifications as a legitimate tool for persuading the public to pursue the policies which his intuition told him were required at the moment"). By contrast, Samuelson approves Keynes's preference for policies over theory, while Friedman mentions it more neutrally: "Though Keynes was a great theorist, his interest in theory was not for its own sake but as a basis for designing policy." Either way, however, whether a vice à la Hayek or a virtue à la Samuelson, the preference for policymaking over theorizing is undisputed, and it is this aspect of Keynes's work that appeals to those concerned with the problems of developing countries. This point is related to what Hirschman[5] mentions as the second characteristic of the nascent development economics, apart from the abandonment of monoeconomics: that it had an appeal—particularly to liberal welfare-oriented economics in the Anglo-

Saxon tradition—in opening the way to improvements and playing positive-sum games (of which more later).

5. *The General Theory* has a streak of "national self-sufficien-
cy"—Hayek[6] draws attention to the essay that Keynes had published in
The New Statesman and Nation in 1933. This can presumably be attributed to the collapse of the 1933 World Economic Conference in London
and the necessity, as Keynes saw it, for "going it alone." Also, the large
size of the British economy in relation to the global economy made such
a policy plausible and kept the import and balance-of-payments problems involved at the level of manageable "leakages" (especially since
Keynes was quite ready to contemplate flexible exchange rates). This
seemed to many people in developing countries to have a family resem-
blance to their desire for greater national autonomy and self-reliance,
national or collective. It also seemed to suit the conditions of India well,
although Rao[7] questions this statement even for India, foreshadowing a
long line of criticism of Keynesian policies as incompatible with the
balance-of-payments position of LDCs and specifically with the depen-
dence of investment on imported inputs; import bottlenecks would set an
abrupt end to the working of the multiplier or, in Harrod–Domar terms,
would increase the capital/output ratio sharply.

Having blasted a trail for a duoeconomics model by distinguishing
between full employment and unemployment economies, Keynes has been
followed by an influential duoeconomics model, a model distinguishing between center and periphery economies. This model, developed particularly by
Prebisch and Seers, has been instrumental in the development of the dependency school. It was also inherent in the Prebisch-Singer hypothesis of a different
position of primary commodities and manufactured goods (or alternatively of
technologically developed and technologically underdeveloped countries) in
world trade. In a sense both Keynes and Prebisch-Seers were preceded by the
duoeconomics models by List and Hamilton, which distinguished between
industrial pioneers (the United Kingdom) and industrial latecomers (Germany,
the United States). The Lewis distinction between economies with limited and
unlimited supplies of labor, superficially closest to the Keynesian model,
could also be listed as a duoeconomics model.

It was, however, soon evident that *The General Theory*, in spite of its
title, still described a very "special case"—in the sense of Dudley Seers. That
special case was that of an advanced industrial country—or perhaps even more
specifically that of England in the mid-1930s—with all the specific features
and assumptions (often more implied and taken for granted than specifically
mentioned) of this particular economy and society, conspicuously different
from those of any developing country. Rao[8] for example lists four such assumptions:

    a. Involuntary unemployment.
    b. An industrialized economy where the supply curve of output

slopes upward toward the right but does not become vertical until after a substantial interval.

c. Excess capacity in the consumption-goods industries.

d. Comparatively elastic supply of the working capital required for increased output.

Rao then goes on to dispute the validity of these assumptions for India, and thus to question the relevance and validity of the basic concepts of *The General Theory* for developing countries. Dudley Seers also specifically criticizes the misleading nature of the "General" Theory.

The four assumptions listed by Rao are by no means a complete list. One could add other important items, such as the availability of data for pursuing Keynesian policies, the existence of a trained and experienced civil service to manage macroeconomic policies and organize public investment, and the existence of a well-established direct-taxation system to help prevent inflationary consequences of budget deficits and to make such deficits "self-financing" as a result of the increased government revenue associated with higher levels of output and employment. In fact, we are coming back here to the point that *The General Theory* is really based on the model of the British economy; referring once again to *The Economist*'s series on "The Keynes Centenary," Hayek once again disapprovingly refers to Keynes as "a great patriot, if that is the right word for a profound believer in the superiority of British civilization"[9]; while Samuelson (in this case equally disapprovingly), after also noting that Keynes was "a British patriot," refers to his "insular background" and calls him "the most provincial of British patriots," paradoxically combined with his cosmopolitanism.[10]

If *The General Theory* is based on the special case of the British economy, the question arises whether a model of the typical economy of an underdeveloped country can be substituted for the Keynesian model. Rao's four items are presumably an attempt to sketch the main features of such an economy, which indeed he proceeds to do in more detail in his article for the case of India, emphasizing the different nature of unemployment in an agrarian economy with a prevailing mode of household production (as India then was); the supply bottlenecks that make the supply curve of output become vertical at a much earlier point than in the Keynes state of full employment; the absence of excess capacity in the consumption industries; the absence of an organized working system of supplying the working capital required for increased output, and more. These features are probably common in some degree or other to all development countries, but are they sufficient to establish an alternative model? Dudley Seers clearly believed that they are not: he would argue that there have to be separate special cases for large and small economies (say, India versus Mauritius), for economies in different stages of development (say, Korea versus Afghanistan), for oil exporters versus oil importers (say, Saudi Arabia versus the Sudan), for centrally planned versus market-oriented economies (say, Tanzania versus Senegal), or more generally for economies exporting manufactured goods versus primary exporters (say, Singapore versus Zambia), or even specifically for economies according to the nature of their main export (copper- or coffee-exporting countries). Thus, there would be no single alternative non-Keynesian model, but a series, perhaps a large number, of such models. This is indeed "abandonment of mono-economics" with a vengeance. Taken to its logical conclusion, this would amount to the position that in the analysis of developing countries there is no place for a "model" approach but that each country must be studied on its own and in the light of its own conditions. A model that is good for all countries is good for no country.[11] Thus there is no scope for any expertise other than knowledge of field conditions, and perhaps such formal expertise as how to collect and organize data and how to present conclusions and policy recommendations.

Technically the situation in developing countries can be described as a matter of lower supply elasticities. But the difference really goes deeper than that. It is fundamental enough to make it doubtful whether the same intellectual apparatus can cover both situations. The market as an operating institution and structure does not really exist in many developing countries in the same sense in which it could be taken for granted in the United Kingdom of the 1930s, which was the background of *The General Theory*. This applies not only to commodity markets but also to factor markets, money markets, government responses, etc; indeed the whole structure of society is such that "indicative planning" of the Keynesian type is neither sufficient nor possible. While the prevailing shortages of foreign exchange intensify such difficulties on the supply side, they would apply even, say, to OPEC countries. The assumption that expanded demand, whether government or private, will be effective in solving employment, growth, and poverty problems will not be tenable. Once again, one could perhaps say that technically this is only a matter of degree, that provided the expansion of demand is large enough at one point, it should be able to move supply. But this would be at the expense of enormous inflation and could not be the basis of sustainable growth. In any case, the only safe assumption is that supply curves become vertical very early in this process. Hence any realistic model for developing countries must start off with the supply side rather than the demand side.[12]

In *The General Theory*, and even more so in the national accounting system and the Harrod-Domar growth model based on Keynesian concepts, investment is identified with production of physical goods different in nature from consumption goods. These goods—by a combination of marginal productivity, multipliers, and accelerators—produce subsequent income and create immediate employment; on both grounds they are particularly desirable in poor economies with unemployed resources. For developing countries, however, this very narrow concept of investment may seriously mislead policymakers.

The point is that developmental investment is to a large extent—perhaps to a dominant extent—investment in human resources or in public services such as health and education. Quantitative studies have invariably shown the great importance of such "human investment" as distinct from the production of physical investment goods emphasized by Keynes. Keynes was of course fully entitled, in a country like the United Kingdom, to assume away the importance of such human investment—further human investment would have come rightly under the heading of consumption or welfare rather than investment. But in developing countries it would be wrong to disregard human investment. While it is true that human investment also has some kind of physical element, such as the construction of hospitals and schools and the production of school books, that clearly is not the essence of the matter.

The Harrod-Domar growth model based on the Keynesian analysis underlines the identification of investment with the production of capital goods. Now it is true that in the Harrod-Domar model allowance can be made for human investment not based on the production of goods through the capital/output ratio by which the rate of investment has to be divided in order to obtain the rate of growth. However, the enumerator (capital investment) has much higher visibility than the denominator (the capital/output ratio not specifically and visibly identified with human investment). This can and has misled development planners using the Harrod-Domar formula to overrate the importance of physical investment and to underrate human investment. The corollary has been that in times of financial stringency, it was human investment that was cut down at the expense of capital investment.[13]

The reasons why investment in developing countries will not be able to rise as much as, or as predictably in response to, increased aggregate demand or increased profitability can be summarized as follows:

1. The technological capacity to produce the required investment goods is not there, and balance-of-payments difficulties may preclude the alternative of importing these goods.

2. The complementary inputs in terms of intermediate products, skills, or market institutions may not be present.

3. The pressure on wage goods, especially food, may prevent the expansion of investment. The expansion of food production in turn may be limited partly by unavailability of such required inputs as fertilizers and partly for reasons of socioeconomic institutions, such as absence of land reforms and lack of incentives due to pressure from landlords or moneylenders.

4. Financing the required investment by additional savings or taxation may be difficult. Savings may come largely from a corporate sector, which may be foreign dominated so that savings flow abroad; middle- and upper-class savers, lacking confidence in domestic institutions, may take their savings abroad; lack of data and of administrative capacity may rule out an effective system of tax collection. Tax evasion may be uncontrollable. In such situations the increase in investment can only be financed by forced savings (inflation which is likely to be of an explosive character).

In all these directions we encounter conditions of cumulative and circular causation frustrating the attempt to increase investment. For example, lack of physical capacity or foreign exchange may prevent the supply of fertilizers to farmers, while food shortages due to lack of fertilizers in turn prevent the expansion of investment in fertilizer production. Where such conditions obtain, the Harrod-Domar prescription of increasing the rate of investment will be of little practical use to developing countries. The solution must lie either in exogenous change (from aid, better export earnings, ample and cheaper financing, foreign investment), or else it must lie in improvements in the capital-output ratio, higher X-efficiency, development of the entrepreneurial spirit, or improved government policies. The former path— improvement in exogenous conditions—is the path pursued by Keynes II, the Keynes of Bretton Woods. The latter path is the one pursued by Schumacher with his appropriate technology, by Leibenstein with his X-efficiency, by Schumpeter with his entrepreneurs, and by the IMF with its emphasis on improved government policies.

The difference between an industrial economy in depression, like the British economy of 1936, and the situation in developing countries may be described in various ways, all of which contain facets of the relevant difference. One way is to say that in the industrial economy with unemployment, the problem is mainly one of demand management, of remedying lack of effective demand, while in a developing country the problem is one of structural constraints on supply; hence the question is much more one of attacking supply bottlenecks than demand management. Another way of describing the difference is to say that in an industrial country the problem is cyclical and the policy task is to move the economy from an unemployment equilibrium to a full-employment equilibrium, whereas in developing countries the problem is structural and the policy task is to change the structure of the economy so that it becomes more responsive to stimulation. This second way of describing the difference also makes it clear that in a sense the policy task in developing countries is pre-Keynesian, namely in the sense that first the conditions must be created under which Keynesian policies could then become relevant and applied with chances of success. This is reminiscent of the thesis that what developing countries need in the first place is not just investment but preinvestment, in the sense of technical training and assistance, research and development, project design, and pilot projects.[14] Translated from the microeconomic level, this means that before an expansion of investment can lead to the desired growth and fuller employment in developing countries, the preconditions of a more flexible and responsive economy must first be created.

The third way of putting the difference is to say that in an industrial economy in recession and with unemployment, it is possible by appropriate policies to create resources out of thin air, since all the necessary resources are already latently present and only have to be given the kiss of life. In a developing country it is not possible to do this; the action required is much more real and in a sense much more micro than overall demand management. Keynes could rightly say that it could be justifiable even to dig holes and fill them up again because of the indirect and multiplier effects of this useless activity; a developing country could not afford to tie up resources in a useless activity since this would preempt them from being available for the expanded investment that is the basis for the desired objective of growth. (It may, however, be justified to dig holes and fill them up again if this seems the only or best way of handing out food or income to idle people to keep them from starvation—but food-for-work projects are not usually justified by such purely humanitarian reasons but are selected for their contribution to investment and growth as well.)

A fourth difference is that the Keynesian problem of moving from unemployment to full employment is of a short-term, cyclical, and once-for-all nature while the problems of development are of a long-term, structural, and continuing nature. This also highlights the importance of technological capacity and of appropriate technology. Both of these could be taken for granted in the Keynesian analysis, and in any case the problem dealt with was a relatively short-term problem of moving the economy from unemployment to full employment; during this relatively short period, technology could be assumed to remain constant. For developing countries, on the other hand, the problem is long-term—one of dynamics rather than comparative statics—and since the technology is essentially exogenous rather than endogenous, the existence of appropriate technology cannot be taken for granted.

Related to the essential domestic production of investment goods, there is also a clear example here of circular causation: the lack of endogenous appropriate technology prevents the domestic production of capital goods, while the lack of domestic production of capital goods and the need to import them from more advanced countries in turn prevents the development of appropriate technology. For developing countries, with too much labor but too little capital and other complementary resources, the appropriate technology is clearly one that substitutes labor for capital, but the capability to substitute labor for capital requires technological power, which is lacking. Moreover, the wide substitution of labor for capital makes food the ultimate "capital" good, and this in turn brings into play the structural constraints (both technological and human as well as sociopolitical) that stand in the way of increasing food production and obtaining larger marketed surpluses.

Yet another reason why the Keynesian model has only limited application to developing countries arises from the Harris-Todaro model of rural urban migration.[15] The essence of this model is that the creation of additional modern-sector urban jobs through increased aggregate demand is bound to attract additional migrants from rural areas. In the conditions typical of many developing countries, especially Africa (where the Harris-Todaro model originated), urban wages are much higher than rural incomes, and there is much underutilized and unutilized labor in the rural areas; in such conditions it can be assumed that for every urban job created by Keynesian policies, there will be three, four, or more rural migrants attracted to the urban areas—another multiplier, albeit of a distinctly non-Keynesian or even anti-Keynesian type.

Thus we would reach the paradoxical result that Keynesian policies would increase unemployment rather than reduce it—a case of having to run fast to stay in the same place. African countries have insufficient capital resources to pursue the Keynesian policies on such a scale and long enough for the rural surplus labor to be exhausted and the Keynesian model to apply. Moreover, in this situation, as Arthur Lewis has shown, real wages would rise rapidly, whereas the Keynesian model assumes that real wages can be kept down or cut in the process of expansion, at least in the short-term cyclical context. The Harris–Todaro model adds another reason to those given by Lewis in his classical 1954 article on why the Keynesian model has severe limitations in poor economies with surplus labor.

Among the factors that Rao introduced as throwing doubt on the validity of Keynes for developing countries, the one that has become a continuing feature of subsequent discussion relates to the inelastic supply of food. Obviously the operation of the Keynesian multiplier where a rise in incomes leads to a simultaneous increase in savings and consumption must depend, in developing countries, crucially on additional supplies of food. In these countries a higher proportion of income increments will go into consumption, even though it may still be true that the marginal propensity to consume is lower than the average propensity. Moreover, at the low income levels of developing countries, much of the additional consumption will be in the form of demand for more food. But if food is produced by traditional small farmers—as [could be assumed] in India—who produce partly or largely for their own consumption, then an additional demand for food may lead to higher rural incomes, which leads to greater self-consumption in the rural areas and may result in no significant increase in marketable surpluses, perhaps even a decrease (backward-bending supply curve). This will bring the expansion process to a grinding halt and result in inflation and intolerable balance-of-payments pressures if the attempt is made to follow expansionist Keynesian policies.

Note that Rao's article was written two years before the creation of the big U.S. food aid program under PL480. Subsequently, in the late 1950s and early 1960s, India became the recipient of a flood of U.S. food aid, which would have changed the picture Rao painted. It has now become fashionable and conventional in development analysis to give top priority to breaking the food-supply bottleneck by means of organizational change, technical progress, irrigation, etc., before the application of Keynesian policies can be contemplated with any chance of success. This priority applies specifically to the poorer developing countries, who cannot hope to pay for food imports by exports of manufactures. The latter was of course the assumption that Keynes could make for the British economy of the 1930s when cheap food was available in unlimited quantities from the United States and the British Commonwealth.

It is of interest to compare Rao's arguments with those of Arthur Lewis in his famous article "Economic Development with Unlimited Supplies of Labour," which appeared two years after Rao in the *Manchester School.*

Lewis also contrasts the Keynesian model with the different conditions in developing countries and regretfully concludes (in the opening pages of his paper) that he must start from the classical model rather than from the Keynesian model, in spite of the superficially attractive analogy between DC unemployment and LDC unlimited supplies of labor. Like Rao, Lewis assumes that the Keynesian expansionist processes cannot operate in the traditional rural sector and do not apply to food production. But he does not derive the same pessimistic conclusion that the expansion process will be brought to a halt by food shortages and inflation or balance-of-payments crises, because he assumes that the transfer of surplus population to the rural areas will reduce the pressure of rural food consumption and set free the necessary marketable surpluses for the towns. In any case, in his model the expansionist process will not raise real incomes in the urban areas because of the competition for jobs from the unlimited rural surplus, so that contrary to Keynesian assumptions the marginal propensity to consume will not increase. This situation will change when the turning point has been reached and rural surplus labor is exhausted, but by that time the development and industrialization process is well established and the LDC has become a NIC and a potential exporter of manufactures.[16]

This view, which has predominated since the days of Rao and Lewis, that the nature of unemployment and indeed the whole nature of the economies of developing countries are sufficiently "different" from those of developed industrial countries with cyclical or even structural unemployment to require a different model is certainly well founded. But there is one important qualification: if the additional investment can be specifically directed so as to eliminate production bottlenecks and increase elasticities of supply and/or can be combined with aid or external investment to supply lacking complementary factors needed for expansion, the Keynesian model of self-financed development, in which additional investment calls forth the additional savings required to finance it, resumes its validity.[17] In the case of aid, food aid would be of special importance, considering that an inelastic supply of food is one of the chief obstacles to the operation of Keynesian multiplier/accelerator types of expansion.

This restoration of the validity of the Keynesian model for developing countries is, however, of somewhat limited relevance because (1) it requires a high degree of fine-tuning, not only of the initial investment but also of the subsequent expansion, to the specific bottlenecks in the economy. Such fine-tuning requires knowledge and information not normally available for the economies of developing countries, and/or (2) it requires external resources— which is a departure from the self-contained Keynesian model for a national economy—external resources equally fine-tuned to the key points among the obstacles to expansion.

It is interesting to note that Rao treats the increase in consumption of food producers—which prevents the Keynesian process—as a "dissipation." In the formal sense that is of course correct, and in fact this increase in consumption by which the multiplier becomes "dissipated" can be treated as a "leakage" in the Keynesian sense. But viewed from another point of view, and specifically if the objective of development is seen as a reduction in poverty and as the satisfaction of basic needs, this increase in rural consumption is a thoroughly desirable thing. A convinced Keynesian might say that if this is the end result of Keynesian policies, so be it. Moreover matters may not stop there; presumably the increased consumption of farmers will improve their health and productivity and make them more willing to accept organizational changes and try new techniques. This is a point Rao fails to consider, and it leads to a more general point of some importance. In the Keynesian model, and in line with the situation in the advanced industrial countries, it is assumed that consumption does not affect the productivity of labor and hence investment; neither does the Harrod-Domar model. Yet as previously discussed, the idea of human investment, which includes a productivity effect of improved nutrition, may have considerable relevance for developing countries. If this is so, the Keynesian process may be to that extent vindicated in its application to developing countries.

The question of unutilized capacity in the consumption-goods industries, which is essential for the operation of Keynesian multipliers as complementary input to unemployed labor, has also been the subject of considerable debate regarding its existence and nature in developing countries. We can distinguish three schools of thought:

(1) There is no unutilized capacity in developing countries, hence the multiplier cannot operate, and vertical supply curves occur not only in food production but also in other sectors of the economy. That is the position of Rao.

(2) There is unutilized capacity arising from structural difficulties and specifically foreign-exchange shortages. These shortages prevent the import of essential spare parts and combine with structural deficiencies and limited local skills in maintenance and manning to idle manufacturing significantly and chronically. The effect of this is similar to the previous case: because of such production bottlenecks, supply curves become vertical and the multiplier cannot operate.

(3) There is unutilized capacity that can be brought into operation by appropriate policies and development strategies. Paradoxically this is the position of the advocates of both balanced and unbalanced growth. In the case of balanced growth, the latent unutilized capacities can be brought into operation by simultaneous expansion of the different sectors of the economy providing the necessary complementary inputs for each other. In the case of unbalanced growth, the latent complementary resources can be mobilized in a more microeconomic way, by applying the right incentives and mobilizing latent entrepreneurship for key sectors of the economy, which then blazes a trail for more general expansion.[18] Under both strategies, Keynesian processes—or rather some thing outwardly similar to them—*would* apply in developing countries, provided

of course such strategies are feasible and can be successfully implemented. The processes are only outwardly similar since in the Keynesian output the flexible element and all the resources required for expanding it toward full-employment levels are readily at hand; whereas in the developing countries expansion requires "strategies," "mobilization," "pressure mechanisms," and "pacing devices" (all terms used by Hirschman) since the resources required are only latently or potentially required.

The mobilization of latent entrepreneurship is of course also a key feature of the Schumpeterian system, where it is linked with innovation. In the Keynesian system, innovation is external or exogeneous to the system. In fact Keynes's theory of falling marginal productivity of investment, which led him to see the future of industrial countries in more leisure and arts rather than in higher incomes, is clearly linked with what some would consider his failure to build the dynamism of technology endogenously into his system. There is no doubt that in developing countries, improvement in technology, either through development of indigenous technology or through successful transfer or adaptation, are key features in economic growth. To put it in Leibenstein's terms, improvements in X-efficiency are an essential part of the development process.[19] Rather paradoxically, the Schumpeter-Hirschman-Leibenstein emphasis on innovation, technology, and entrepreneurship, while it takes us outside the Keynesian system, at the same time leads to the conclusion that the Keynesian expansion process has some, albeit modified, applicability in developing countries. In other words, Keynes was relevant for developing countries in spite of his model rather than because of it.

We have discussed Rao's views about the relevance of Keynes to India. Much of the subsequent discussion has also related to India, sometimes with different results from Rao's.[20] While this is understandable in view of the strong links between the Indian academic tradition and Cambridge and the high degree of sophistication of Indian economists, the results can be misleading in that India is not a typical developing country. It is noteworthy that in 1964 Burmese economist Hla Myint complained about this exclusive concentration of the discussion on India at the Manchester conference on Teaching Development.[21] It is quite true that, at least in the theoretical literature, there has been little direct discussion of the applicability of Keynes outside India. On the other hand, as far as the international aspects are concerned, the Latin American School and the related Prebisch-Singer analysis of deteriorating terms of trade and unequal exchange are at least indirectly a refutation of the validity of Keynesian analysis to developing countries. These can be interpreted as stating that external factors prevent the successful application of domestic expansionist policies due to the resulting balance-of-payments pressures. Or to put it in Dudley Seers's terms, the proposition says in effect that there should be a separate model of countries relying on the export of primary products subject to deteriorating terms of trade and unequal exchange. But the policy prescription of ISI (import-substituting industrialization) amounts to an attempt to reconstitute the conditions in which Keynesian processes *can* function.

In one sense the criticism of *The General Theory* as being written in terms of a closed economy and hence inapplicable, or even dangerous, for developing countries because of their precarious balance-of-payments position is not fair to Keynes. It must be remembered that Keynes was firmly in favor of international commodity price stabilization. Professor Kaldor has quite recently reminded us of Keynes's advocacy of buffer stocks in primary commodities in his article in the *Economic Journal* of 1938.[22,23] During the war Keynes prepared his proposals not only for an international clearing union but also for an agency for international commodity control, which would set up buffer stocks for all the main commodities. This proposal was never properly acted upon although Keynes attributed the utmost importance to it. The subsequent negotiations for an International Trade Organization (ITO) were only a pale shadow of what Keynes had intended, and in any case turned out to be futile since the U.S. Congress did not ratify the ITO. It is clear that Keynes thought he could improve on the market mechanism, not only in the macro sense of maintaining full employment but also in the micro sense of improving on the working of commodity markets. If the Keynesian system is mentally adjusted to include commodity price stabilization at a high and satisfactory level, thus guaranteeing profitable investment in primary commodity production, it certainly begins to look much more feasible and applicable to developing countries.

In addition to the Keynes I of *The General Theory*, there was, of course, the Keynes II of Bretton Woods. If the removal of deflationary biases in the world economy, financial flows to developing countries, and commodity price stabilization through buffer stocks—or even more reliably through a world currency based on a bundle of primary commodities such as Keynes wanted—are all assumed to have been achieved, then the balance-of-payments objection to Keynesian policies looks distinctly weak.

The Keynes II of Bretton Woods also planned and pleaded for an International Monetary Fund that would have the power to put pressure on balance-of-payments–surplus countries to take measures of adjustment in an expansionary direction. Instead, we have an IMF that puts all the pressure for adjustment and ''discipline'' on the countries with balance-of-payments deficits and, in practice only, on the developing countries. This is understandable because in the twenty-five ''golden years'' of full employment with little inflation that followed Bretton Woods, there was no need to put expansionist pressures on balance-of-payments–surplus countries; by the time this would have become right again, we had gotten an IMF that, in spite of the rhetoric of its charter, was neither willing nor able to do so. In that sense the Keynesian system was hoist on the petard of its own success. But once again if we go through the mental exercise of imagining the existence of a Keynes II-type IMF, expansionist policies in the developing countries would have become much more relevant and feasible.

In appreciating the importance of Keynes II for developing countries, we return once again to Hirschman. In his essay he suggests a second foundation stone for development economics, in addition to the abandonment of mono-economics by Keynes I.[24] This is the assertion of the mutual-benefit claim, creating the possibility of international macroeconomic interventions raising global welfare to a higher equilibrium level. Although Hirschman does not specifically mention Keynes in connection with this second foundation stone, yet his role in proposing just such a global system inevitably comes to mind. One can argue whether Hirschman was right to include the assertion of the mutual-benefit claim as a precondition for development economics, thus condemning all dependency school, unequal exchange, and neo-Marxist thinking to an existence outside his defined boundaries of "development economics." However, if one does accept this second precondition, then one is also bound to argue that Keynes played a crucial role in both these respects.

This paper has already provided some examples of how the inclusion of Keynes II enables us to give a much more positive answer to the question of his relevance to developing countries. I think it is a tragedy that Keynes's original ideas were not more fully accepted and did not prevail at Bretton Woods. I am thinking here particularly of his proposals for a world currency controlled to satisfy liquidity needs and based on primary commodities; the creation of an IMF imposing expansionary "discipline" on balance-of-payments–surplus countries, but much less contractionary discipline on balance-of-payments–deficit countries; the creation of an international clearing union, which would automatically have worked in that direction; the creation of a full ITO. The Marshall Plan was a truly Keynesian measure and Keynes would have acclaimed it. But perhaps he would have preferred that it be slightly less generous, that it exact some repayment from such balance-of-payments–surplus countries as Germany and Japan during the 1963–73 decade, and that these repayments be channeled into developing countries with balance-of-payments deficits. Similarly, if oil prices had been stabilized at a satisfactory level prior to 1973, the oil shock would not have disrupted the system and measures to develop other energy resources, and more oil resources would have been taken earlier and in good time. This is an imaginary reconstruction of the world as it could have been according to Keynes II, but it may serve as a testimony to the power of his thinking and to his ultimate relevance for developing countries.

If we return more soberly to Keynes I, I cannot do better than quote the conclusion reached recently by Sukhamoy Chakravarty in his previously mentioned article:

> Keynes teaches us that given the problem of time and uncertainty, the job [of using surplus value constructively for development] is likely to be badly done by the market mechanism and the economy may remain caught in a low-level equilibrium unless an all-round and judicious investment effort is launched. It is, then, quite appropriate to conclude that the relevance of Keynes to developing countries is not merely methodological in nature, there are substantive

economic insights as well which help us understand better the functioning of the economic mechanism in developing countries wherever a large number of investment decisions are made on a decentralized basics in an uncertain environment. While in some respects the classical model of development retains its primacy as a conceptual device, we understand this model much better including its merits and deficiencies if we take full note of the contribution that Keynes made on fundamental questions of economic analysis, even though his policy preoccupations were quite different.[25]

There is only one amendment I would make to this conclusion by Chakravarty. I do not agree that "the classical model of development retains its primacy." On this point I would go along with Dudley Seers. Our choice is not limited to the classical or the Keynesian model. Both are special cases and neither is fully relevant. What we need is a conceptual device, or rather conceptual devices, which are new and which supplement both the classical and the Keynesian models. We have many elements of such a model available, and a number of them have been mentioned in this paper. But they are still waiting for a synthesis that is as convincing and relevant as the Keynesian system was to the Western industrial economies with unemployment and surplus capacity. Will there ever be a General Theory of Development? If so my own feeling is that it can only be built up from the many different special cases that Dudley Seers has discussed.[26]

We can make a distinction between the precise assumptions and simplifications of *The General Theory* on the one hand and the way of thinking and concepts underlying its framework on the other.[27] The former, the precise assumptions and simplifications, are broadly inappropriate for conditions in developing countries; the latter, the framework and concepts, remain relevant, especially when we include the Keynes of Bretton Woods. If he had had his way, the scope for growth in the developing countries through increasing the rate of investment based on increasing effective demand for their products abroad would have been immensely greater than it is today. The relevance of Keynes I is, to a considerable degree, a function of the acceptance of Keynes II.

Notes

1. D. Seers, 1967, "The Limitations of the Special Case," contribution to *The Teaching of Development Economics*, edited by Kurt Martin and John Napp (London: Frank Cass).
2. A. O. Hirschman, 1982, "The Rise and Decline of Development Economics," contribution to *The Theory and Experience of Economic Development: Essays in Honour of Sir W. Arthur Lewis*, edited by Gersovitz, M. et al. (London and Boston: George Allen and Unwin).
3. V. K. R. V. Rao, 1952, "Investment Income and the Multiplier in an Underdeveloped Economy," *The Indian Economic Review*, February.
4. M. Friedman, 1983, "A Monetarist Reflects," *The Economist*, June 4, pp. 35–37. F. A. Hayek, 1983, "The Austrian Critique," *The Economist*, June 11, pp. 45–48. P. Samuelson, 1983, "Sympathy from the Other Cambridge," *The Economist*, June 25, pp. 21–25. These contributions to *The Economist* appeared in a series, The Keynes Centenary.

5. Loc. cit.

6. Loc. cit.

7. Loc. cit.

8. Loc. cit.

9. Loc. cit.

10. Loc. cit., p. 22, but Samuelson's sole explicit evidence for calling Keynes "the most provincial of British patriots" is that "he never really cared for Americans." Is not this perhaps an example of American provincialism?

11. Michal Kalecki took the same position in *Theories of Growth of Different Social Systems*, *Scientia* (Italy), May–June 1970. (I am indebted to Jerzy Osiatynsky for pointing this out to me.)

12. This point is clearly argued by Michael P. Todaro, *Economic Development in the Third World* (London and New York: Longmans, 1977), pp. 177-79.

13. The point made in the preceding three paragraphs is also made by Andrew M. Kamarck, *Economics and the Real World* (London: Blackwell, 1983), pp. 108-115. Kamarck writes: "The present situation, in which economists spend their time measuring what is easy to measure (durable capital goods) instead of trying to measure what is less precise but what really matters, is like the story of the drunk who had lost some money. He hunted for it under a street light because the light was better, rather than looking for it in the dark alley where he had really lost it. If economists truly want to be useful, we have to look where the problems are, and not where it is easiest to look." For the same criticism of the Harrod-Domar formula, see also H. W. Singer, "Keynesian Models of Economic Development and Their Limitations: An Analysis in the Light of Gunnar Myrdal's 'Asian Drama' " in *The Strategy of International Development: Essays in the Economics of Backwardness* (London: Macmillan), 1975.

14. For the development of the concept of preinvestment, see H. W. Singer, *International Development, Growth and Change* (New York: McGraw-Hill, 1964), Chapter 2, "Toward a Theory of Pre-investment," pp. 18-25.

15. J. R. Harris and M. P. Todaro, 1970 "Migration, Unemployment and Development: A two-sector Analysis," *American Economic Review*, March 1970.

16. W. A. Lewis, 1954, "Economic Development with Unlimited Supplies of Labour," *Manchester School*. The paraphrase of this paper given in the text is my own, and Arthur Lewis must not be held responsible for it. His original paper has, of course, since been developed and modified in many different ways and by others.

17. This point is also made by A. P. Thirlwall (who has devoted much attention to the subject of this paper). In the most recent edition of his book on *Growth and Development with Special Reference to Developing Economies* 3rd ed. (London: Macmillan, 1983), p. 274, he quotes credit for fertilizers, transport facilities, land settlement, and irrigation as examples of such bottleneck-breaking investments, and quotes evidence from Ecuador and Morocco for high rates of return and short gestation periods for such investment.

18. This position is broadly that of Hirschman as is also indicated in his previously quoted essay on "The Rise and Decline of Development Economics."

19. H. Leibenstein, 1966, "Allocative Efficiency Versus X-Efficiency," *American Economic Review*, June.

20. The two most recent contributions are by S. Chakravarty, "Keynes, 'Classics,' and the Developing Economies" and K. N. Raj, "Keynesian Economics and Agrarian Economies," both in *Reflections on Economic Development and Social Change. Essays in Honour of Professor V. K. R. V. Rao*, edited by C. H. Hanumantha Rao and P. C. Joshi (New Delhi: Allied Publishers, 1979).

21. H. Myint, 1967, "Economic Theory and the Underdeveloped Countries," in *The Teaching of Development Economics*, edited by Kurt Martin and John Knapp (London: Frank Cass).

22. N. Kaldor, 1983, "The Role of Commodity Prices in Economic Recovery," *Lloyds Bank Review*, July, pp. 21-34.

23. J. M. Keynes, 1938, "The Policy of Government Storage of Food Stuffs and Raw Materials," *Economic Journal*, September, pp. 449-60.

24. A. O. Hirschman, 1982, "The Rise and Decline of Development Economics," loc. cit.

25. S. Chakravarty, 1979, "Keynes, 'Classics,' and the Developing Economies," loc. cit.

26. In an earlier paper dealing with a related subject, I have taken the same position in drawing a parallel between the universalism (Hirschman would call it monoeconomics) of both the classical and Keynesian systems in speaking of an aggregate "investment" as the source of growth imperceptibly leading to a belief in a universally valid "efficient" or "modern," "superior" technology versus the disaggregation of the investment concept into specific inputs leading to an emphasis on "appropriate" and indigenously developed or adapted technology. H. W. Singer,

Keynesian Models of Economic Development, and their Limitations: an Analysis in the Light of Gunnar Myrdal's "Asian Drama." U. N. Asian Institute for Economic Development and Planning, Occasional Papers, Bangkok, December 1969. Reprinted in H. W. Singer: *The Strategy of Economic Development. Essays in the Economics of Backwardness* (London: Macmillan, 1975), pp. 22-42.

    27. This distinction is very similar to the one made by John Fender in *Understanding Keynes. An Analysis of "The General Theory"* (Brighton: Wheatsheaf Books, 1981), pp. 149-50. Fender deals with the relevance of Keynes to current conditions in industrial countries, but his distinction is equally valid when asking ourselves questions concerning his relevance to conditions in developing countries.

11

Keynes and the Postwar International Economic Order

John Williamson

I would like to start by recalling an incident that occurred in September 1941, three months before Pearl Harbor. At that time Keynes had already spent the better part of two years directing the external finances of one of the principal belligerents engaged in total war. He had done the same thing during World War I when he was in his thirties. It's a part of his career that has been understudied: if aspiring historians of Keynes read this, I think this part of his life might repay scrutiny.

At that time, Keynes was already beginning to turn his thoughts toward the problem of reconstructing an international economic order after the war. The first memorandum he wrote on this subject asserted that history recorded only two periods of notable world prosperity up to that time: he remarked that these happened to have coincided more or less with the reigns of the two great English queens, Elizabeth I in the sixteenth century and Victoria in the nineteenth. If one makes a similar comparison today, one has to add that there has now been a third period of notable world prosperity which, as it happens, coincided with the first twenty years of the reign of Queen Elizabeth II of England.

The postwar boom, as James Tobin has said, was notable not just for the rapidity of world growth but also for its generalization to the furthest corners of the globe and, for the best part of twenty years, for its stability. There was much more price stability in those postwar years when Keynesian techniques of demand management were dominant than there was either in the previous period of world prosperity back in the Victorian era or than there has been in the subsequent period. It is interesting to note that this latest boom coincides, as did the Victorian era, with a period in which there was a recognizable international economic order, in which countries recognized certain rules of the game as governing their economic conduct. One of the questions that I want to ask is whether the existence of that international economic order contributed to the postwar boom or whether it was as much of a coincidence as (presumably) the sex of the English monarch.

A condensed version of "Keynes and the International Economic Order" in Trevithick and Worswick (1984).

First, however, I shall consider a prior question: To what extent would we be right in regarding Keynes as an architect of that postwar order? To the extent that we can conclude that Keynes was an architect of the order and that the order was a significant factor in contributing to the postwar prosperity, we are led to ask the question: If we attempt to redesign an international economic order, what should we learn from Keynes?

Keynes and the Design of the Postwar Order

So my first question is: What did Keynes contribute to the design of the postwar international economic order? That order, I suggest, can be characterized in the first place by adherence to what James Tobin has referred to as the neoclassical synthesis. I understand by that a combination of conscious macroeconomic management in order to stabilize the level of economic activity, with a willingness to leave microeconomic decisions (in general) to the market. I shall refer to the latter as "microeconomic liberalism," though I have to ask you to understand that I am using the term "liberalism" in the nineteenth-century European sense rather than in the twentieth-century American sense as James Tobin used it.

Let us turn first to the microeconomic liberalism. The postwar order was one of relatively liberal trade in industrial goods. We saw more or less free markets in commodities, or at least in tropical commodities—there was, in fact, a great deal of restriction of trade in temperate-zone commodities, as American farm interests have constantly complained. And we saw growing capital mobility. In all those respects the international system has come to institutionalize microeconomic liberalism.

My reading of Keynes is that he was deeply ambivalent about the wisdom of that course of action. For example, during the war James Meade led an initiative in the British economic service to negotiate an international union to liberalize trade. In the end this was not successful, because the proposal for an International Trade Organization was thrown out by the U. S. Congress. What survived was the General Agreement on Tariffs and Trade (GATT), and that organization in its rather ad hoc way has over the years been spectacularly successful in liberalizing trade in manufactured products. Keynes was not, however, one of the great forces behind that initiative. On the contrary, he would sometimes write memoranda that appeared dismissive, or even overtly hostile, to the idea of liberalizing trade. I find it very difficult to be sure to what extent that really reflected his beliefs, as opposed to his enjoyment in teasing those with whose views he disagreed. If he found conservatives were placing a great deal of importance on trade liberalization, I think he just enjoyed pulling their legs. When it came to decisions on the crucial issues, for example, whether James Meade's proposed commercial union should receive the blessing of the British Treasury or not, he finally came down in support. But he did it in awfully grumpy terms:

. . . if all the other countries in the world agree to fall in with the stipulations of his Commercial Union (which, in my judgment, is extremely unlikely), we shall gain more on the swings than we shall lose on the roundabouts. That we shall lose something on the roundabouts is, in my judgment, indisputable. Nevertheless, I am ready to be persuaded not to oppose the scheme, on the ground that our discretion is only restricted if others also are conforming to a strict code, and that the latter, if by a miracle it does come about, may be to our very considerable advantage. (JMK XXVI, p. 284)

On commodities, he was looking for a system that was by no means one of unfettered markets. On the contrary, he supported a general system of buffer stocks for commodities, both temperate and tropical. He was defeated through inaction; the overt hostility came from a curious combination of the Bank of England and the British Ministry of Agriculture, both of which were afraid that the regime for temperate agricultural products that Keynes envisaged was far too laissez-faire and would result in the ruin of British agriculture. In consequence, none of that initiative reached fruition, so that in the postwar period we came to have far more liberal trade in tropical agricultural products and far more controlled trade in temperate agricultural products than Keynes favored.

Finally, on the question of capital movements, Keynes was openly hostile to the restoration of capital mobility. In the 1930s he had observed flights of funk money from continental Europe destroying any possibility of economic management—the sort of phenomenon that has become all too familiar in Latin America in the last two years. He therefore favored the permanent maintenance of tight restrictions on capital mobility. He recognized that such restrictions would leave a gap in international arrangements, since capital movements do have a legitimate role in contributing to the economic development of poorer countries. For that purpose a new public-sector institution was created—largely at the initiative of the United States rather than of Britain, though certainly with the enthusiastic support of Keynes and the British Treasury. That institution is still with us today in the form of the World Bank, but the sums it disburses are trivial compared with those handled by private markets.

The conclusion that I draw is that Keynes really cannot be considered a driving force behind the microeconomic liberalism that finally characterized the postwar international economic order. The initiative came rather from the distinguished group then serving in the U. S. Treasury and from those English colleagues with whom he was working at the time—an outstandingly talented group that included Marcus Fleming, Sir Roy Harrod, James Meade, Lionel Robbins, and Dennis Robertson. It is difficult to recall an equally illustrious group of economists having served in government together, with the possible exception of the Council of Economic Advisors in the early Kennedy years.

The other leg of the postwar international economic order was the idea of conscious macroeconomic management. The belief that this was necessary because the system is not self-stabilizing over any interesting time horizon was embodied in what came to be known as the Bretton Woods system. This is the corpus of conventions and rules implicit or explicit in the Articles of Agreement of the International Monetary Fund, which were agreed on at the conference at Bretton Woods, New Hampshire, in July 1944. That conference came together to finalize the details and ratify the outline of an agreement hammered out over the two previous years between the British and the Americans (who at that date dominated the economic planning of the Allies).

Both Keynes and White drew up their own very different plans for reconstructing the international monetary system. Keynes's proposals envisaged the establishment of an international clearing union, involving the creation of a new international reserve asset, which Keynes called ''bancor.'' Countries would have held most of their international reserves, not in the traditional forms of gold or foreign exchange, but rather in the form of bancor deposits with this new clearing union. The proposal of the U. S. Treasury—the White Plan—was essentially that the existing system based on the gold exchange standard be retained, reinforced by the creation of a stabilization fund. It was that stabilization fund that eventually emerged as the International Monetary Fund.

It was well known that when the initial views of Keynes and White were in conflict, White almost always won. But there was one significant exception. This concerned the extent to which the fund was to be a passive observer of the policies of its member countries. The original White Plan would have had the fund hold deposits in the central banks of its individual member countries, which could have been shifted at its discretion, thus giving the fund a direct influence on the internal policies of its member countries. The Keynes Plan, which insisted on fund passivity in the policies of the member countries, was ultimately accepted.

But even in this context there is a qualification, for a similar argument concerned the extent to which countries ought to be able to draw automatically on the resources of the stabilization fund when they were in balance-of-payments deficit. The British held that such drawings should be automatically available within the agreed limits, whereas the Americans increasingly insisted that drawings be conditional upon the adoption of approved balance-of-payments adjustment policies. This argument about the appropriate extent of fund ''conditionality'' started as far back as 1944 and continues down to the present day. The British thought they had won that battle at Bretton Woods and, in fact, everybody else seems to have thought that the American side had agreed that drawings would be essentially automatic. But it turned out that the decision not to fight everyone else together was tactical, and U. S. dominance on the fund's executive board was subsequently used to insist on fund conditionality. The fund's policies involving a high degree of conditionality, for anything other than minimal drawings, were accepted, and built into the operational procedures of the fund in the 1950s.

This was only one of several issues on which Keynes was defeated. Let me mention four other instances.

Keynes had envisaged his international clearing union as settling bilateral imbalances between a series of central banks. He had assumed that all exchange market transactions would be channeled through central banks, as under the wartime British system. White, on the other hand, envisaged a return to competitive foreign-exchange markets, as was eventually written into the agreed arrangements.

A second instance is provided by the contrast between Keynes's suggestion of a clearing union that would have held the accounts of individual countries in the form of the new reserve asset, bancor, which would then have been exchanged between member countries, and simple maintenance of the gold exchange standard supplemented by a stabilization fund. Keynes again lost out.

The third instance involved the proposal, embodied in Keynes's system, that interest be charged on excessive credit balances of bancor. A country that ran too big a cumulative balance-of-payments surplus would run up its balances of bancor, but, instead of being rewarded for that by earning interest, it would have had to pay interest. This was intended to contribute symmetry to the adjustment process by placing pressure on surplus as well as deficit countries to help restore balance-of-payments equilibrium. That idea was denounced at the time as penalizing what was bound to be the permanent surplus country, the United States, and in due course it had to be withdrawn. Some of us found it rather amusing, therefore, that thirty years later, in the early 1970s, during negotiations on international monetary reform, the U. S. delegation came out with a similar proposal to penalize chronic-surplus countries that built up overlarge cumulative surplus positions. I refer to the reserve indicator proposal put forward by the United States in 1972, which by then had come to see itself as a permanent chronic-deficit country instead of its earlier vision of itself as a permanent chronic-surplus country.

However, although Keynes's proposals for interest penalties on surplus countries were rejected, there was in fact a proposal with a similar intent inserted into the IMF agreement. That was the so-called scarce currency clause. Each country puts into the fund a limited amount of its currency, which can be lent out to other members. If a country were in chronic surplus, then eventually the fund would exhaust its holdings of that currency. The U. S. team proposed that in such a situation the fund should be authorized to legitimate discriminatory trade controls against imports from the surplus country. Potentially, the proposal was directed specifically against the United States and was therefore greeted by the British (Sir Roy Harrod in particular) as an extremely important and generous gesture. It was built into the IMF agreement but has never been used.

Finally there was a big difference in the size of the fund. The original American proposal was for a fund of some $5.5 billion. That was eventually talked up in the agreement at Bretton Woods to $8.8 billion. Keynes, on the other hand, proposed initial overdraft rights summing to a total of $26 billion. The difference is even greater than that suggests, because the United States could have been called on to finance something like $23 billion (as everybody else would have been eligible to draw against the United States). Twenty-six billion dollars in 1944 amounts to something like 780 billion in today's dollars! To make the comparison another way, if the fund had been set up on the scale that Keynes proposed, and if it had maintained that size relative to the world economy over the years, then the U. S. Congress would currently not be asked for a mere $8.4 billion quota increase but perhaps for $50 billion more. The scale on which Keynes was thinking was not acceptable to the United States.

Why did Keynes support Bretton Woods? Hence, on almost all the basic issues, both microeconomic and macroeconomic, Keynes's proposals were rejected. Yet despite that, Keynes fought passionately for British acceptance of the Bretton Woods agreement, which was by no means a foregone conclusion in the political circumstances of the time in Britain. The question therefore arises: Why did Keynes put so much effort into struggling for something that did not reflect his own views? There seem to be three possible explanations.

First, it is conceivable that he was under a misapprehension about the nature of the agreement. In a whole series of important respects, one can argue that in 1944 Keynes did not understand where the postwar world was heading. He did not believe, to begin with, that Meade's proposals for trade liberaliza-tion would get anywhere. He thought that everyone had agreed that capital mobility would be permanently suppressed. He did not understand the nature of the convertibility commitment into which Britain had entered at the Bretton Woods conference; when he came to realize that this was an active obligation on monetary authorities to make available foreign exchange at the official exchange rate for any current account transaction, he fought bitterly, first with Dennis Robertson and then with the U. S. Treasury, to try and get that obliga-tion changed. He assumed that the scarce currency clause would be worth something, whereas it has never been invoked, despite the fact that for many years the German mark was about as "scarce" a currency as one can imagine. Finally, in the early days of the fund, there was a general understanding that the fund would make its finance available more or less automatically, not subject to the high conditionality that subsequently became the practice.

Nevertheless, I do not know that one can push this explanation very far because Keynes clearly did come to realize—maybe not in 1944 but certainly by the Savannah Conference in early 1946—just how wrong he had been on most of those topics. There is an account by Lord Kahn (1976) of just how bitterly Keynes reacted after Savannah, even writing a memo (no copy of which survives) urging that Britain withdraw from the IMF because it had been subverted from what he had understood to be its original purposes. Persuaded to suppress that memo Keynes went back to England and made an eloquent speech in defense of the IMF in the House of Lords. So even though there may have been misapprehensions and though he may have been bitter,

Keynes nevertheless clearly believed that there were some very important elements in this postwar deal that deserved to survive.

I think the second hypothesis one has to entertain is that Keynes recognized that the Bretton Woods system was based on a set of ideas that he had helped develop in the interwar period, in particular in *The General Theory*, even though it rejected the specific proposals that he had conceived during the war. According to this line of argument, what commended itself to Keynes was the fact that the Bretton Woods system was set up in order to implement some of the basic ideas of Keynes's earlier teaching. Even though all sorts of details with which he sought to embellish his ideas were rejected, nevertheless he had a commitment to the fundamentals.

For example, there is an explicit endorsement in *The General Theory* (JMK VII, pp. 378–79) of what later became known as the neoclassical synthesis. Another central idea is that internal balance should be the dominant aim of macroeconomic management. Keynes had pioneered this in the early 1920s in the days of the *Tract on Monetary Reform*. In the *Tract* Keynes's formulation of the internal-balance objective took the form of price stability rather than full employment. But as the nature of the macroeconomic problems facing Britain changed in the interwar period, so Keynes's formulation of the idea of internal balance shifted gradually to full employment. (There are some amusing instances in the interim period, when Keynes had changed his policy advice and recognized full employment as being the appropriate policy target but had not yet managed to adapt his theory. Citations can be found to the *Treatise* in support of Keynesian ideas that demand the analysis of *The General Theory*.) There is a clear evolution, first in terms of policy advice, subsequently in terms of theory, of the form the internal balance target should take. The implicit, and to some extent explicit, agreement at Bretton Woods involved each country's managing its own internal demand to secure full employment, while modifying its demand policies to some extent if it came up against its reserve constraint or accumulated excessive reserves.

In the event of a large imbalance, a nation should be prepared to change its exchange rate. That again is consistent with the position that Keynes arrived at in the interwar period. He had urged a managed exchange rate rather than either a free-floating or a rigidly fixed exchange rate as a result of the gold standard. James Tobin has mentioned how Keynes fought against Britain's decision to repeg to gold in 1925, looking instead to exchange management as something that would give a country a degree of policy freedom to combine internal and external balance. Keynes even discussed in much of his interwar writings how this should be done by limited flexibility of exchange rates, a wide band (relative to what was agreed at Bretton Woods), coupled with a crawling peg. Although I have preached the crawling peg for about twenty years now, until I came to read Keynes's interwar writings more extensively in preparation for this paper, I had never realized that it was John Maynard Keynes rather than Sir Roy Harrod who first invented the idea of the crawling peg. It is there in his recommendations for the Genoa conference in 1922

(JMK XVII, p. 364). It is there again, even more explicitly, in *The Means to Prosperity*, the work he wrote at the time of the world economic conference in 1933 (JMK IX, p. 362). The only time he didn't talk about crawling pegs and wider bands was during the period between Britain's decision to go back to gold in 1925 and its decision to suspend the gold standard in 1931; in these years he took the view that it was unpatriotic to do or say anything that might undermine confidence in the currency and therefore cost the public money. Quite deliberately in 1931, he went out of his way to refuse to speculate, even though he knew that Britain was about to go off gold, a moral position that, I suspect, few economists would practice at the present day.

But I have to say that, despite my admiration for Keynes's interwar position on managed-exchange rates, when it actually came to designing the postwar system he has to bear a large measure of responsibility for the decision not to adopt a system of limited exchange-rate flexibility, but instead to legislate an adjustable peg with a narrow band (JMK XXV, p. 97). Only when a chosen exchange rate became incompatible with the simultaneous achievement of internal and external balance would one change it. On such occasions the change would be large. Keynes seems to have rationalized his support for the adjustable peg by his belief that because everyone would have exchange control, there would be no significant capital mobility in the postwar world. That was not to be; once capital mobility returned in a significant way, the adjustable peg became unworkable. The repeated exchange crises of the late 1960s led to the breakdown of the Bretton Woods system in the early 1970s.

A third respect in which the postwar system reflected Keynes's ideas was in accepting the need to ensure sufficient liquidity to maintain global demand. This was a preoccupation that Keynes first manifested in the *Treatise on Money*; it became a central theme in *The Means to Prosperity*, where he urged—in the middle of the Great Depression—simultaneous economic expansion by all the major countries. To make that possible, given the reserve constraints that almost all countries were suffering, he proposed to issue paper notes acceptable to everyone as equivalent to gold. As I have already indicated, the postwar system did not go nearly as far in the direction of expanding liquidity as he had wanted, but it did go some way toward supplementing liquidity. And so once again, I think, one can postulate that Keynes may have felt that something of those ideas for which he had been pushing was being incorporated in the Bretton Woods system.

The final reason that seems important to me in explaining why Keynes supported the Bretton Woods agreement was that he passionately believed in the need for an international economic order of some form. In particular, he felt there was a need to have United States participation, and indeed leadership, in that order. I think one can see this if one goes back to his writings in *The Economic Consequences of the Peace* (JMK II, pp. 6–7), written during the Versailles conference, where he sketches movingly the benefits that had accrued from the pre–World War I international economic order. One can see it also in the evident trauma with which he observed the irresponsibility of the

Council of Four, the leaders of the major victorious Allied powers in World War I, in their total disdain for economic questions, their unwillingness to make any effort to reconstruct the economic life of Central Europe. One can see it again in his repeated criticism of United States isolationism in the interwar period, the refusal to wipe clear the burden of debt from World War I, a sword that dangled over such prosperity as was achieved in the 1920s and that helped lead to the catastrophe of the 1930s. And one can see it in the continuous stream of proposals to reform the international monetary system, starting at Genoa, going on to the *Tract on Monetary Reform*, the *Treatise on Money*, *The Means to Prosperity*, and finally emerging in the international clearing union proposals drawn up during World War II.

Keynes was therefore confronted with conflicting pulls: personal pride of authorship in certain rejected proposals versus a hope that what was acceptable would contribute to a better world. He decided to accept defeat on particular issues for the sake of furthering cooperation. As a result of this statesmanship, the world got a liberal international economic order after World War II.

The Postwar Order and Global Prosperity

That leads me to the question: Was that statesmanship worthwhile? Did that international economic order contribute in an important way to the postwar boom?

I think most economists would judge that microeconomic liberalism was important in contributing to postwar prosperity, although there are some of us who are not quite sure whether we wouldn't have been even better off if Keynes's proposals for commodity price stabilization had gone through. In terms of bringing the United States into leadership of the system, clearly that was successful, so far at least. We saw Marshall aid. We saw the growth of development aid. We saw the United States taking the lead in opening markets, which played a crucially important role in generalizing the world boom. We saw the U. S. provision of a convertible dollar, which was an essential part of the financial background for the postwar prosperity.

I think that many people have had doubts whether the Bretton Woods system per se really mattered that much to macroeconomic management. Did the IMF contribute in a significant way to world prosperity? I had some doubts about that myself twelve years ago. I recall that I snickered along with others at the thought of Pompidou and Nixon arguing passionately about the price at which the United States should not sell gold. But, in fact, there were important issues at stake in those discussions: issues about whether one had a set of conventions guiding national economic policies, about whether one should limit the freedom of monetary policy to create exchange-rate misalignments.

If one compares the exchange-rate misalignments that arose in the final breakdown phase of the Bretton Woods system after 1968, and those that have arisen under floating exchange rates, with the rather orderly exchange-rate system of the earlier postwar period, there is a dramatic change for the worse. I certainly believe that large exchange-rate misalignments—that is to say, overvaluations and undervaluations, deviations of exchange rates from underlying sustainable levels of competitiveness—impose real and major economic costs. Those misalignments have come about in recent years because current international monetary arrangements do not impose any effective constraints on the way countries manage their economic policies.

The Bretton Woods system, I would argue in retrospect, produced a degree of policy coordination via the existence of reserve constraints on countries' behavior that was important in contributing to the impressive performance of the world economy. The classical model of this process comes from the gold standard. When one country has a balance-of-payments surplus, it gains gold, and simultaneously another country must be having a deficit and losing gold. Under a gold standard the second country will therefore have to tighten up, as the first one, according to the gold standard rules of the game, expands. So there is no reason for balance-of-payments disequilibriums to destabilize the overall level of world activity.

In retrospect, it is reasonable to argue that something of the sort was going on under the Bretton Woods system as well. With the exception of 1958, when the recession was mild, there were no world recessions during the period from the early 1950s until 1971. What we had were a series of national recessions against a background of continuing world prosperity. There was a recession in France in 1959, in the United States in 1960, in Britain in 1961, in Canada in 1962, in Italy in 1964, and so on. Precisely because the world as a whole remained prosperous, it was easy for individual countries to adjust. During this period a balance-of-payments deficit provided both an early warning that demand was excessive and that deflationary action was called for and a safety valve that allowed the country to avoid building in inflationary inertia.

Consider the contrast between Britain in 1964, when there was an unsustainable boom, which then had to be capped, and Britain a decade later in 1972–73, when the exchange rate was allowed to float and inflation went through the roof, thereby building inflationary inertia into the economy for a decade. Contrast the picture of a prosperous world economy in the 1960s with a series of individual national recessions produced by the balance-of-payments constraint, with the two global macroeconomic disasters of the last decade, namely the inflationary acceleration of 1972–74 and the depression of 1980–83. In the former, U. S. monetary expansion was generalized to the rest of the world because everybody was trying to defend their fixed exchange rates against the dollar. The more recent disaster—the depression of 1980–83, with its associated debt crisis and the virtual halting of growth in the developing countries—was again initiated by an abrupt switch in American monetary policy, which was magnified through the attempt of other countries to prevent their currencies depreciating to the point where the control of inflation would be jeopardized. Both of those events were caused by the breakdown of the monetary order constructed by the architects of Bretton Woods.

Keynes and International
Financial Reconstruction

A first moral I would draw from the above discussion is that there is a need for a greater measure of order than we have at the present time. We really do suffer, as I think Keynes saw we would suffer, from the breakdown of any agreed-upon set of international conventions governing the way countries conduct their policies, enjoining them to take into account either explicitly or—in my view preferably—implicitly, the interests of the rest of the world. We should be thinking about how we can redesign the system to function better.

A second conclusion is that we need to restore the neoclassical synthesis, which gives markets their just due in guiding microeconomic questions, provided there is enough management to keep the macroeconomy on course. That is a consensus which, as James Tobin makes clear in the earlier paper in this volume, we have lost at the present day.

I think also that we should extend the consensus about the underlying objectives to accept the basic premise that lies behind Third World demands for a new international economic order, the premise that there should be some measure of international income redistribution built into international arrangements. That is not something Keynes ever pushed for because it was not an issue in his day, but it is a natural extension of his thought.

The third area where I think we can learn a great deal from Keynes is exchange-rate policy. If one contrasts the rather sterile debate between the improbable alternatives of permanently fixed exchange rates on the one side and freely floating exchange rates with no intervention on the other side, which is the way that most of the debate on exchange-rate policy has been conducted over the past twenty years, with Keynes's discussion in the interwar period of how to manage exchange rates, Keynes walks away with the honors. He enunciated the basic principle that the exchange rate should be engineered to fit the domestic economy, rather than that economic policy should be targeted on trying to maintain a particular exchange rate, e.g., in the belief that inflation will then fall automatically, as was attempted in Argentina and Chile in recent years. He urged that, in selecting an exchange-rate target, one should look both at interest rates, which are important for the internal economy, and at competitiveness. He argued that, if one wants to combine a decent measure of exchange-rate stability with enough flexibility to allow the exchange rate to fit the domestic economy rather than vice versa, then in a world of high capital mobility one is driven to something like a crawling peg, deliberately avoiding big changes. In *The Means to Prosperity* he even presented the idea that a useful rule of thumb in deciding how to manage a crawling peg might be provided by inflation differentials.

There is, however, one area in which I do not believe we should be too sympathetic to the position that Keynes took in the later years of his life: his perception of a chronic and semipermanent deflationary bias in the world economy. This fear concerned him deeply in the late 1930s and early 1940s, though it became muted as discussions with the Americans progressed during the war. There is an account at a fairly early stage in these discussions, in 1943, of how Keynes had already abandoned the fear of a return to slump in the immediate postwar period (JMK XXVII, pp. 320–25). Despite the change in views, Keynes continued to press for a degree of liquidity creation that in retrospect one has to say could only have been inflationary and that would surely have prevented the postwar boom being sustained for over twenty years.

If one is thinking of designing an international monetary system, one has to worry not only about the exchange rate mechanism that is going to hold the countries together but also about the anchor that is going to prevent the whole system from taking off into inflation. Keynes did not really address himself to that question. He endeavored rather to rip up the anchor of gold without putting into place an adequate alternative. Gold could not be expected to provide an adequate anchor under present circumstances; rather, we have to borrow something from the monetarists, along the lines of Ronald McKinnon's ideas for coordinating credit-expansion policies among the major countries.

I conclude that, while Keynes did not provide a blueprint for international monetary reform that could be adopted at the present day, there is nonetheless a great deal that we can and should learn from Keynes about how to go about reconstructing a more ordered international system.

References

Kahn, R. F. (1976) "Historical Origins of the International Monetary Fund." In *Keynes and International Monetary Relations*, edited by A. P. Thirlwall. London: Macmillan.

Keynes, John Maynard, *The Collected Writings of John Maynard Keynes* 30 vols. (London: Macmillan, for the Royal Economic Society, 1971–)

Trevithick, James, "Keynes and the International Economic Order" in *Keynes and the Modern World*, David N. Worswick, and James Trevithick, eds. (Cambridge: Cambridge University Press.)

About the Contributors

Peter L. Bernstein is President of Peter L. Bernstein, Inc. and the editor of *The Journal of Portfolio Management*.

Robert Boyer is *Maître de Recherche* CNRS-CEPREMAP. His most recent book is *Accumulation, Inflation, Crises*, published in Paris in 1983.

Dudley Dillard is Professor of Economics at the University of Maryland. His "Keynes and Marx: A Centennial Appraisal" appeared in the Spring 1984 *Journal of Post Keynesian Economics*.

John Eatwell is a Fellow of Trinity College, Cambridge and Professor of Economics at the New School for Social Research. His *Whatever Happened to Britain?* was published in 1984.

John Kenneth Galbraith is Professor Emeritus at Harvard University. His most recent book is *The Anatomy of Power*.

Robert Lekachman is Distinguished Professor of Economics at Lehman College and is the author of *Greed Is Not Enough*, which was published in 1984.

H. W. Singer is Emeritus Professor of Economics, University of Sussex and Professorial Fellow at the Institute of Development Studies, Sussex, England. His most recent book is *The International Economy and Industrial Development*.

Paul M. Sweezy is co-editor of *Monthly Review* and the author of *Four Lectures on Marxism*, published in 1982.

James Tobin is Sterling Professor of Economics at Yale University. The third volume of his *Essays in Economics* was published in 1982.

Norman B. Ture is President of the Institute for Research on the Economics of Taxation and the author of "The Accelerated Cost Recovery System," a contribution to *New Directions in Federal Tax Policy for the 1980s*.

Harold L. Wattel, the editor of this volume, is Professor of Economics at Hofstra University.

John Williamson is Senior Fellow at the Institute for International Economics.